THE LIFE REVAMP

KRIS RIPPER

carina
press

If you purchased this book without a cover you should be aware
that this book is stolen property. It was reported as "unsold and
destroyed" to the publisher, and neither the author nor the
publisher has received any payment for this "stripped book."

carina
press®

Recycling programs
for this product may
not exist in your area.

ISBN-13: 978-1-335-42455-6

The Life Revamp

Copyright © 2021 by Kris Ripper

All rights reserved. No part of this book may be used or reproduced in any manner whatsoever
without written permission except in the case of brief quotations embodied in critical articles and
reviews.

This is a work of fiction. Names, characters, places and incidents are either the product of the
author's imagination or are used fictitiously. Any resemblance to actual persons, living or dead,
businesses, companies, events or locales is entirely coincidental.

This edition published by arrangement with Harlequin Books S.A.

For questions and comments about the quality of this book, please contact us at
CustomerService@Harlequin.com.

Carina Press
22 Adelaide St. West, 41st Floor
Toronto, Ontario M5H 4E3, Canada
www.CarinaPress.com

Printed in U.S.A.

THE LIFE REVAMP

Chapter One

Tim was perfect. He was everything I looked for in a partner: employed (hello, *doctor*), stable (no crazy exes lined up around the block or stories about how he wanted to punch people), and kind. He didn't drink too much or spend all night fighting with strangers on the internet or say passive-aggressive things and then gaslight me when I called him out about it. He had a retirement fund. He always found interesting things to talk about.

He was *perfect*.

We'd been dating for almost six months and it seemed like now was the appropriate time to Get More Serious. To be honest, at this point in my not-quite-disastrous but also not-quite-fruitful dating life I wasn't even sure what getting more serious was supposed to look like. I guess we'd go exclusive and, having done that, we'd make more of an effort to see each other? Move in together eventually, get married, combine our finances, buy a house, adopt a kid or two?

It was a little heteronormative and cookie-cutter, but that didn't trouble me much; whoever it was who said that thing about no battle plan surviving contact with the enemy could have said it about relationships. All of my friends had fallen in love and paired off, and their relationships took whatever shape made sense to the people involved—not necessarily the shapes they would have predicted.

Tim and I would find our way. That's how it worked, at least judging from observational data.

Which is why, when he said, "Should we discuss where this is heading?" over wine at a fancy restaurant, smiling at me with all the assurance in the world, I should have been elated.

Wasn't this what I'd been waiting for? Wasn't this exactly what committed adult dating looked like? Two grown-ups, fancy restaurant, having a Serious Conversation About Their Relationship?

So why was there a heavy sensation in my gut, a weight that held me back from all the excitement I'd expected to feel in this moment?

"Yes," I said, or forced myself to say, pushing down that feeling and willing it to disappear. "Let's do that."

"Well, Mason." Tim lifted his glass. "I really enjoy what we've been doing and I'd like to do more of it."

"Me too," I echoed, clinking my glass against his. He was a busy doctor, I was a less-busy-but-still-working-full-time-with-a-solid-social-life bank sales associate. We saw each other once a week. It's not like he was going to give up his doctoring to see me more—and I wouldn't want him to—so I guess that meant... I'd be giving up things in my life?

But no, I was just being paranoid about this after the many, *many* times I'd dated people who expected me to make all the allowances for them without getting anything in return. Tim wasn't like that.

Tim was the perfect guy. Who was now looking a little uncertain.

I was officially screwing this up. "Sorry, a lot on my mind. Let's definitely do more of this, um, of everything." I smiled at him, which wasn't hard, because Tim was the guy you smile at. We'd met through a dating app and from the first texts back and forth he was always easy to smile at, even when he was just words on a screen.

He shook his head slightly. "I'm doing this all wrong. I was so caught up in having this conversation I skipped over all the usual catch-up things. How was your week? Is everything all right?"

"Yeah, everything is all right, sorry. Just having an off night, I think?" I wasn't going to compound my weirdness by inventing a crisis. That was a thing younger Mason might have done, and while I slightly envied his willingness to make something up when he didn't know what to say, I was no longer that careless with the truth. At least that's what I told myself as the silence grew awkward.

"My timing is terrible," Tim said. "I apologize. Let's table this for right now and revisit it when we're both fully present. But for the sake of my future reference, this *is* something you want to revisit, isn't it? It's completely okay if it's not! Only I would appreciate knowing that now."

"Definitely." The relief of being let off the hook made my voice firm. "Very definitely."

"Okay, good. Now let's pretend I never brought it up." Self-conscious laugh. "I just signed up for a training I thought you might find interesting. If you want to hear about it?"

I did want to hear about it. More than that, I wanted the conversation to return to something completely neutral, which didn't demand I have or think about my feelings.

We went back to my place after and had exceptional sex— Tim wasn't just a pretty face, let's be clear, he had the skills to back it up—and then he went home because he had early appointments the following day.

And I nominally went to bed. By which I mean I stared at the ceiling for a long time. And then sent a snap to my best friend. I was too lazy to turn on the lights so it was just a shifting pattern of darkness and less darkness while I spoke, though I turned on a sparkle filter to give Declan something to watch.

"Okay, date recap, I fucked everything up? He wanted to talk about our relationship and I froze like—" I paused, trying to come up with a really good metaphor. And failing. "Like a freaking deer in headlights, Dec, what is *wrong* with me? He's perfect. He wants all the things I want. He's a doctor. He's nice. He's stable. Why am I not over the moon right now with an exclusive boyfriend, picking out table toppers for my wedding Pinterest board?"

And send. That's how I'd pictured this moment, when I'd imagined it, but now that it was here I couldn't even be happy about it.

I expected Dec to be asleep and get back to me in the morning, but a few minutes later my phone buzzed.

He was using a filter that gave him a cowboy hat, which was a funny juxtaposition against the rainbow shower curtains in what was clearly his partner Sidney's tiny apartment bathroom. "Wait, what happened? I'm confused. Also oh my god, make Sid stop editing, I'm sooooooo tirrrrrrrrred. But tell me what happened, because I don't know what you fucked up and I want to be supportive." He pointed. "Supportive face, now tell me how I'm supporting you."

I was just about to reply when a new series of snaps came through.

"Also, nothing's wrong with you. You say he's perfect when you know there's no such thing. If I'd drawn a picture of who I thought was perfect for me it'd be a picture of you, which is obviously not true, and I'd have never been open to Sid, and then we'd all be super sad. Romance is not a formula in a spreadsheet, Mase!"

One more snap, this time no cowboy hat, just Dec with his hair mussed in front of a plastic rainbow.

"This is me not apologizing *again* for leaving you at the altar. Please note my emotional growth." Then he stuck his tongue out at me and added, "I haven't grown *that* much."

I flipped on my lamp and said very solemnly, "I see your emotional growth and I appreciate it." I left a long pause where I did not stick my tongue out in return even though he'd be waiting for it, just to mess with him. And I really didn't need him to apologize again for leaving me at the altar when we were twenty-two. "But seriously, why am I like this? I've been hoping that dating Tim—or anyone—would get to this point and now it has and I can't even be happy about it? Am I self-sabotaging? Should I call him right now and propose? Ahhhhh."

Snapchat is like a super-sped-up version of the telegraph, where you send a message and then wait for the other person to watch it and record their own, then they wait while you do the same. Sometimes I kind of like all those pauses. The lack of immediacy can be perfect and allow me to virtually chat with my friends throughout the day while actually hearing their voices.

Right now the lack of immediacy was super annoying because I wanted Declan to tell me how to fix this thing with Tim.

Which he didn't. He did send four entire series of snaps, this time from Sid's kitchen, with a chicken on his head. Not an actual chicken, a filter of a chicken, which was one of his favorites and also let me know that he was trying to reassure me with a calm, meditative chicken filter, even though he himself was pacing and gesturing and couldn't stay still.

"Okay, first, you are *amazing*. You are an amazing human being, there is *nothing* wrong with you, you're wonderful, and of *course* Dr. Tim NoLastName wants to lock that down, because you're a fucking catch, Mase, okay? So stop acting like he deserves better than you! He doesn't. Literally *no one* deserves better than you, you're the fucking best, and I say that as an authority on the subject."

New snap. "Second, you should definitely not call him up and propose, oh my god, don't even *say* that." He shook his head violently and the chicken filter glitched trying to keep up. "Seriously, take it from me, that is the exact wrong thing to do. I know ambivalence is scary when you think you have everything you want, but *listen to it*. You're not doing anyone any favors if you pretend you're more into something than you are."

New snap. "And Sid totally backs me up on that, FYI, but anyway, I don't think it's self-sabotage. You just need some time to think about it, and you're allowed to need that. Just because a guy seems 'perfect'—" aggressive air quotes "—doesn't mean he's perfect *for you*. Like maybe he is? But you don't have to decide that tonight."

New snap, with his face closer to the screen. "Ummmm also Sid's done editing so we're kind of on our way to bed—or going to do something bed-related anyway—but I'm totally here for you—both of us are here for you—but don't propose to Tim, just take a bath and read a book or something, okay? I love you sooooooo much! There is *nothing* wrong with you." He got even closer, his eyes slightly out of focus. "Mase, you're incredible. I'm so lucky you're my bestie." He blew me a kiss.

By the time I'd seen all the snaps I had a text that read, *Also if you need me, we can phone?*

In other words, he'd put off having sexy times with his partner if I was freaking out. Which was sweet, but no. *I'm fine, you two kids go have a good time*, I sent back.

And I was fine. Mostly. Just confused.

Ambivalence? Was that what this was? This...this feeling of *meh* when I expected feelings of *yay*? But I liked Tim. We had fun. I respected him. He respected me. Sure, it wasn't a formula in a spreadsheet, but when you added up all the good things, shouldn't that still equal *hell yes, let's take this to the next level, baby, I'm totally in*?

Chapter Two

The night after Unnatural Disaster Ambivalence hit, I went out on a blind date. Not, like, *because* of the ambivalence. The blind date had been scheduled two weeks earlier when I finally caved and told my friend Claris I'd go out with her and her husband. Not in a threesome way. (I'd checked.) In a "my friend Claris is in an open marriage with her polyamorous husband and she thinks he and I would hit it off, which I know because she's mentioned it no fewer than every other time I've talked to her in the last year" way. They had tickets to an art gallery opening and I said I'd come along. No pressure, plenty of things to talk about, no big deal.

I really liked Claris. I'd liked her ever since the first time she showed up at the bank where I worked to sell us on supporting some incredibly wholesome community improvement event she was planning for some incredibly wholesome community organization. Claris was an organizer and grant writer for local nonprofits, the kind of person who could juggle a dozen projects at once and never show up without all of her notes in perfect order. It was admirable as hell, to be honest. And beyond that, she had a whole *way* about her, like one of those old movie stars, a sprinkling of Mae West attitude—flirty and funny and clever, but always like she was bringing you in on the joke. It went without saying that her husband would also be interesting and smart, since those things tended to run in couples. But since I'd always pictured getting married as part of my own future, which I couldn't very well do if the dude was already married, I'd said no to her attempts to set us up. Until either she wore me down (likely), I got increasingly desperate (somewhat likely), or she came up with a meet-up that was so low pressure it actually sounded kind of fun (pretty likely).

And okay, maybe I was a *little* bit curious. Diego—the husband—was a fashion designer. He was one of Claris's favorite conversation topics, and even after running what she'd said through a filter of *is married to him and therefore not objective*, I was still left with a pretty intriguing set of characteristics. He was Claris's age, so only a few years older than me. He'd gotten a degree in fashion design and then went out into the world and worked at an entry-level customer service job like the rest of us. But he'd never stopped designing clothes, and had been designing his own clothes since childhood. (Which, not gonna lie, was charming AF.) He apparently specialized in tailored suits and casual "menswear," though Claris had said it with the air quotes and clarified that Diego didn't believe in gendered clothes.

Diego Flores, she'd said, in that tone that meant someone else might recognize his name, though I hadn't. And I didn't go digging around for info. Because I was not a creeper. Even though when someone tells you her husband is a rising star in the local fashion scene, every neuron in your head is screaming to google. I am a man made of self-control, so I hadn't.

Which, in retrospect, was kind of dumb because if I'd googled I might at least know what the guy looked like, instead of standing outside the gallery scanning everyone who approached, waiting to see Claris and A Husband-Like Figure, whose clothes would probably be unique and on point, who'd probably be handsome and have a good laugh. I couldn't imagine Claris with anyone who didn't have a good laugh. Maybe I'd at least make a friend out of this deal. Not that anything was technically stopping me from going out with other people. Tim and I weren't exclusive—yet. At least not until we revisited that getting-serious conversation.

I refocused on the present instead of some imaginary potential future. No couples in sight. I checked my phone again. Where the hell was Claris? I'd just started to text her when I was jolted rudely out of my huff by a dude staring down at his phone as he walked and bumping into me.

There's this moment when something like that could go a few different ways. Was I going to be a dick about it? Was he? Were we going to launch into dueling apologies until one of us abashedly walked away? I was already annoyed that I'd been standing there like a dunce looking for Claris, so at the slightest hint of aggression I probably would have taken this random klutz down.

But he didn't give me aggression. He gave me a wide-eyed blink, from under long eyelashes. "Oh no, was that my fault? That was my fault, wasn't it? I'm so sorry, I was distracted and—"

I waited, but he didn't follow it up. Just kind of stood there, brows slightly tilted down, like a kid had been playing with an avatar designer and matched the "mad" eyebrows with the "slightly embarrassed" mouth. "No problem," I said. "I'm actually just waiting for people." I wasn't totally sure why I felt the need to justify standing outside the gallery, but there it was.

"Are you?"

Something about his tone—curious? dubious?—made me want to further justify myself. "Blind date, to be honest. I have fewer than zero hopes, if that's possible." *Liar. You wish you had fewer than zero hopes.*

"Oh no, one of those? Let me guess—you were set up by

someone you didn't feel you could refuse, but it's obvious to you that it will never work so you've resigned yourself to wasting your evening?"

"Exactly. I did *try* to refuse, but my friend is very persuasive." I made a show of sighing so it would be clear I was mocking myself more than anyone else. "This sort of thing happens more and more as I age out of 'attractive and unattached' territory and into 'destined to die a spinster' territory. I used to have to fight the rakes off with a stick, but sadly even they've stopped paying attention to me."

He smiled, lighting up exactly one dimple, on the right. The asymmetry was oddly compelling. "Oh dear. You'll end up living with a poor relation out in the countryside somewhere, a topic of pity and derision, unable to manage your own affairs unless someone very rich dies and leaves you their fortune."

"And *then* I'd have to fend off the fortune hunters," I agreed solemnly. "It's really a terrible life, so you can see why I'm on another blind date, despite my track record of not being good at blind dates."

"Indeed. As a matter of fact—"

But whatever he was about to say was cut off by the flurry of Claris arriving, her curly hair having broken free of its severe braid to form something of a mane around her face, her voice slightly panicked. "Oh thank god, you found each other. I'm so sorry I'm late! The freeway was a parking lot, I swear I could have gotten out of the car at University and walked here faster. Hello, darling," she said to the man beside me, kissing him. "You've met Mason, then?"

"Not exactly." He turned to me, his smile a little mischievous now, and held out his hand. "I promise I'm neither a fortune hunter nor a rake. Diego."

"That is cold, man. Seriously cold." I shook my head and took his hand. "Mason, as you apparently already knew."

"I had an inkling."

"So you *didn't* meet?" Claris frowned at each of us in turn. "Leave it to two people on a blind date to fail at basic introductions."

"To be clear, I figured out who I was talking to when he mentioned becoming a spinster." Diego paused before adding, "I hope it isn't *too* cold? I couldn't find a good place to interject. And we were kind of…riffing."

My desire to remain disgruntled was at war with my desire to find him charming. "You're on probation," I told him. "And you, Claris, are fifteen freaking minutes late to a date you've been haranguing me about for months. What the hell."

"I know, I'm sorry. It was the damn traffic. And the fundraising meeting ran long, which I did warn you it was likely to do, but I honestly did not expect it to run over by forty-five minutes. Who on earth does that? Plus, I had no idea I could have called in, and there people were, on the little spaceship speakerphone." Her hands strayed to her hair and she turned back to Diego. "Oh dear god. Tell me it's not as bad as it feels like it is."

"I promised I would never lie to you, so…" He let the thought trail off, lips still curved, humor in his eyes.

"Damn. Let's get inside so I can find a bathroom. Today has been a mess." She started resolutely marching toward the doors.

We followed after her. Diego called, "Yes, but did you get the money?"

Claris turned and beamed at him, hair forgotten. "Of course we did, silly boy. You know I always get my way." Then off she went.

"She's going to get there first and she has the tickets," he observed. "She'll just end up having to wait for us anyway."

"It would be undignified to run," I said primly.

He laughed. "I am sorry about before. I didn't mean to deceive you, kind sir."

I couldn't help playing along. In any other circumstance—like if I was out on a real blind date, with a person who wasn't married, whose wife wasn't also on our date—I probably would have held back. People tend to be attracted to my Cool, Calm, Have It All Together persona, which doesn't leave a lot of room for romance novel banter. But this was Claris's husband, so I had literally nothing to lose. "Intentionally deceiving me would be fiendish indeed."

"Fiendish! Perish the thought."

Claris was gesturing madly to us as she held out her phone to the person scanning tickets. "I'm so tempted to slow down just to see what happens," I confessed. "It would serve her right if they made her wait."

"They won't. She really does get her way most of the time."

And sure enough, with a glance at us, the ticket-scanner waved her through.

I sighed. "There's no justice in the world when rude people are rewarded for their behavior."

"But she's so *charming* with it is the problem. Have you ever tried to be mad at her? It doesn't take."

"Only once, and not mad so much as disgruntled because she'd written the bank's participation into a grant before we'd had a chance to actually finalize our contribution. So I read her the riot act about professionalism and responsibility and blah blah blah."

He smiled, pushing his hair behind his ear. "You lectured *Claris* about professionalism? That can't have gone well."

"Oh, but see, that's how she got me. I was sure she'd be

pissed but instead she apologized and told me I was right, and she wouldn't do it again, but she just *knew* I'd want the opportunity to support a queer youth center, wouldn't I? She could hardly send out the grant without acknowledging the bank's support, could she? And somehow by the end of it I was *thanking* her." We'd only known each other a short time at that point, but I remembered walking away from that meeting knowing that A) I'd been played and B) I admired the hell out of the play.

Which... "All right, I grant your point. I cannot be mad at that woman, even when she's clearly in the wrong. But you're married to her. Aren't you supposed to be bemoaning the chore split and crying about how the sex is boring?" Not that I was prying exactly. But not that I wasn't.

Ticket-scanner waved us through and we entered the gallery together, making our way through the small crowd toward the back. "Oh, the sex is never boring with Claris," he said, when we'd wandered to stand before a display of photographs, black and white, all mounted in black frames with wide mats. I was still thinking about sex with Claris, but Diego had apparently moved on, because his next comment was, "This is a bit...on point."

They were all forced-perspective pieces with humans looming over what I could only describe dryly as "the effects of climate change"—acres of burnt forest with looming blackened trunks, eddies of trash overwhelming a shoreline, an actual garbage dump site. Which, you know, yes, humans are responsible for the collapsing global climate. I agreed. But there was something a little annoying about the photos.

"I think the problem I'm having," I said after a minute of study, "is that the voice my brain has assigned the photographer is basically the voice of the person who holds up the line at Starbucks to ask about the origin and pasteurization process of the milk."

"Exactly. It's not quite to my taste, to be honest. I suppose I like my art like I like my sex partners."

Hard as I tried, I couldn't pick up the thread. "Um. Not looming over you looking terrifying?"

He grinned, the dimple flashing again. "In the right mood I might not mind that in a sex partner, but no, I meant *subversive*. The last thing you want in sex or in art is to be bored." He tilted his head to the side. "Do you think we're missing something? It can't be this obvious. Can it?"

"Missing something. Hmm." I stepped back. Then to the side. Then to the other side, shifting around him and appreciating how his hair brushed the top of his collar. Just the kind of hair you'd want to run your hands through if you were kissing...

Begone, random, unwelcome thought.

I viewed the nearest photo from the other side, up close, looking for...well, okay, I wasn't looking for anything really. But it did give me a moment to realize just how aware of Diego I was, his body, his attention, which was confusing since if I hadn't choked on my date with Tim I'd be standing here in an exclusive relationship with a doctor I already knew I liked. Yet... Diego was not a doctor. But I did seem to, uh, like him. If that's what this was.

"You look like a spy," Diego whispered. "Are you trying to find a secret code embedded in the surface of the image?"

"Maybe I am." I leaned in closer. "You never know. There could be a microchip for me to scan with my spy tech. Or a tiny bar code or something."

"Bar codes are so nineties, it's all QR codes now."

I shot him a raised eyebrow. "Now who's the spy, my dear sir?"

He moved slightly closer to me and lowered his voice. "Don't shout about it. But yes, if you must know, I'm a trained agent with the Art and Espionage Service."

I also lowered my voice. "I've never heard of it."

"Well, *obviously*. If you'd heard of us we'd have a much harder time doing our job, now wouldn't we?"

"And what is your job? I mean, in broad strokes."

"To ensure hostile forces are not transmitting state secrets via the visual arts. That's my department, of course. There are other departments for music and film and…" He paused to flesh out the story. "Um. Podcasts? Maybe they're embedding things in podcasts."

I nodded very seriously. "Verbal triggers, right?"

"Yes, that's exactly it. Trying to take control of the populace via verbal triggers implanted in seemingly mundane podcasts."

"It's probably *The Moth*," I said. "I've always been suspicious of *The Moth*."

He tilted his head closer confidentially. "Our technicians have gone over every millisecond of that show and so far detected nothing. But the analysts agree there's something fishy about it."

"This is cozy," Claris said, stepping up beside Diego.

I suddenly realized we were basically two grown men playing make-believe and felt myself flush.

But Diego, without changing his tone, said, "I've had to bring Mason in on the secret nature of my intelligence work, but you did say he was trustworthy."

"Ah. Yes. Your…intelligence work." She nodded. "I am comfortable vouching for Mason in this capacity."

"You don't believe he'll be a liability to my work investigating art and its use by spies to buy and sell vital intelligence data?"

She bit her lip as if trying to control a rogue smile. "Oh,

no, in fact I think Mason could be an, er, asset. To your important work. He's *very* observant." She winked at me. "I'll leave you two gentlemen to it. I have some contacts of my own to develop." And away she whisked.

I let out a breath I didn't realize I'd been holding.

"You okay?" he asked.

"Sure. I just had a meta moment of thinking that playing pretend wasn't exactly normal behavior for a blind date."

Diego reached for my hand, clasping it between both of his. "Mason. If you can't play pretend with your date, then why are you dating them?"

The question, teasing as it was, knocked me back a moment. I would never have talked like this with Tim. It wasn't that he didn't have a sense of humor, just that he wouldn't have understood *art gallery* as an appropriate venue for pretending to be spies. I didn't allow myself to be bothered by the fact that I couldn't think of any venue Tim would find appropriate for playing spies.

I brought myself back to the moment. "According to my friends I'm usually *fixing* them more than dating them, so maybe that's your answer."

"Oh no, that's not good. Fixing never works out well in the long run, though I suppose it does form the basis of a lot of marriages. Let's go find some other possible security exploits." And then, as natural as anything, we were holding hands. Walking through the gallery, looking at the next display, fingers loosely intertwined.

It didn't last long. Maybe two minutes. Four or five at the most. But since most of the people I'd dated expected me to initiate all the contact, it stood out to me as A Thing. Not forced, not entirely casual.

Since we weren't on a serious date, I wasn't exactly running my usual program of balancing my outgoing appearance with an internal checklist of ways Diego did and didn't meet up with the kind of person I saw myself with. Still, without The Usual First Date Questions, we ended up just…talking. A little about our jobs, but since Claris had told him that I worked in marketing and sales at the bank, and she'd told me that he designed clothes, we were robbed of/saved from the general chitchat.

And honestly? It was fun. If I didn't have a well-established friend group already, or if we'd been younger when we met, Claris and I would have probably had a non-work friendship from the beginning. But something about being in our thirties made that kind of thing more complicated than it used to be, so it had never exactly shaken out until now, and if this semi-sham of a blind date was the thing that made it happen, I wasn't complaining.

It might have been easier if I liked them just a little bit *less*. They were obviously so into each other, so delightful together, so damn #relationshipgoals. It was almost intimidating to watch, except each time I started feeling slightly alienated, one or the other of them would find a way to pull me in again. And Diego didn't take my hand after the first time, but he did find other ways to touch me, brush against me, stand close beside me to study the crooked beak on a painted parrot and quietly debate whether the hooked end of it might in fact be a disguised arrow, and if so, was it pointing to the location of a hidden microchip lower in the painting?

I left them outside the gallery at the end of the night, exchanging cheek kisses. Claris teased Diego about how she'd really just set us up to encourage him to finally separate his business and personal finances, adding to me that creatives were notoriously bad at doing so. Diego promised to come by the bank where I worked to set up a business account. Claris promised he would have all the necessary information to do so, with the kind of sidelong couple-look that should have made me feel excluded, and would have, except she followed it by saying, "We don't want Mason thinking you keep poor records, darling, so we'll try to hide that from him as long as possible."

"I don't keep *poor* records," he told me in his defense. "I just don't keep a picture of every single receipt in a database cross-referenced by purchase, company, tax year—"

"That's hot," I interrupted.

He groaned. "Oh no, not another one."

Claris laughed. We said goodnight.

I sent my post-date recap to Dec, as usual. This time it took me longer than ten seconds to figure out how to summarize. *NGL, I really liked him. Too bad he's super married and I'm sorta taken.* True statements. I added, *Also we pretended to be conducting a counter-espionage investigation. So FYI, you're covered if you need any help with that.*

He sent back a toothy emoji—the happy one, not the eek one—and *That sounds amazeballs. You liked him?*

Me: *Yeah. Like I said. But I'm in the market for a serious boo and he's already got one.*

Declan: *I'm just glad you liked him! At least it sounds like you had way more fun than you usually do!*

Me: *I've definitely never gone out on a date and had my date's wife along for the ride before. Look at me, trying new things. :P*

He replied with an entire rainbow of hearts. I sent the same back and put my phone away, trying not to take it too personally that Dec didn't think I sounded happy after dates with the guy I was actually dating. I couldn't worry about that, not tonight, not while I was still thinking of things Diego had said and smiling. And the way he'd held my hand, just for a minute or two, the warmth of his palm in mine.

I'd been right, by the way. He had a great laugh.

Chapter Three

You know how every now and then you look around and see the normal, everyday things in your life in this entirely new (and usually unflattering) light? That was me after meeting Diego.

It wasn't *Diego* exactly. It was him and Claris and their whole…thing. The partnership-and-happy-marriage-and-open-communication-and-successful-careers thing they had going. Adulthood plus relationship equaled what I always saw in my future but had never attained, and spending the evening with people who'd managed to get it made me look at my own life through a very different lens.

Not that I was unhappy. I was dating a doctor. I had a solid job, great friends, and a nice place to live. I'd moved into the apartment after Declan left me at the altar when we were twenty-two. In the wake of abandoning the life I'd meant to have with Dec I'd moved into this apartment I couldn't at all afford, and had hooked up with a girlfriend-slash-roommate I'd rebounded with largely out of financial need (not that I realized it at the time; at the time I'd just needed to feel wanted again, and like I was worthy of being someone's boyfriend). Thankfully she was rebounding too so while we didn't part as friends, at least neither of us had gotten our heart broken.

I poured coffee and sat down on my ratty old post-college futon, where I'd spent many a night with a controller in hand, or a book, or my computer, feet propped on the small coffee table I'd grabbed when a friend of my mom's was getting rid of it, my butt firmly planted in the place where the cushioning on the futon had molded into a butt-shaped divot.

How had I become *that guy*? The guy with the futon and the butt divot. I used to go out. Hell, I used to be the guy other people went out in the hopes of seeing, and I'm not even saying that like I'm just that hot. It wasn't about being hot, it was about being *fun*. Back in college I was the one always rallying the troops to do something on a Friday night, which was often followed by rallying them to do something on a Saturday afternoon, like drink a gallon of water and eat "breakfast." But even being hungover used to be kind of...not fun, but an acceptable part of life. Which, again, not like I missed waking up with a mad headache, but at least it meant I'd *done* something, gone somewhere, been around people. Post-left-at-the-altar-me had been even wilder for a while, like I was subconsciously making up for that near miss by partying twice as hard. I'd settled down though, and still spent most of my twenties having a good time, making people laugh, being The Guy You Like Hanging Out With At The Club (TM).

Man. Now I couldn't even claim to be The Guy You Ever Saw At The Club. Because I was too busy with the very serious business of butt-divoting. Until recently at least I'd had single friends who empathized, but now they'd all paired off and it was just me, alone, in my apartment, with my cup of coffee and my Xbox controller, only going out one night a week for drinks on a date pre-determined by a literal Doodle poll because we were those people now.

Part of my current environmental ennui was definitely Dec's fault. Technically he rented a tiny little in-law unit in someone's backyard, but he house/dog sat for them so much that most of the time he had the run of the bright, spacious main house, giving the impression that Dec had leveled up when actually he hadn't.

Not that it was a competition, obviously.

But not that it *wasn't*.

Well, okay, it wasn't a competition at all. Not as far as Dec was concerned. And don't get me wrong, I was super happy for him. Being left at the altar had been horrible, but when it came down to it, he'd saved our friendship and I'd way rather be friends than pissy divorced people.

Plus, we would have lost the Marginalized Motherfuckers, which has been our mutual friend group since college. In the terrible six months after Dec and I were supposed to get married, I'd had this realization: either I could forgive him, or the whole group would fall apart. They would have sided with me, obviously, but we would have drifted away from each other, the rift widening the way things like that did. While I'd always had friends, I'd never had real friends until the Motherfuckers, people who will clean up your puke if you drink too much after a breakup or who will agree that your boss is a monster and your professor missed your genius—while also being the people who will point out that you *had* been kind of a jerk to that customer, and maybe just one more revision of that paper will make it slightly more clear what it is you're saying?

They were my family and I didn't want to lose them. Which meant I had to forgive Declan, so I did, which is how he's still my bestie. Even if he does sort of have a way nicer place than me, and even if after years of refusing to date anyone he immediately fell in love with a really wonderful partner. Totally not bitter about that.

Here I was. Sitting on my futon. Obsessing over the past. Being definitely, completely not bitter *at all*. So I did what all normal people do when feeling lost in my own head: I checked social media. #totallyreasonable.

Dec had made some kind of fancy salad for dinner and posted roughly seventeen pictures of it on Instagram, plated perfectly for him and Sid, so obviously I had to both heart and comment. Our friends Ronnie and Mia—The Cutest Lesbian Couple You Know (TM)—were on vacation in Hawaii and had posted a number of adorable vacation photos featuring bright floral print wraps and plenty of gazing lovingly into one another's camera lenses. Hearts all around. There were also a few short videos that I squeed appropriately at while legitimately missing them.

Drinks with the MFers was a longstanding tradition. Without Ronnie and Mia, the brunt of the happy feels had been on Dec's shoulders. He'd done his best, but between me being The Guy With The Butt Divot, Sid being super low-key by nature, and our other friends—Oscar and Jack—generally never bringing The Happy, it had been a big job. Speaking of Oscar, I messaged him to see if he wanted to play *7 Days to Die*, where we currently had a world we'd entirely mapped, mines and tunnels connecting our hubs in every climate zone, and a network of roads and bridges that resembled the California highway system. Basically, it was badass. And a good place to go when life was…less than badass.

Not that there was anything wrong. My life was solid. As previously noted. I checked the time, but it was moot; Tim was on call and didn't like doing things while on call. I mean, technically he was always willing to go in to deliver if one of his patients was in labor, but he also had shifts where he was The Dude Who Delivered Your Baby If Your Doc Wasn't There. There might be a different phrase for that; he didn't always go into work details. I'd asked him once why and he said he didn't see how it would be interesting to other peo-

ple and I hadn't wanted to seem, like, weirdly interested, so I
hadn't asked any more.

Oscar messaged back to say he was at work, so I fired up
Skyrim. Nothing like playing a decade-old computer game to
make you feel…stuck in the past. No, I meant comforted, at
home, like watching old movies or reading old books. Basically, *Skyrim* was the game equivalent to picking up a book
you've read a thousand times. For me that was these old romance novels by Georgette Heyer, which I'd been reading
since I was fifteen, partially because some of them were just
these great romantic stories about characters who shouldn't
really be together who fall in love, and also because I relished
the way people had no idea what to do with a young Black
man reading historical romance novels as if he didn't care
what anyone thought.

True confession: I did care, at least at first. But I made
myself act like it never occurred to me that people might be
judging, and by the time I got to college (and made my way
through all the best and worst historical romances) it was no
big deal. Also, I got Ronnie super hooked on Heyer, which
was one of my life's great achievements.

I'd told Claris about my love for the genre at some point
early on in our friendship, after we'd moved past the "work
colleagues" part and I actively looked forward to her projects
(her grant-writing work brought her to the bank to solicit support, and since the amounts were usually low, we often said
yes). Since I'd taken on being the point person for that kind of
community outreach work back when I was young and spry
and excited to go to my adult job and do adult things, I was
Claris's main contact. By the time we were meeting at coffee shops to talk about her next big thing, I was comfortable
enough to bring a book to read while I waited, and after teas-

ing me about my old-fashioned habit of "reading on paper," she'd asked about the book.

That was a few months before she mentioned how well I'd get along with Diego. Which was itself a few months before she mentioned the, ahem, open nature of their relationship. Which was a few more months before she suggested he and I go out.

I hadn't even met Tim yet when Claris first told me about Diego. Now here we were, Tim and I in the limbo of non-exclusively dating, while Diego, although married, felt totally at liberty to date. What even was my love life?

I got another cup of coffee, which I set in the same coffee ring I usually set it in (which had been part of the table longer than I'd owned it), settled my butt in the same divot I usually settled it in, and picked up the controller, which my fingers knew so well that I hadn't had to actively think about the buttons in years. I stared down at it for a long moment, realizing that I probably hadn't *seen* it in years, not even when I periodically took a bleach wipe to it because controllers got nasty.

Look, at least I was also the guy who kept his Xbox controller clean. That had to count for something. Still, after going out with Legitimate Grown-Ups I felt more than usually conscious about how I'd basically fossilized in my post-Declan ruts. How much deeper they'd gotten since. I still got laid whenever I bothered to try, at least most of the time. And this thing with Tim seemed good. Steady. Predictable. He was way better than my past non-exclusive dates, most of whom my friend Oscar referred to as "fixer-uppers." Which was, in retrospect, pretty fair, though I remember being pissed at him when he first said it. To be honest, even hooking up with people and acting like having sex with them more than once was "dating" felt like one of my post-Dec ruts, which was only obvious now that I was dating a legit grown-up.

But it wasn't the same as what Diego and Claris had. What they seemed to have. Who knew what people's relationships were actually like, you know? But I knew that at least some of what I'd seen made me sort of yearn. They laughed together, teased each other, enjoyed hanging out. I knew she adored him, and brief exposure made it clear that went both ways, and man, I really wanted someone to look at me the way Diego looked at Claris. That mix of amusement and affection and love and attraction and... Meanwhile, I was just floating through my life, going to the same job, the same grocery store, the same coffee place, driving the same routes, coming home to the same butt divot. Certainty was good, right? Had I somehow managed to reach the point of diminishing returns on having a perfectly decent life? How was that even a thing?

It was almost enough to depress a guy.

Thankfully I didn't have time to get too involved in self-pity because Oscar got off work and felt like playing *7 Days*. With a text addendum that read: *But no voice. Can't talk anymore today. Too many customers. Customers bad.*

I'd been kind of hoping for the distraction of conversation, but I fired up an audiobook instead. We were building Elsa's ice palace—or as close as we could get to it—and having something on in the background was nice.

So yeah, I guess I was that guy: the one who reads Georgette Heyer and cleans his game controller and doesn't have a decent couch and builds Disney palaces in video games. You know. *That guy.*

Maybe I needed to view this confrontation with Claris and Diego and the life I'd always wanted but never gotten as a much-needed splash of ice water right to the face. An opportunity. To take some action, set some goals. I'd been waiting for Tim to make a move in a more committed direction, but froze up when he did. Maybe I needed to do it myself. Then

I could be *that* guy: the one with the doctor boyfriend and the path that leads to the future he's always wanted, with all the assurances and comfort that come with it.

Alternately, I could play video games until the wee hours in an attempt not to think about the rest of that stuff. Damn.

Chapter Four

By Monday I felt totally normal and not-self-pitying again.

I'd had fun with Diego, but I'd decided to see it as a wake-up call. A reminder of what dating could be, when it wasn't terrible. If we're being real honest, my last couple of boyfriends/girlfriends (and I use the terms advisedly) were just hook-ups who'd lingered awhile. Long enough for me to get used to having sex with them, but never long enough for me to fool myself into thinking it would be anything permanent. Tim was the first person I'd been with who hadn't started off like that. We'd met on an app, but we'd talked about more than just how we got off and when we could meet up. He was interested in politics and the socioeconomic implications of GMOs and how to improve health care for people in poverty.

At least, those were the things he'd listed on the app. In practice we saw each other once a week and only for long enough to catch up over dinner and, when we were lucky, have sex. Not that I was complaining. Even in the aftermath of my bungling The Relationship Convo, Tim had been gracious. He'd sent a text the next morning that only said, *Please don't feel any pressure about anything!* Which I really did appreciate. He was a good guy. And he was available. To be in a relationship. With me.

But Diego was an entirely different situation. He didn't tick any of the boxes I'd been looking for in a partner. He had a job in fashion design, which was awesome, but weren't jobs in creative industries a notoriously unstable way to earn a living? He was fun to hang out with, but didn't that mark a sort of…frivolousness? I didn't know how to classify our playful evening in terms of my previous experiences, and maybe that was fine. After all, Diego was in a committed long-term relationship already, so tricky feelings would not be involved. That should make everything so much more relaxed. He might come in to open an account, he might not. There was nothing at stake except amusing banter and, bonus, Claris could stop trying to set me up with her husband now. Maybe this was the upside to having bungled things with Tim: I was entirely free to live out a little fantasy with a grown-ass man who could talk about art and could also pretend to be a spy while talking about art.

I didn't skimp on Monday morning. Deep purple shirt that looked fucking amazing on me, a diamond-point bow tie studded with little glitter bits like stars (which I'd bought from a local tie designer, #supportlocalartisans), all grooming meticulous. Maybe he wouldn't even show, but if he did, I planned to look irresistible.

This was not a date. This was a man I'd met at an art exhibit who needed to open a bank account. And that's *if* he showed up.

Spoiler alert: he showed up.

I'd been hired as a teller, way back when having a job where I wore a tie was basically peak adulting. These days I worked on the sales and marketing side of things, so I was the one who'd help with new accounts, investment options, basically anything we had a glossy pamphlet for. At first I'd loved it. I'd actually really *enjoyed* being the person customers talked to when they had no idea what they wanted. I liked being the one with the answers, the guy you could trust with your retirement savings or your kid's college fund.

Maybe everything gets old eventually, or maybe I'd just gone stale myself. For the last few years it had felt a lot more like going through the motions than enjoying my job. I had some work friends who were decent—for work friends. And I didn't mind my direct supervisor (though the general manager was the kind of blowhard my mother would call a "shit for brains" under her breath and then swear she'd never said any such thing). The benefits were great, the schedule was forgiving, my 401(k) looked good, and I had no logical things to complain about.

I was just, like, bored.

At least usually. Not so much on the day Diego came in. Make that: not after I looked up and saw him stepping tentatively through the door and looking around. Nope. He was a regular boredom eliminator, and not always in the way I expected.

I'd taken care with my appearance. Diego...looked like he'd just come out of a knock-down fight with a crafting room, and the room had won. I must have done a whole thing with my face because he was shaking his head as he approached me, already apologizing.

"This is the worst possible second impression. It's a costume. Something like a costume. That is, I blame small children." He shook my hand before sinking into a chair in front of my desk. "Sorry, I really wanted to go home and change but it's nearly one and then I thought I'd be late and I figured it would be better to come here right after school or else I wouldn't know when you were working tomorrow." A pause for breath and I watched his eyes glide over my...something. What was he looking at? The shirt? The tie? It wasn't the straight up-and-down appraisal I was used to from people checking me out, more of a meandering appreciative assessment.

"After school?" I asked, instructing my brain to ignore the look. "Do you have children?" How had I missed that? Married to a smart, gorgeous spouse, passionate about his career, volunteering at the kid's school—the dude was basically my dream come true except *I* was supposed to be the smart, gorgeous spouse.

"Oh my god, no. Claris prefers kids to be someone else's responsibility. I mean, we babysit sometimes, but in general, no. Not our kids at all. Not that I wouldn't have kids, which I would, I think, but that it hasn't happened at this point in my life and it may not? But it still could." He seemed deeply flustered. Enough so I grabbed a mini bottle of water from the bottom drawer of the desk and passed it over. "Thank you. This is really not how I'd planned to—ah—be. When I came here."

I raised my eyebrows and smiled, hoping the combination came off slightly—but not intrusively—teasing. "No? How did you plan to be?"

"I had an outfit picked out that would make me look quite dashing," he said, voice low, leaning forward as if we were sharing a secret. "I was going to wear a scarf, because I have deduced that you enjoy playfulness. And colorful socks for the same reason. But well-made shoes because I think you appreciate quality." His eyes held mine. "Well? Would I have passed muster?"

There was something seductive about the way he drew me in, the way he kept my attention. The way I could picture what he was saying as he spoke, and even the insinuation that he knew what I'd like didn't bother me like it might have, coming from a less earnest person.

No man who shows up with dreams of dashing in his head

but in reality wearing a paper doily glued to his shirt could really come off that skeevy. I gestured to the doily. "I think you're losing some of your accessories."

He laughed and, instead of pulling it off, which is probably what I would have done, he tried in vain to press it back into place. "I sometimes do a thing with one of the local elementary schools where I spend a morning talking to the younger kids about clothing and design and self-expression. It's technically part of the anti-bullying campaign, and the teachers tell me it's a good thing, but I'm really in it to mine the ideas of the youth."

I tweaked a cluster of plastic googly eyes that had been attached to his watch. "Yes, I think this will be everywhere next season. You could call it 'The Eyes of Time.'"

"Exactly! You get the youth, Mason."

Since I was at work I couldn't make any colorful allusions to how much (appropriately aged) youth I could get, but the obvious joke shimmered between us and both of us laughed.

"I will now endeavor to make up for my sartorial sins by arriving prepared for all manner of account opening." He placed a binder on the desk and turned to a black folder at the front with silver writing on it that read: *Personal Checking Account.* "Not to give you the impression that Claris does all of my financial everything for me, but if you did have that impression, you wouldn't be entirely wrong. I try to hold up my end by keeping the bathroom clean, which she says is more than an even trade."

Swinging between flirtation and odd domestic asides was giving me social whiplash, but I reached for the papers he'd held out. "You don't need all of this to open an account," I mused, taking a look. "Oh, I see. Money order for the opening funds as well."

"Right. Precise amounts. We—by which I mean I—had

planned to do all this in November, you know, start the new year off right. But then here we are, and it hasn't been done yet. One of these days my personal finances will be separate from my business finances. Or so I keep promising Claris, whose financial life is in perfect order."

"It's still January, I think it counts." He probably hadn't needed to show me the entire folder, which had spreadsheets and bank statements from the business accounts and a profit and loss report that I did not allow my eyes to linger on, because it was none of my beeswax, as my mom would say. "So you keep your two businesses separate, then?"

"It makes the most sense. Claris is a consultant and makes oodles of money. I design quirky waistcoats and barely scrape by." He paused, and there was a sense of awkwardness to it, a slight hesitation that made me look up, to where Diego's eyes were staring quite intently at the folder in my hand. "I'm starting to do better than that. Don't tell anyone, but it's beginning to feel like I might someday make real money as a fashion designer, which is exhilarating and also unsettling because I didn't think dreams actually came true in real life."

The baldness of the confession, the near-reverence of his tone, touched something in me I'd almost forgotten existed. The part of me that also once believed dreams came true. I cleared my throat and said, "Your secret is safe with me. Even if I get taken by a hostile foreign power, I will never tell."

"Thank you. I do like working with people who understand that the future of the world is at stake."

"And it all comes down to this account." I grinned.

"If you heard Claris talk, you might genuinely think that was true. I'm lucky she introduced us at last, Mason. Or else my finances might have never been sorted out."

I felt weirdly exposed, his playfulness almost jolting me out of myself. "Speaking of which," I said, a cowardly subject change I justified because I was, after all, at work. I began to page through screens and ask him questions, occasionally checking the folder again. I'd worked with Claris on enough bank-sponsored fundraisers to know how well she managed projects, and this was no exception. She'd picked out the exact type of account that I would have selected for him, which, coupled with the spreadsheets and organized file, made me feel an odd sense of intimacy with her.

It didn't take long to finish the details and open the account. I let him know how to set up the online portal and gave him the usual rundown on our services. Blah blah blah, don't hesitate to contact me, you might find X, Y, Z interesting, here's a big packet of things you won't read. I set his own folder on top and settled it on the desk in front of him.

"That's it? That was…relatively painless."

I couldn't help allowing the hint of a smirk into my expression. "Did you think it would be pain*ful*?"

"Not exactly. But when you put something off for years before doing it, I think it tends to collect an…air of morbid dread around it. When it's then accomplished in thirty minutes sitting across from, uh, *you*, I guess it seems a little silly to have worried about it for so long. Of course until recently I wouldn't have had a *you* to take the edge off."

"I'm…glad I could help. In all the ways." Which felt true. All the ways. The account. The alleviation of dread. The… mutual appreciation.

He patted down his pockets, pulling out a crumpled receipt, keys tangled with a piece of jewelry made of red yarn and Cheerios, and finally a wallet. "I hope I'm not being too forward, but I realized after the other night that we hadn't even exchanged phone numbers. And I do love Claris, but I'd rather not leave her in charge of arranging *all* of my playdates. If you will." He didn't immediately hand it to me. "That is—

as long as you are also in favor of potential future playdates. No pressure, of course."

If he'd straight up asked me out, I would have known how to react. But phrasing it like that, like it was all in good fun, disarmed me. "Playdate" and "future" were both concepts I thought I understood…until you put them together. Wasn't the future for seriousness? Maybe, with Diego, it wasn't. And maybe I wasn't mad about that. "I am open to potential future playdates," I said after a moment of deliberation. Realizing he now looked like he regretted saying anything, I leaned in very slightly and lowered my voice. "The question is: would it be too forward of me to write my cell number on the back of my card? You might think I'm something of a tart. And I'm already concerned for my marriage prospects so I wouldn't want word to get around that I was fast."

His lips twitched while I kept my expression as serious as I could. He placed a hand over his heart. "I promise not to think you…unappealingly tarty if you give me your number. And me? What if I give you mine and you're terribly turned off by the impropriety of my doing so while you're engaged in your job?"

I mimicked his hand-over-heart. "I promise not to be turned off." After considering a qualifier of some sort and deciding against it, I just let the statement stand.

Diego lost the battle with his Serious Expression and grinned. "Oh good. I would hate to be responsible for that." He began patting down his pockets again while I picked one of my cards out of the container on the desk and wrote my number on the back. Since he was still searching for something, I offered him my pen.

"Thanks. I try not to bring a lot with me when I'm being made over by little kids." He used the pen and handed both it and the card to me. "Respectfully, sir, my card."

"And mine in return." He tucked mine away immediately but I glanced at his. I have a thing. About handwriting. There's something intimate about it, about someone's imprint on paper. Almost like in a way you could touch them through the shapes of their letters, the pressure of their pen.

I realized I was just sitting there staring at his phone number and quickly pocketed the card. "Thank you."

"Of course, of course." His smile was full of mirth. "It has been a very good meeting, sir. I hope to renew your acquaintance as soon as is convenient for us both."

"As do I, as do I." I held out my hand, which he grasped in both of his. I didn't know if that was an old-school handshake, or just the thing that felt natural in the moment, but whatever it was, I liked it. "Let me know if you have any questions about the account."

"I will...call the bank if I have questions about the account. I will call you for other things. If that's all right. So as not to further mix business with pleasure."

I knew I was blushing. It seemed ridiculous to be blushing, but I was. "That is acceptable," I said with dignity.

He stood. I stood. We stood there.

"I'm resisting the urge to walk you to the door like a gentleman," I confessed, keeping my voice low.

"It's the thought that counts. Until we meet again." He bowed. Legitimately. Bowed at me before turning and walking regally to the door, and somehow without losing a single doily.

Maybe I couldn't lead him out, but I could certainly appreciate the view.

I looked around, expecting everyone to have seen the whole thing, to be ready to rib me mercilessly for a dude bowing at me over my desk. But no one was paying attention. This is what happens when you have the Motherfuckers as your friends: you expect everyone to tease you as a way of showing their affection. Not that my coworkers had affection for me. Not that they didn't.

Not that it mattered. Diego Flores had just flirted with me in the manner of a hero from an old romance novel. And he'd *bowed*. Like. That was a little bit wacky.

And I was a little bit swoony over it. *Le sigh*. Swooning over Claris's husband was potentially dangerous, but what the hell, he was fun to talk to and I definitely wanted to do more of that. Talking. Not swooning. Well...maybe swooning. It was practice swooning. Preparatory swooning for some eventual person I'd date who wouldn't already be married. Like Tim. Who would be an excellent candidate for swooning.

I pushed the thought away. Tim could be swoony, too. Probably. This was just new-person-swoon. It was a different type of swoon. No pressure. All fun. Charming. With that one dimple. A little new-person-swoon never hurt anyone or damaged any boyfriend prospects.

At least, that's what I was telling myself as I waited for my post-Diego flush to fade away. He really was charming, though.

Chapter Five

I did not count on Diego calling. At all. I hardly gave it another thought for days.

Liar. I didn't obsess over the possibility he would call, because that would be dumb and self-defeating. But I did, after holding out for an entire twenty-four hours, Snapchat Dec to tell him about the whole thing. I sent a melodramatic wide-eyed snap with a sparkly pastel filter (Dec was roughly seventy percent more likely to actually respond to something I said on Snapchat if I used a filter), and sure enough he came back with *What happened??? R U OK????*

Since Dec had his headphones in pretty much all day long, I recorded a snap to say yes, I was fine, and oh, also, the hot, creative, fashionable, married guy I'd sorta been on that blind date with had stopped by the bank to open an account and we'd exchanged phone numbers and *OMFG WHAT AM I DOING MAKE IT STOP.*

Dec: *MAKE WHAT STOP THAT SOUNDS AWESOME HE WAS SO CUTE AND FLIRTY OMG I LOVE HIM ALREADY!!!!*

Dec's absolutely my boy, but his messaging can leave something to be desired. Then again, all-caps-no-commas! Dec was exactly how he'd be in real life if we were having this conversation, so it did add to the sensation I was actually hearing his voice.

I sent back a brief message about how this was Not A Thing, I had no hopes to get up about it, whether he called or not, and no hope meant no disappointment. My response sounded measured and even-toned and completely normal.

And Dec saw through it because we've been best friends since we were eighteen, and we'd legit been close enough to plan a marriage to *each other*, which now seemed batshit to me, but there you go. We were young and dumb. Now we were older and wiser, but I guess my tells hadn't changed at all because the next message was a snap taken in a bathroom with a filter that gave him cat ears and whiskers. Dec's sense of decorum wasn't his strongest quality. "*You* can pretend you aren't getting your hopes up. I will get my hopes up for both of us! Diego seemed super sweet! Keep me posted! Love you!"

I replied with a heart because, well, I didn't have any defense to that. I should mention that I had a steady dating thing already, but why bother saying something he already knew? Judging by the way my insides got all floaty when I entered Diego's number into my contacts, if he never called me, I was going to be very slightly *crushed as fuck*.

And he didn't. For two more days. Two days I definitely did not spend thinking about how I could call him, how usually I was The One Who Did The Calling but somehow this felt different. Because of the context, maybe? Because I was also usually The One With The Solid Life And Career, but next to Diego, I didn't feel like either of those things was as solid as I wanted them to be. Or maybe it felt different because I'd liked him a lot, but it didn't seem rational to have expectations about it, so in the end, I did nothing.

And then, while I was doing laundry after work, my phone rang. I'd just thrown the first load into one of the dryers in my apartment building's laundry room and the ringtone almost made me jump out of my skin. Then I saw it was Diego and not only did the bubbly feeling in my stomach show up again, but suddenly I was sweating. I slammed the dryer door, shoved quarters into the slots, and hit on before scrambling (with no dignity whatsoever) up the stairs because every call I'd ever answered in the basement had been cut off before I made it to ground level as if they'd lead-lined the stairwell.

"Hello?" I said breathlessly, even though I knew it was him.

"It sounds like I'm interrupting something important," came his warm, humor-filled voice. "Are you on the run from agents sent to burn you?"

"If I say yes are you going to sell me out?"

He fake-gasped. "How could you think that? I would never double-cross you. I swear on...um...actually I have no idea what spies swear on."

I tried not to huff and puff into the mic as I went up two more flights of (friendlier to cell service) stairs. "I think they're usually quite loyal to the government they're spying for?"

"True. I haven't figured out enough of my backstory for this. Should I call back? You sound busy."

"No! I mean no, you definitely don't have to call back. Was in the basement doing laundry, just getting back to my apartment. I guess if I say I'm breathing hard because I had to climb some stairs quickly that probably doesn't make me look swole?"

He laughed. "I know what you look like already. Swole: check."

And, well, if a man's right. "True. I'm a fucking catch. Is that what you called to talk about?"

"I'm not against your swoleness as a topic of conversation, but actually, I'm in your area kicking my heels while Claris has a meeting and was wondering if you wanted to get coffee?"

It was said so lightly, so casually, that I couldn't be certain if the slight tension I heard in his voice was real or just a projection of the tension I felt. Did I want to have coffee with Diego? Hell yeah. Was it possible to want something like that too much? Because if so, I was in trouble.

Coffee was just coffee. Any two people could go out to coffee. Single, married, whatever. "Sure, sounds fun."

"It won't get in the way of doing laundry? Because I have respect for laundry day, Mason."

I ignored the little thrill that went down my spine to hear my name spoken like that, in that warm, teasing tone. "One of the many things I love about my building is that I've never had anything stolen from our laundry room." Of course, usually I set an alarm for when the cycle would be done and immediately retrieved my stuff, but I was in the mood to live dangerously. "Where do you want to meet up?"

He was at a local chain called Sobrantes that was only about a ten-minute walk from my apartment, so I definitely did not take twenty extra minutes trying on clothes to go to coffee with someone I considered not relationship applicable. And I for sure definitely did not call Declan, who lay on his bed to watch me get dressed on video the way he used to lie on his bed to watch me get ready in the dorms before a night out.

After I'd tossed the third shirt into a pile on the floor he made a somewhat theatrical throat-clearing sound and said, "Mase, what's up with you right now? You never agonize over, like, *a shirt*."

"Yeah, but I never go out with locally famous fashion designers. What if he judges?"

"I mean, what if he does? He's seen you in clothes before, it's not like he'll be newly offended by your choices."

"This is different," I insisted, pulling up the fourth contender—a fun, quirky red, with slightly puffed sleeves—and turning to the side. "At least my ass looks good in these jeans."

"Your ass looks good in *everything*. But so does the rest of you."

"Diego's only seen my ass in boring work clothes." I assessed my reflection again. Okay, the shirt could stay. Aside from being comfortable and a good color on me, it was also slightly playful. "Fuck it, I'm wearing this. Decision made."

"Yay! You look great."

"Dec, you literally always say that."

"You literally always look great."

I rolled my eyes at him. "I need to go to my non-date coffee thing now."

"It's gonna be great! I can tell."

"You cannot tell something like that. Not a thing."

"SORRY GOING THROUGH A TUNNEL CAN'T HEAR YOU!" he shouted and blew me a kiss as he hung up.

I surveyed my reflection again. I looked very much like myself. The me I showed to the world, in a looser-than-usual shirt. I finished the look off with a pair of Chelsea boots and grabbed my purse. I'd started by calling it a "murse" until Mia pointed out that there was already a perfectly good word for that, and we really didn't need a new gender-specific replacement unless I thought having a purse was a threat to my masculinity.

Which it wasn't. And calling it "my purse" made all the right people uncomfortable, so score.

Diego was sitting at a table outside and waved as I walked up from where I'd parked. "I would have bought you something but I wasn't sure what you drank so I've been awkwardly sitting here without having made a purchase because I also didn't want to drink a whole latte before you arrived. Not that you took that long, just that I knew I'd be drinking faster than necessary." He shook his head. "I have clearly overthought all of this, sorry."

"Not at all." Maybe it was because he seemed flustered and I was generally good with flustered, or because he looked so cute sitting there on a café chair in the last bit of low sunlight coming over the bay, but whatever it was, I kissed his cheek. "Sorry I took so long, I overthought my clothing options."

He'd come in close for the (friendly, casual) cheek kiss and hadn't moved very far away. He looked down at my outfit with obvious approval. "My good sir, you look splendid. May I escort you inside? And I love your purse."

An entirely unfair twinge of attraction hit me all at once. "Why thank you." There, that sounded good, right? Totally normal? Totally not choked by *oh shit I like this guy way too much*?

We went inside and—after a slightly awkward hesitation at the counter during which I registered that he wanted to buy my drink, but also that I wasn't sure I wanted it to feel that date-like—Diego got himself a latte and I got myself an iced coffee. The table we'd had before was now taken by a person in a low bowler hat with an enormous, scarred-faced, ridiculously friendly dog we stopped to pet on our way to a free table around the corner.

"I've always wanted a big, brutal-looking goofball of a dog like that," I said as we sat down. "A hulking pit bull with a heart of gold."

"Yes! The kind that uptight people would turn their noses up at, but who actually you could leave your baby with and the dog would protect it?" He flushed. "This kid in my neighborhood growing up had a dog that used to follow her around everywhere and I always envied that."

"That's exactly it, though. Dog with a vicious bark, but the sweetest temperament."

"Seeming duality that's actually harmony." His dimple flickered and our eyes held way too long.

"Harmony is good." I took refuge in swirling the ice in my drink, hearing the familiar, comforting sound of it hitting the glass. "I love that this place still gives you real glasses if you're staying here."

"It's a nice touch."

Was this getting weird? Whatever happened, I did not want this to get weird. "So, what's Claris's meeting about? I mean, if it's not confidential."

"Oh, definitely not. It's a monthly get-together with one of the agencies she works with on housing resources. She took off like she was riding to war, so I gather the partners on this project have not necessarily been meeting their deliverables deadlines." He smiled, this time no dimple. "Whipping people into shape is one of her favorite things so I'm sure it will go well."

I couldn't help an eyebrow waggle. "This is where I definitely do not make any insinuations about the, uh, marital bed. And whipping."

He laughed. "Oh, that too, when the mood strikes us. It strikes her more than me, so she enjoys indulging with any number of playmates."

So. That meant. Claris. Huh. Open relationship, so it made sense that Claris could go out and find someone to whip. Didn't it?

Diego leaned forward just slightly, a lock of hair falling against his cheek but not quite in front of his eyes. "Questions, sir? Have I scandalized you with my frank talk?"

He kind of had, but I wasn't about to admit it. "Not the frankness. I guess I always thought I'd basically explored all the options—top, bottom, romantic, casual—but maybe I haven't."

"Consider me your Google. I can't speak for every polyamorous person, but I'm one of two leading experts on what it means to me." Pause. "And I have something of a vested interest in your comfort with the subject. Wink wink, etc."

"Is that right?" I knew my way around a *wink wink*. "And what, pray tell, would that be?"

"I could tell you, but once you know, Mason, you can't unknow. And what if the information poses an unexpected hazard to you?"

"You mean if I'm abducted and forced to spill all my secrets?"

He nodded gravely, eyes twinkling, but beneath the humor I sensed something much more real. "There are plenty of risks with this kind of confession."

"I see what you mean." I took a contemplative sip of coffee to cover my own deliberation. Maybe this could never become what I imagined for my future, but I liked him, and there was no reason we couldn't have fun in the present. "Having considered the risks, I am now prepared to be, uh, read in on the situation."

"In that case." His voice lowered. "The thing is, my dear sir, I find myself in the position of wishing to pursue a gentleman, but without having accurate data about whether he's even interested."

I swallowed, mouth dry. "That does sound potentially hazardous."

"Oh, it is."

"And this gentleman. Has he given any indications about his…" I trailed off, realizing that I didn't actually know what I was asking.

"That's where it gets complicated. I have a reliable source who reports that this gentleman's interests are, shall we say, harmonious with my own, but of course that's not the same as hearing it from him."

"No," I agreed.

We sat there for a long moment, both of us clutching our glasses, eyes locked. He licked his lips, a move that immediately captured my attention. What would it be like to look at Diego and think about kissing him? To think about tucking his hair behind his ear, or sharing the kind of smile you can only share when you've seen each other naked?

"Mason." He inhaled and—because mirror neurons or shared risk—I held my breath too. "I would very much like to date you. We can talk about what that would mean to both of us, of course, but first—*are* you interested?"

The bare, raw vulnerability of it shook me. I didn't want to send mixed messages, but I couldn't stand to see him open and exposed like that question must have left him. I reached out a hand and before it had moved halfway across the table he'd already grasped it. "I... I'm not sure..." I couldn't leave him out on this tenuous limb all alone. "I've been seeing someone and I... I thought it might be getting serious, but... It's not exclusive."

He nodded. "Okay."

"I don't know what Claris told you, but I've had a lot of somewhat lousy relationships. If you could even call them that. I'm trying to put my energy more into...functional connections with people. If that makes sense. And you're, you know, taken. I don't see how, with things being as they are, we could really...what that would even look like."

His fingers tightened on mine. "Do you want to hear what it would look like for me? I mean, not that I'd be dictating anything, obviously relationships are what you build with the other person or people, but I've given it a little thought— maybe more than a little thought—and I have some ideas about—" A car honked right in front of us and he huffed a laugh. "Saved by the horn. Sorry, I'll shut up now." He closed his mouth, then immediately opened it again. "Okay, one more thing, I am not trying to pressure you *at all*, it's just I have some experience with this, and I know what I like, and it's possible there's a middle ground, even a big one, where both of us would really enjoy ourselves, but now I'll let you talk, this time I'm really shutting up."

And he did. Which left a lot of no one talking in the wake of Diego's somewhat adorable rambling. Also, when did I get so bad at having conversations like this? When did I start relying on the momentum of sex to carry me into "relationships" without even discussing what I was looking for with the other people in those relationships? I swear, I used to talk about this stuff.

"Um. Okay. So." I shifted back in my chair, realized that might seem distancing, shifted forward again, too far forward, dammit. Why hadn't I just stayed in the same position I'd started in?

"Hey. If this is too heavy, we can talk about it some other time. Or never! Never is also fine."

"No, I…" I closed my eyes for a second. When I opened them, Diego was looking at me with all the compassion in the world. "I'm sorry, you just took me a little by surprise. Claris said we were harmonious?"

"I think the phrase she used was 'astonishingly compatible, darling.' Um. The 'darling' was Claris, not me. I'm not calling you 'darling.' Not that I wouldn't, but I'd get consent first."

"I don't object to 'darling.' I just. I mean." *Get it together, mister*, I heard in my mother's voice. I took a deep breath and got it together. "The kind of relationship I'm ultimately looking for is serious and committed. You know? I want to fall for someone, and I want to hold their hand in public, and I want to sit across a table at a fancy restaurant with them and know that they're just as into that as I am. And a true partnership, maybe with a dog, maybe with kids. That's the dream, I guess. I know the white picket fence thing is clichéd, but I wouldn't mind moving to the suburbs. That actually sounds good to me."

"The suburbs are not as bad as people act like they are, I promise." His thumb brushed across the sensitive skin between my thumb and forefinger and I fought an uneasy tide of longing. "I love your dream. It sounds wonderful."

I pulled my hand away. "Not to most people. And you've already got it. Don't you?"

"Some aspects of it, like the house in the suburbs."

Right. It was time to nip this in the bud. If he thought we could be fuckbuddies while he went home to his wife, that wasn't gonna happen. "Honestly, I'm pretty demisexual. I've tried to do the hook-up thing, but my friends inform me that serial monogamous hook-ups are not quite living the spirit of hook-up culture. It's just, I want to have all the feels for the person I'm banging. Not just some of the feels."

"I get that, I think. I don't know if I have *all* the feels for anyone. I don't want to have sex with my colleagues or fall in love with my favorite cashier at the grocery store. But I know a lot of people do want to exclusively have sex and fall in love with one person, or at least one person at a time."

Which, while obvious, kind of knocked me back a bit. "That's true. I've only been in love, for real in love, once before, and it was years back."

"I've only been for real in love twice, I think. There were one or two other people I thought…might be building in that direction. But things always happened and then they were gone." He paused. "The way this works for Claris and I is that our marriage doesn't close us off to dating other people, and that looks *way* different for her than it does for me."

"Yeah, man, and I respect that. But I'm looking for something stable and long term, you know?" Five years ago? Sure, I'd have gone for it. But now, when it seemed like I might be heading toward…something?…with Tim… Hell, I had no idea. And sitting across from Diego wasn't making it any clearer.

"And I completely respect that, but listen." He tapped lightly on the table, as if he wanted to reach out but didn't. "I love Claris. She loves me. We're really *good* at being married. But she also loves casual flings with people, whereas I don't want that. I love the *relationship* part of being with someone. The deep conversations, the way you build something together, the way that over time more things tie you to each other. I have that with Claris, but that doesn't mean I…don't also want it with other people. I'm perfectly capable of feeling love for— even of being in love with—more than one person. Long term, and committed, and serious. And it is completely fine if that's a deal breaker for you. But if it's just something you haven't tried, or even considered, well." His eyes cut away for a second. "I'm here for you thinking about it, if you're interested."

It seemed to me like he should be, maybe not indifferent, but at least not that invested in my reply. He had Claris, right? And that house in the suburbs? Plus whoever else he wanted to propose dating to. But looking at him, the way his fingers were pressed against his latte, it appeared to be the opposite. "Can I ask you something?"

A glimmer of a smile. "I did volunteer to be your Google for all things, well, me."

Our eyes met. I pretend-coughed. "Let's just say I reserve the right to revisit using you as my personal search engine. See, I don't even know why that's dirty, but it is."

"Agreed. And I consent to those terms. But yes, to return to the point, you can ask me anything."

And even that, surely casual, felt like a big responsibility. As if Diego were opening himself to me and I needed to honor that. Which I did, but also, I had questions. "I don't want to say anything offensive, but I'm not sure how to phrase this. Definitely tell me if I get it wrong. But you don't feel like it…cheapens your love for Claris that you can also love other people?"

He shrugged. "Not even a little. Like I don't think it cheapens my love for one friend to love another, or that loving my sister cheapens my parents' love for me. Love as a limited-quantity item has never made sense to me."

"Yeah, but…isn't that part of the…specialness of it? Of romantic love?" I wished I knew how to better express the question I'd had in the back of my head since I first agreed to meet them at the art gallery. "I don't know, it's just that's how I always thought of it. As a special thing you saved for one person."

"But people can fall in love more than once in a lifetime. And for me it's always a little bit different. The way I felt about the first person I ever fell for is different than the way I'll feel about the next, which is different than the way I feel about Claris."

I couldn't help smiling ruefully. "I believe that. I've only really been in love with my friend Declan. Which lasted right up until he left me at the altar."

His eyes widened. "He didn't."

"He really did. Literally. All dressed up, standing there in front of this big crowd of people, our parents, our friends, everyone. I'd had this vision in my head of him pulling up in a limo, walking down the aisle with Mia, one of our besties, while I'd walked with Ronnie, another one of our besties. And the limo pulled up. The music swelled. The door opened. I saw his face." I paused dramatically. "The door shut, the limo pulled away, and I became a jilted lover."

Diego covered his mouth with his hands and said, the words muffled, "Oh my god. I can't believe that actually happened. Were you okay?"

"Hell no. I was devastated. And also I wanted to freaking kill him for a while."

"I can only imagine. Or no. I can't really imagine. You forgave him?"

People always asked that. And I understood it. But it also made me feel like they saw me as the victim in a way I didn't really feel I had been. "I mean, yeah. But I'd been moving way too fast and gotten swept up in this super-serious lifelong-commitment thing before we were anything close to ready for it. Sure, I forgave him for hurting me. I also realized that as fucked up as it had been, it was probably better than having to get divorced later. Plus, I wanted our friends to keep being our friends, so I got over myself."

He looked at me for a long moment. "It's a hell of a thing to 'get over.'"

"Well, I didn't have much of a choice. And like I said, he was right."

"Was it right? Or did it simply turn out all right? I think there's an important distinction there."

I considered it more than I would have if someone else had said it. "Maybe. It *did* turn out all right, though. And that's what I prefer to focus on."

He nodded. "Your perspective is so interesting to me."

"Um. It is?"

"Yes. A lot of people don't think about things from different angles, but you do."

"I try to, anyway." I took a sip of iced coffee. Weird that talking about Dec flipping out on our wedding day had sort of calmed my nerves. "Polyamory is all pretty new to me, or at least thinking about it in the context of me being involved is. But I'd like to…keep thinking about it. This. You. Me."

"There is a *this*, though, isn't there?" His eyebrows drew together in concern. "Or have I invented the entire thing?"

"No. I mean, no, you haven't invented it."

"Okay. Good. I…thought I felt something. Feel something. With you." He cleared his throat. "It seems only fair that I let you know I am powerfully attracted to you and would like to go out on another date. This time *without* Claris, as much as I enjoy her company."

"What, she's not already waving around tickets to something else, strongly insinuating that you should invite me?"

He shook his head. "I give her three more days before she resorts to that. There have been *emphatic hints* as to just how I should be approaching you. Which I told her to stop because I really don't need a dating coach." A frown crashed over his brow like a wave, leaving his mouth curving downward. "Oh no. Mason. What if I *do* need a coach? What if I try to plan a date and it goes horribly awry because I'm fundamentally bad at dating? But then, what's the alternative? Let my wife plan all my dates? I might be *terrible* at this."

"I have good news and bad news," I said, fighting off a smirk because it seemed unsporting.

"Bad news first."

"Everyone feels terrible at dating. My friend Sidney has a whole YouTube channel about that very subject."

He wrinkled his forehead even more. "Not helping."

"The good news is that since everyone's terrible at dating, everyone else is used to it?" I ended on a question mark because as the words were coming out I realized they may not, in fact, be good news.

"Unacceptable. I will not be brought down to a widespread

level of terrible dating." He lifted his glass. "I will persevere, sir!"

"Will you now." I clinked mine against it. "I look forward to your efforts." And damned if it wasn't nice to see someone treating dating as an equal opportunity endeavor, and not just leaving it all up to me.

"It occurs to me that I have now set the dating bar uncomfortably high for myself," he said after a minute. "Can I, perchance, take all that back?"

"Not even the slightest chance, no." I raised my eyebrows at him. "Are you giving up already?"

"Don't you even suggest it or I will call you out!"

I laughed. "Okay, okay, don't call me out. My dueling pistols are getting polished or something."

He looked quickly around and lowered his voice. "By god, man, don't say that so loudly! To think you'd be at such a disadvantage!"

"Couldn't I just...borrow your pistol?" I asked innocently.

"Why, are you asking to polish my pistol, Mason?"

"Maybe we could polish our pistols together."

This time he laughed, and the sound of it made my chest fill with light. "Indeed, but not on our first real date. I'm not a *rake*."

"Perish the thought. Also, don't you have to pick up Claris or something?"

His eyes widened. "Oh no! What time—shoot—she's probably—" He pulled out his phone and winced. "Yep, that's why I should never put this on silent, oops. Gotta go!" He stood up, taking my hand and bowing over it. "Until next time, my good man."

"Until next time."

And then he was off. I sat there awhile longer, trying to wrap my head around it all. A date. With a married guy. Who enjoyed committed relationships so much he wanted to have more than one. Could I be someone's second-best? That probably wasn't how Diego (or Claris) would think of it, but how could I think of it any other way?

There was no reason to get ahead of myself. Focus on the important things: I was free to date whoever I wanted. So was he. We liked each other. We laughed together. We were communicating clearly. We had appropriate boundaries. All good so far.

And damn, that one dimple. That soft hair. Mmm.

Chapter Six

I don't hate my job. At all really. It's just not super satisfying anymore. And that whole thing about Millennials being whiny babies for wanting to *gasp* feel fulfilled at their jobs is a bunch of crap. It's actually healthy to want to feel good about the thing you spend a huge portion of your time doing. Which I know because I used to feel that way.

Now I mostly try not to be too obvious when I'm sneak-scrolling Instagram and zoning out.

I was watching some paint-pour Reels when a text came through the Motherfuckers thread relocating our weekly drinks night to Ronnie and Mia's house instead of the queer-ish bar affectionately known as The Hole. *Got off plane yesterday, can barely lift water to mouth, not leaving house* was Ronnie's message. Followed by Mia's eternally perky *Plus we have so many pictures to show you!*

Man, I needed to get out. Travel. Do something worth taking pictures of. At the very least so I'd have stories to tell my friends. Until then I'd have to live vicariously through others.

I stopped by my place to get changed and then headed over with a bottle of wine I knew they'd like, primed and ready for a massive photo tour of Hawaii complete with many colorful asides and envy-inducing adventures.

What I got was Mia exclaiming, "You're here! Ronnie,

Mase is here! Come in and tell us everything about the new boyfriend-guy, we're dying to hear the story!"

Ronnie, coming up behind her, took the wine. "No one technically used the word 'boyfriend,' we're just extrapolating from gossip."

I sighed theatrically, though at this point if the friend group *didn't* spread all of my business I probably wouldn't know what to do with myself. "Nothing's happened with Tim. He started talking about our relationship, I choked, and we've been avoiding the subject ever since, the end."

"Not Dr. Tim NoLastName! The new guy!" Mia frowned and glanced at Ronnie. "Isn't there a new guy? Didn't Dec say—"

"Yeah, but that doesn't mean—"

"Are you guys talking shit about me?" Dec called from the kitchen.

"No!" they shouted in unison. Mia hooked her arm through mine. "Living room, c'mon. Dec's bringing out food. I think he imagines we haven't eaten since we left. To be honest it's amazing, but don't tell him I said so."

"I heard that!" Dec poked his head out of the kitchen. "Just sit, we'll bring stuff out. Are we waiting for Oscar and Jack?"

"I vote no," I said. "You snooze you lose in this family."

"I'm with Mase," Ronnie agreed.

Mia already had her phone out. "I'll just text them to see where they are."

"Our whole vacation was this." Ronnie gestured, smiling, at her wife. "Mia being kind and me being grumpy. At one point this very white, very straight middle-aged woman asked her if she minded dating Americans."

"Did not." I looked at her. "They did not."

Mia's eyes were bright and viciously delighted. "Right? Apparently in her part of America they don't have Asians. I should have done my dad's I-can't-speak-English-telemarketing accent, but instead I turned to Ronnie and said, 'Oh, wait, you're American? Well fuck me directly in the ear and call me Susan.'"

I cracked up. "You didn't."

Ronnie kissed her. "She really did, and then smiled all sweetly at the lady and pulled me in the other direction. It was epic."

"It sounds epic!"

Dec, loaded down with a tray of…basically everything, walked into the living room and made a beeline for the coffee table. "Don't get epic without us!"

"We already told you this one."

He grinned. "Oh, the one where we're calling Mia Susan? Super epic. Here, finger foods. Sid has all the—" He moved aside so Sidney could set down a massive bowl of fruit. "Fruit salad!"

"Yummy yummy!" we called. Because when you get into The Wiggles in college, they never go out of fashion, am I right? Enjoying kids' stuff ironically as a young adult is evergreen.

"Is that the whole spread?" Mia asked. "I want to interrogate Mason about his new romance, if there is one, which you led us to believe there was, mister."

Dec bit his lip. "Um, I only mentioned he met a guy. That's literally all I said."

"Lies!"

I waved a hand at both of them. "No one's interrogating me and there is no new anything, we're supposed to be interrogating you guys about your trip!"

"Later! First, you tell us—"

A knock, then Oscar's voice calling, "Somebody open the fucking door, my arms are full!"

A few minutes later, after Oscar's offerings (supplies to chocolate-dip things) had been dispersed to where they needed to be and everyone was arranged around the room, Mia nudged me again. "So?"

"Uh. Well." I shot a dark look at Dec, who made a face at me. "I did meet a human. But it's not like all that."

"He's married," Oscar said.

"Non-monogamously," Dec added. "Legitimately, not just to be a cheating jerk."

"But definitely married. And also successful."

"Hey, Mase is successful!"

Oscar snorted. "Not like that."

Mia clapped her hands like a kindergarten teacher. "Thank you, riffraff, but I'd really like to hear about Mason's dating life from Mason."

"Um," I said. Expansively.

"He's not actually dating a somewhat successful fashion designer who's married non-monogamously to that fundraiser he did that thing with that time," Oscar said on my behalf.

I glanced at him. "Thanks?"

He shrugged. "It's true. She did that thing that time. And *he's* somewhat successful. I had Jack look him up."

Jack waved a hand. "I don't have some kind of magic wand I can wave and find out how much money someone's worth. I googled and followed a couple of links."

"*Again*," Mia said. "Mase?"

"I...like him. His name is Diego Flores. Though we are not dating, that's, um, accurate. I mean. We decided to be open to dating maybe? But in reality we just went to coffee one time."

"For which you tried on like seventy-three different outfits," Dec put in.

"It wasn't that many."

He pursed his lips meaningfully.

"But can we go back to the guy has a last name?" Mia lightly smacked Ronnie's arm. "Did you hear? The new boyfriend-guy has a last name!"

"I can't wait to google him later!" Ronnie whispered back.

"He's definitely not my boyfriend. He's a guy. With a wife. And I've been dating Tim."

"Dr. Tim NoLastName," Mia clarified, nodding. "Yep, we're all familiar with Dr. Tim NoLastName, aren't we?"

Since this level of trolling should never be rewarded, I ignored it. "Maybe I just made a friend. Y'all don't need to make it into a whole thing."

"Technically it's Dec making it into a thing." Oscar focused his attention on carefully dipping a graham cracker into chocolate. "Though for the record you like the wife and you never tried on seventy-three different outfits to see her."

I shot a look at Dec. "You are the weakest link."

"I know! I'm sorry! But also I'm not because I already like this guy."

"That makes no sense. I've met him like twice."

"Three times because he also came into the bank, remember?"

As if I could forget. "That doesn't count."

Mia held up a hand. "Did he know you worked there when he went in?"

"Not only did he know Mase worked there, but he went in to see him!"

"He was opening an account."

"Spontaneously, shortly after meeting a super-hot guy who works at a bank." Dec's eyebrows did all sorts of jumping around.

Mia giggled. "Okay, okay, let's let Mase off the hot seat."

"But—" Ronnie looked at me as if she was trying to decide what she wanted to ask. "But *did* you like him? Is this a thing we should never mention again because there's no way you'd date a married guy, or…?"

In the grand scheme of things it wasn't that complicated a question. Except I realized I couldn't answer it. Not directly. "I like him. He's smart—both of them are really smart—and creative. He technically designs menswear, but he does it with this emphasis on gender fluidity, and fitting traditional pieces on people of all different shapes and expressions, at least that's how Claris describes it. And in person, he's…he volunteers at schools, and he's so thoughtful. I really…like him." Oh my god, why did I sound like such weak sauce right now?

"Good. Right?" Mia glanced at Ronnie, then back at me. "Why are you acting like there's a huge *but* at the end of that sentence?"

Oscar sighed loudly. "Because the guy is *married*. And all Mase has ever wanted is to get married and live happily ever after like a damn Disney princess, but this time his prince is already married so he can't commit to being happy about it. Obviously."

Ronnie tossed a paperback at him. "Thank goodness we have our resident expert in relationships to explain this to us so succinctly."

Jack smirked and Dec laughed out loud, but Oscar stood his ground. "I'm not judging, I'm just calling it the way it is."

"Is that true, though?" Mia's voice had grown softer, like she was being gentle with me. "It seems like things could be kind of good?"

I wasn't going to answer that. "Why are all of you so obsessed with this person I met like less than a month ago when I've been dating Tim for half a year?"

No one met my eyes.

"Hello?" I allowed the annoyance to creep into my tone. "Anyone?"

Mia and Ronnie looked at each other, Dec looked at his hands, Sidney didn't really look anywhere (but that was their normal thing), Jack was looking at his phone, and Oscar— sighed heavily. "We don't like him."

"That's not true!" Dec immediately objected. "I have never, ever said that."

"It's not about *liking* him," Mia said carefully. "Obviously we've never met him."

"Which is part of the problem," Ronnie added.

"Or," Oscar said, "we just don't like him. He sounds like a paper doll, not a person."

"Okay, what the hell does that mean?"

Mia put her plate down as if she was about to give someone bad news. "It's really not that we don't like him. You seem to like him, which is all that matters. It's just that it feels a little like you're…buying the first decent house you've ever walked through instead of shopping around for the one that works *for you*. You know?"

I blinked at her. "Um. No?"

She cast about at the others. "Dec, you explain it."

Dec started to demur, but I stared him down until he wriggled like a fish on a hook. "Just, you know, for a long time you dated people who were…not great. People who needed your help, or needed your support, or needed you to be checking in with them, like, all the time. And it's really good you're moving away from that! That's so good!"

"But?"

"But like…you don't have to settle down with the first person who's kind of a grown-up. You can wait until you find one you really like, who makes you feel something. That's all."

"I feel things for Tim. I feel all kinds of things for Tim." Sure, I hadn't seen him in two weeks and he wasn't that good at texting, but I felt things for him. I must. We'd been dating for months.

"Right," Dec said. "Yeah. Of course you do. I'm sure it'll all make more sense when we meet him. Right, guys?"

"Yes! That's so true." Mia smiled widely. "So when will you be bringing Dr. Tim NoLastName to drinks, Mase?"

"Oh no. No way. I am *not* subjecting Tim to the Drinks Curse."

"Oh, hey, Sid has a theory about that!" Dec sounded almost excited about the theory, but he was probably just relieved to be switching subjects. "They think it's a myth."

Sidney winced. "I would not have put it like that."

"Yeah, but you literally *did* put it like that."

"I mean, in this context."

Jack raised his hand. "It must not work all the time since I'm still here."

"You don't count," I said. "You were already coming to drinks when you two hooked up. Sidney too. The Drinks Curse only applies to people who come to drinks as a date, none of whom have ever lasted long after that, so I don't see how it can be a myth."

"Yeah, but Sid said it's a what-do-you-call-it, selection bias. Right?"

Sidney didn't look super thrilled to be explaining this. I could completely imagine them floating a theory to Dec in the spirit of, like, academic inquiry, but really not ready to present their analysis for all of the Motherfuckers.

"Just, um, that if you...if someone was under the impression that taking a certain action would lead to a certain result, one might—subconsciously—choose to take that action in order to achieve that result." Their eyes darted around at all of us, then lowered to study the food. "That's all."

"I'm still confused," Ronnie said. "The action is what?"

Mia, though, was nodding her head. "The action is bringing someone to drinks, right? You think maybe Mase subconsciously brought people to drinks only when he wanted to break up with them?"

"Hey!" I said. "Wait."

"Not...not break up with." Sidney's cheeks were now pink and despite their theory undermining The Truth About The World I felt kind of bad that Dec had brought it up. "Just it might be that thinking there was a supernatural reason for a relationship dissolving after bringing someone to drinks might make it attractive to bring...someone with whom you wouldn't mind the relationship dissolving. But it's only a theory based on what data I have, which isn't at all scientific."

"I think you're right." Oscar scratched his head and tugged on his shirt before speaking again. "I brought one person to drinks ever and I think I probably did that because I wanted to give myself permission to be done with him. Anyway. It's an interesting idea."

Jack's eyes narrowed. "Are you having feelings right now? Do I need to get a pillow for you to punch?"

Oscar flipped him off.

"Oh good, glad everything's functioning normally." Jack had mad smirk game, let it be said. "Selection biases are real, though. If you want to study the effect of television on children and then the majority of subjects are from one economic, racial, or class demographic, you're not taking into account a lot of other variables there, thus skewing your results. If you—" he gestured at me "—are exclusively focusing on 'has gone to drinks' as the cause of the breakup, then you're probably missing some of the variables that also contributed."

I shook my head. "Um, thanks, everyone? But I'm not trying to be a scientist, I just know that since every single person I've ever brought to drinks has no longer been dating me within two weeks of doing that, I'm definitely not bringing Tim to drinks."

Sid opened their mouth, then closed it again.

"Oh what?" I snapped. "Sorry. Just it looked like you were about to say something."

"Just…you're choosing *not* to bring him. Because you don't want the relationship to end. I think that might…kind of validate the theory a little?"

"Holy shit, Sidney broke the Drinks Curse." Ronnie lifted her glass. "To Sidney!"

The others called, "To Sidney!" while Sidney blushed and clearly wished they were somewhere far, far away.

Me? I just sat there. Thinking. Wondering. Worrying. Had I been doing that? Like. Seriously? Had I really used drinks with my friends as a reason to end relationships? Had I really subjected people I no longer wanted to date to the, like… sideshow act of "We're so serious, come to drinks with my friends"? Because if I had done that, I was an ass.

And if I hadn't…then was I really saying there was a *supernatural* connection between drinks and breakups? That sounded all kinds of "thing a guy tells himself because he's living in denial."

My friends had always called me out about stuff when they needed to, and I'd done the same for them, but having new people around truly did change things. For the better, mostly. Except on days when you kind of wished you could just keep going on with your old misconceptions. About relationship-ending curses. Uh, everyone had those, right? And anyway, this was proof that everything was fine with Tim, since I'd already said I wasn't bringing him to drinks. So there.

Chapter Seven

My first official date with Diego…was not at all what I'd been expecting.

"Manicures," I repeated.

"Unless you don't like manicures," he said quickly, probably sensing just how unexpected the proposal was.

"It's not that. I keep my nails looking good, but a little pampering never hurts. It's just that I've never been asked out to a manicure before. I've only had two—one before my friend's wedding, and one before what was supposed to be my wedding."

Diego coughed into the phone. "I hope this isn't bringing up any bad memories? And we don't have to! It's just that it's casual, which I thought might appeal to you, and I'm busy this week, so I thought that would be a chunk of time we could spend together. Which actually sounds like I'm multitasking our date, and that's not *at all* the impression I'm trying to get across to you right now."

I laughed. I couldn't quite stop myself (and didn't try that hard). When a man asks you to his house for a manicure in order to double-book your date alongside his professional grooming services and then immediately realizes how bad that sounds and is genuinely contrite about it…well, you either hang up on him or laugh, and I wasn't about to hang up.

Call me easy, but I do like a man who takes care of himself. Ahem.

"Oh god, forget I even asked, I am the worst. Mason, please forget this whole conversation. I'm going to hang up and call back and start completely over, okay? Okay. That's— I can't—" He made a sort of tortured sound, which cut off as he legit hung up.

Man, this dude. I obediently waited for the phone to ring again and answered brightly, "Hello?" as if we hadn't just done this whole thing.

His voice was deliciously formal. "Greetings, my dear sir. I would like to invite you out riding with me sometime next month when opportunity will bring me to your general environs."

"Next month?" I echoed, grinning stupidly. "That seems like a very long time to wait for a ride, sir."

He choked. "Ah—ehm—you see—"

"I prefer to ride my men sooner than that," I added helpfully. "Sorry, I meant *ride with* my men. Of course."

"Of course. Yes, I can see where, um, you would…not want to wait. For a ride."

"I'm not averse to waiting for an especially good mount, if you will. Some horseflesh is worth waiting for."

He giggled. Diego Flores, rising fashion designer, giggled in my ear. "Oh god, I can't. Fess up, you've read a lot of old romance novels, haven't you?"

"Didn't Claris tell you that? I got hooked on them when I was a teenager. I'm also down for lying in bed with a bowl of popcorn and a box of tissues watching Jane Austen movies. I'm open to book recommendations if you have them."

"I'll share my BookNook with you. And my historical romance shelf link because I've read everything. Back when I used to read more."

"Send me the link. And I'd love to come over for mani-cures, honestly. A manicure date sounds like fun."

"I'll also provide lunch! It's not just come over, get your nails done, and I kick you out."

"That would be rude as fuck," I agreed, mostly to hear him giggle again.

Which he did. "This is the worst idea I've ever had. I try not to run all of my dating ideas by Claris, but she would have vetoed this one, and she would have been so right."

"Not really, since I'm agreeing to it."

"Yes, but I'm *multitasking* you into my manicure appoint-ment, though you will actually get a manicure out of it? So maybe that... Does that help? I can't tell."

"I'm completely open to a manicure date."

"Good! Thank you. I wish, I desperately wish, that I was asking you to dinner, but we have a project planning meeting scheduled for Gentlemen's Fashion Week, and even though the event isn't until September, I'm already feeling late."

"Gentlemen's Fashion Week?"

"It's this whole—this whole thing. But if you're serious about not minding a manicure date, why don't I tell you about it then?"

"Deal."

"Good. I will see you soon, sir."

"I look forward to it."

"As do I."

We hung up. I was still smiling down at my phone when a snap from Declan came in. He'd picked a filter that distorted his features, but he still looked adorable. Something-some-thing-cooking-something. I picked a much better filter—with a top hat—and recorded one to send back. "I don't know what you're talking about but if it means you're making food, I'm here for it. Also I just got off the phone with Diego and he asked me over for manicures, which should make you happy."

I got back a row of exclamation points followed by *AHHHHHHHH.*

I laughed and returned to thinking about Diego.

Manicures, I never would have guessed. What did he have in store next? And how was I going to keep up?

I brought a bouquet of irises to our manicure date, which made Diego blush.

I can romance a man. Even over manicures, let it be known. I appreciated what he'd said about keeping things on the casual side of dating, but that didn't mean I couldn't bring my "A" game.

"Oh, these are—they're beautiful. Let me find a vase. Come in." He led me inside and worked on the flowers while I looked around at the frankly gorgeous kitchen.

"This place is straight out of a showroom. And not an Ikea showroom either." I ran my hand along one of the marble countertops. I was pretty sure it was marble, anyway, not like I do a lot of shopping for stone, but it looked marble-like. "Impressive and veiny," I said with appreciation, caressing it and smirking at him.

"I aim to please with my impressive veiny-ness," he replied with gravity, setting the vase by a window where it picked up the sunlight and scattered it like jewels. "Thank you for the flowers."

I bowed. "I also aim to please."

"You are quite pleasing."

A cough from a doorway leading to another room. "If you're ready?"

"Sorry! We are. At least, I think we are. Mason, bring your hands."

"My hands are ready. And am I late? I didn't think I was…" I definitely was not. I make it a point to never be late. I can't stand lateness as a thing.

"No, but I'd given you a time that was slightly early for our appointment, and then our appointment got moved up to exactly the time I'd given you." He gave a flustered hand motion I found incredibly endearing. "So technically everything is right on time, but we have less wiggle room than I'd hoped. Also, this is June and her sister Yolanda. June, Yolanda, this is Mason."

We all exchanged hellos, and then I took a seat on one side of a dining table while Diego sat at the other side, both of us surrendering our hands. Diego went with a holographic dust clear polish and I opted for a simple guy-manicure. I didn't think the bank would go for me showing up with rainbow nails.

"I used to be self-conscious about manicures, but Claris pointed out that one of the perks of being one's own boss is unlimited self-expression. Usually I go to the shop for them, but more and more we've been experimenting doing them here or on location."

"This is better anyway," June added as she filed. "Claris doesn't like touching things at salons."

"True. And this way we get to support June's business and she doesn't have to pay a rental for her station."

I glanced around as if Claris was going to materialize from the ether. "But Claris isn't having her nails done today?"

"She's otherwise engaged. But Yolanda was free, and you were free, and now here we are." He smiled ruefully. "I was right, by the way. She was *appalled* when I told her about our manicure date."

June made a snorting sound. "Claris has a lot to offer, but I'm not sure I'd want to date her."

"It wasn't that bad! Well. There was a night when she took a conference call in the middle of a movie, in an actual theater, then spent the rest of it huddled over in a corner of the arcade, hissing at any children who dared attempt to play *Pac-Man*."

"Not that bad, huh?" June laughed. "Stop trying to gesture, I'm working here."

"Sorry." To me, he said, "We make better spouses than we did people who were dating each other."

"I really don't mind the manicure-as-date thing. It did seem a little strange at first, but I've gotten used to it now. And I do value personal grooming." If we didn't have company I might have gone in for an eyebrow waggle, but as it was, I just smiled.

He smiled back. "Thanks for entertaining the idea."

Topics moved away from Claris's dating deficiencies and toward other things. Yolanda didn't talk much, but clearly Diego and June had known each other for some time, and looped me into their various conversations—politics, art, celebrity gossip. Our manicures finished at the same time and while it wasn't something I did frequently, it was nice having a professional shape and file my nails, push back the cuticles, do all those…small touches that made my hands appear somehow more capable.

"Do you think perception leads to ability?" I asked as we entered the kitchen after saying goodbye to our nail technicians. "I was thinking about how my nails look neater and thus I perceive my hands differently."

"I'm a fashion designer—I think perception is, or at least can be, important. Maybe it doesn't lead directly to ability, but there's a connection there or humans wouldn't bother trying to influence perception. I think there are studies and things that prove it. Here, please sit. I got a sushi platter for lunch, so fingers crossed it's good."

"Sounds delicious."

"I hope so. I almost went with sandwiches, but that wasn't quite the vibe I was going for, and then I became slightly obsessed with finding fancy sandwiches, which is not how anyone should spend their time."

I grinned. "What, Subway wasn't good enough for you?"

He put a hand over his heart. "I *love* Subway. The artificial fluffiness of the bread is everything. Like on some level I know it's probably made with horrible preservatives and it's what people will be eating twenty years after aliens invade and we're all living in bunkers, but I don't care, it's delicious."

"Same. Totally the same." I waited for him to come back to the peninsula and take the barstool beside me before asking about the evening. "It sounded very top secret when we were on the phone."

"That would be much more exciting. This will be Claris, her assistant, and me sitting around with notebooks and they'll both have laptops and spreadsheets will be created, and probably conditional formatting will be involved and—" He shuddered. "But all that aside, the project is a really good one. It's called Gentlemen's Fashion Week, which is meant to be a nongendered approach to a certain aesthetic, including designers from all backgrounds."

I raised my eyebrow. "Meant to be." Though honestly, focusing was a challenge since watching Diego eat sushi was apparently all-consuming. It was just in the way he moved, the ease of it. The angle of his wrist, the way his fingers held chopsticks, how he balanced them as he picked up a piece, delicately dipped it in soy sauce, then brought it to his... I should not be staring at the man's lips. Probably.

"In retrospect, calling it 'Gentlemen's' might have been a misstep. This significantly more influential designer came up with the idea because there aren't that many menswear-focused events and asked me to help him, uh, get the show up and running. I gathered together some other designers on the local scene who I liked and thought had shared values. We wanted to focus on that kind of dapper, waistcoats-and-neckcloths style, and give people who weren't normally invited into that space a starring role."

"That seems positive?"

"It does. It did. But then the guy who'd originally had the idea backed out and he was the 'big name,' if you will, so now the whole thing kind of hinges on...well, me." He clicked his chopsticks together a few times, as if fidgeting. "And I'm not sure sticking with 'Gentlemen' in the name was the best decision. For the people who understand our intention, it's wonderful. One of my designers called it empowering, to be able to own the word 'gentlemen' in the sense of that style. That's what I was hoping for—empowering. But the wider world..."

"Doesn't get it?"

"Some don't get it, which is a problem I can address. But others...actively misinterpret it in a damaging way."

I grimaced. "That's disappointing. Is it a matter of changing the name? The messaging?"

"You and Claris think alike, very focused on fixing the problem, which I appreciate. I get mired down in like... I should have seen this coming, I should have prevented it, how foolish I was to think people would understand, I'll let everyone down, I can't possibly manage this, no one even knows who I am, it will all fail and it'll be my fault, blah blah blah."

"Not that there isn't a place for processing all that," I said. "But they're two different conversations. To be clear, I'm open to processing, but I'm still trying to get a handle on the basics."

"Thank you, Mason. For saying that. I mean, for treating feelings as if they are equally important." He swallowed. "Well, you know Claris. It's not that she doesn't realize feelings are important, it's just that she doesn't have much patience for them when there are things to fix."

Oh, awkward. I was there as his date. But I was only his date because I was her friend. "I get that temptation for sure. Fixing stuff seems so much more satisfying. But I think sometimes it's easier to see the solutions once you've processed the emotions."

"That's a good way of looking at it. Claris and I process so differently I forget there's room for things that can't go on a to-do list or a Gantt chart."

Wary of treading into dangerous waters, I made my tone lighter. "I must admit, I do love a Gantt chart."

"Why sir." He fluttered his eyelashes. "Are you coming on to me?"

"Talking about Gantt charts really turns me on. I hope that doesn't bother you."

He laughed. "You're so damn clever. Thank you, truly, for fitting me in this afternoon. It's been lovely."

"I agree."

We finished our lunch and decided to have a cup of tea before I left. He was just beginning to pour it when footsteps approached from the far side of the kitchen. "Do you want tea?" he called.

Claris entered, looking as good as always, a skirt flowing around her ankles and a loose tank over it, her hair attractively tousled. "No thank you, darling, but take your time. I just got a text from Perri telling me our strategy session's been rescheduled for next week." She kissed my cheek. "Mason, I'm so glad you're here! And your nails look lovely."

It seemed like a playful dig at the date, if it was a dig at all, so I fanned out my fingers for her perusal. "Thank you. I should get that done more often, I feel extra groomed."

"It's always good to treat yourself." She inclined her head.

"I ribbed him mercilessly about it, but the truth is one finds out the make of one's partner in moments like this, don't you think?"

Before I had time to say—or *think*—anything about it, she'd moved to Diego's side. "My love, let's order something in tonight. Mason can stay, we can have a fun evening together, and then I think I'll go out. May as well get all of our recreation in now, before the show really ramps up." A pause with a significant glance across at me. "Perhaps the two of you would like to…stay in?"

It was one of those mutual-glance-mutual-blush-mutual-look-away moments, the kind you see in movies that make you feel vicariously embarrassed. "Oh. I mean." He pushed my tea over to me. "Only if you want to."

"I can stay for dinner," I said.

Claris opened her mouth and Diego plastered his hand over it. "Ignore her. Not everyone wants to immediately have sex with each other."

She said something that sounded like "But why not?" and I laughed.

Diego bit down on what clearly wanted to be a smile and unhanded her. "Go away, you. We don't need a matchmaker."

"Clearly you *did*, but all right. You two figure out dinner and let me know when it arrives!" She kissed the air at each of us and swept off to the rest of the house.

"God, sorry. Or maybe I'm not sorry. I'm definitely not sorry Claris played matchmaker, but I am kind of sorry she won't back off now. Except when it's helpful. The trouble is knowing when it will be helpful versus when it just feels kind of overbearing."

I nodded. "It takes a lot of effort to sustain annoyance at Claris. She always makes me laugh before I can really figure out how to tell her how rotten she's being."

"But is she being rotten right now? That's the relevant question."

"I think she can be forgiven this one time."

"Well, if you say so, then that's what we shall do. I officially forgive my wife for trying to pressure you into having sex with me."

I raised my eyebrows. "Is *that* what was happening there? I don't think anyone's ever pressured me to have sex with their husband before."

He flushed like a schoolboy. "Just hearing you say it, *sex*, does something to me."

"Sex," I said. "Sex, sex, sex."

"Oh my. My good chap, I cannot begin to express my emotions upon this occasion."

"The occasion of me saying the word *sex*?"

This time he hit my arm. "Sir! I insist you stop using that language around me this instant! You will offend my tender sensitivities!"

"My gravest and most sincere apologies." I pulled his hand to me and bowed over it, holding his gaze as I did so.

He flushed, if possible, even darker. "I…we…oh god. Um. We. Food. Order."

What was I doing? I let go of his hand and sat back on my stool. "I got carried away, sorry."

"No, no, it was great! Don't apologize! Plus, we should definitely blame Claris."

"Speaking of—what will she want for dinner?"

"Anything. The woman has an appetite for any food you put in front of her. Won't cook it, but loves eating. How do you feel about Ethiopian food?"

"Excellent."

"Good! We have a favorite place. Let me find the menu."

We pored over the various dishes like children given leave

to go to their favorite candy store and buy whatever they liked. It was fun. Talking to Diego, standing next to him at the counter, our heads together, our freshly manicured fingernails drawing invisible lines under this dish or that, light glittering off his holographic flakes.

Chapter Eight

Once a month I go to church with my mom. It's our tradition, ever since I went to college, and I very rarely miss a church date. It wasn't the church we went to when I was a kid; she found a more friendly church after the youth minister took her aside when I came out to let her know that he couldn't have me around the other teenagers anymore because I might "corrupt them with sin." For two weeks she muttered darkly about how ridiculous the idea of me corrupting anyone was, almost to the point where I took offense.

I was fifteen. I kind of *wanted* to be at least a little bit corrupting. I definitely didn't want to come off as some kind of naive innocent. In actual fact I wasn't exactly Casanova back then, though I dated with the same eagerness and awkwardness of any other pansexual teenager trying to figure things out.

After the youth minister thing we'd gone to a different church, a more progressive one, and it took a long time to feel like home. She'd abandoned her whole church life, which was a big part of her world, because some jackass was a homophobe. And also, yes, the church as a thing was homophobic. But still, I'd felt pretty guilty about it until she found her place at the new church.

I think part of the reason I kept going is because she did it for me. I felt tied to the people who'd given us that feeling of home again so I drove out once a month and picked her up and off we'd go to church. It was almost always just the two of us, but this time Declan was coming along because he and Mom had a cooking date afterward.

Dec looked good in his Sunday best and Mom enjoyed having two escorts. She called him "my paler son" when she introduced him to people and he loved being able to have a mom-like relationship with someone. His own parents were, y'know, not the worst, but not close. They were extremely neutral as figures. Always really nice to me, but I'd never call them "Mom" and "Dad" the way Dec had been calling my mom "Mom" since the third time he met her.

Usually I loved their close relationship. Not always.

"So Mom, did he tell you about his date?"

I made a Quite Displeased face at him, though it was hard to take him seriously with raspberry jam spackling his shirt and some kind of creamy filling on his fingers.

My mom, who'd been doing some mid-bake washing up, turned to eye me over her shoulder. "Did you have the kind of date you should have told me about? What's all this?"

"Nothing. I mean. No." Never say *nothing* to my mother, it only piques her interest more. "We got our nails done, that's all."

Dec leaned toward me but facing her, like he'd forgotten he was in person and was trying to get his head in the frame. "*And* they had dinner! He's the most interesting guy, he's a fashion designer! Isn't that cool?"

I shoved him. "Would you go knead something and get out of my business?"

"Um, lemme think." He tilted his head to the side in an exaggerated thinking pose. "Nope. I'm good."

"You're an ass."

"Boys," Mom said. "You, Declan, go back to work, we

need to get that chilling so it'll set before you leave. And you—what date?"

"It was casual," I said. "Manicures. Dinner in his kitchen. Pleasant conversation. That's all it was."

She narrowed her eyes. "Really."

"Yes. Really. Plus, he's married. So there."

I knew that would get her. Her expression snapped shut. "You did *what*?"

"Oh my god!" Dec obviously couldn't help intervening. "It's so not like that, his wife set them up! Mase's friend Claris is in an open relationship where she and her husband can date people other than each other and she thought that he and Mase would get along, and they totally did, so everybody wins." He elbowed me, leaving a flour splotch on my shirt. "Don't make it sound seedy!"

"All right, fine, it wasn't *seedy*." I get more emphatic when Dec's around. "But he is married, so it probably can't work out. I'm just saying, no matter how nice he was or how well it went, that's a pretty hard limit."

Mom was looking at me in a way I didn't like. Almost as if she were…analyzing my words and facial expression and running them through some kind of database in her head to see what I was actually saying.

Or, okay, that was pretty elaborate. Maybe I only felt that way because I…wasn't saying some important things. Like how much I'd liked talking to Diego. Or how possible it had felt to do more of that when we were sitting together and his hair was falling across his face in a way that made me want to push it back behind his ear. Definitely wasn't saying *that* to my mother.

"It went well, then?" she asked, still Terminator-eyeing me.

"I mean. Yeah. He's pretty cool. Which makes sense be-cause Claris is cool."

"Hmm." My mom's *hmm* game is on point. Her *hmm* can mean anything from *there's no way I'm buying that and you darn well know it* to *I've already moved on in my head and am now planning my to-do list for tomorrow.* Somehow in this case I was pretty sure it wasn't the second one.

"I think it went really well and the next date will go even better if anyone wants my opinion," Dec said as he delivered the pan of... I had no clue, just that they were making something they'd seen on the *Great British Baking Show*...into the fridge.

"No one wants your opinion," I told him. "Plus, I am *dating* Tim."

Dec shrugged. "Since you've never introduced us, I don't even know if Tim is real. Diego's real because he has a website."

"Oh my god, Tim is obviously real! And you googled Diego? What is *wrong* with you?"

"I wanted to see the clothes he designed." He turned to my mom. "And they're *fabulous*, very cute, but not nutty. Like they're classy but you can imagine actually wearing them, not just seeing them on a runway."

"Hmm," Mom repeated, still looking at me.

"I'm gonna go bag weeds," I mumbled and made my escape.

This was how I'd pictured our future when I'd thought we were getting married: us going to church with Mom, coming back to the house to drop her off. Me doing yard maintenance or fixing stuff while Dec baked with her in the kitchen. Not in a heteronormative way, but because he's always loved baking and I don't, so I'd just find other things to do. I could hear their laughter occasionally and it made me smile to myself. Mom had waited a long time to officially forgive Dec for breaking my heart, but it was only the fact that we hadn't gotten married that made this kind of future possible at all. If we had, we'd have made each other super miserable.

Granted, there were about a thousand better ways to tell a guy you don't want to marry him and think it's a bad idea than leaving him at the damn altar. Ask me how I know. But still, ultimately that really awful experience got us here, and here was a good place. The sun was warm but not too hot, the work was physical and satisfying, and I could smell good things coming from the kitchen window.

It was a little hard to imagine where Tim would fit into a scene like this. Would he be stiff and awkward with my mom? Not that he was awkward in general, but he could come off a little stiff before you got to know him. It was just that he was serious, that's all. Obviously I couldn't bring Declan with us if I was taking Tim to church. I didn't know why I knew that, but I did. The picture wouldn't resolve in my head. Tim's parents were still married, and it sounded like he genuinely liked them, in a sort of formal way. It didn't seem like he'd done a lot of baking elaborate TV show pastries with them, in any case. Which wasn't a prerequisite for good in-law behavior, of course. My dad had left us when I was a baby, so it had always been Mom and me. She'd never had a serious boyfriend, which meant we'd always just relied on each other. She must have been lonely at times, though she seemed happy enough now. But what about in ten years? Or twenty? I didn't want to be alone. When I was Mom's age, I wanted to wake up next to someone. I wanted that security.

Which I could never have with Diego, I reminded myself. How would that even work if your partner had more than one partner? Did you switch off days or something? If church fell on my day with him, would he come with me to Mom's? Actually, Diego would probably have fun doing stuff around the house. Something about him made it easier to imagine him covered in flour than it was to imagine him standing on a stage showing off his designs. Which…was that even a thing fashion designers did? I had no idea, since a hundred percent of my knowledge about fashion design came from *Project Runway.*

Not that this was a real possibility. Tim was the guy I'd been dating for months. Get it straight, brain. If there was a future with anyone, it was him. Not my new, yes, delightful, but also, yes, married friend.

Mom came out to find me later, after they'd chilled and glazed their creation, ostensibly to let me know dessert was ready and the coffee was brewed. Not that she kept the pretense up for long. "Declan doesn't usually tell me when you've been out with people."

"Oh yeah?" I kept working at clearing a couple of years' worth of leaf and weed debris, packaging it up for one of her friends to use as mulch. Since there was bound to be leftovers, Mom had some plans for what she might want to grow if she ended up making the time to garden. With my mom it was always that she was *making* time. She'd jump down your throat if you told her you didn't have time for something because if there are people in the world who can become brain surgeons and astrophysicists, you can surely get your butt to the gym.

"Every now and then, if he thinks it's gone well, he might mention it. But this is different."

"It's really not." Except…but no. I couldn't let it be different. Not in the way she meant.

"Okay, son. If you say so." Code for *we both know you're lying, but I'll let it pass this time.* "Thank you for doing all that, I can finally get Marybeth off my back. 'I could really use some mulch,' she says to someone else while I'm standing right there. 'Oh, mulching is so good for the soil!' Like she's a walking lesson in how to grow plants."

I smirked up at her. "Go on, you're jealous of Marybeth and her garden."

She swatted at me. "You know that's not true. What's the point in being jealous of a woman who thinks you should be jealous of her? But I will say I wouldn't mind growing some greens back here. They're so much better when they haven't been sitting in a produce section for days."

"If we get all this cleared maybe we can put in some raised beds or something." I didn't know how to put in a raised bed, but it was one of those things I said, in my role as Man of the House. I could google it. Pick up some lumber and nails, hunt down a hammer. How hard could it be?

This time I got a pat on the shoulder. "Well, I don't know about all that. We'll see. Come on inside before the coffee gets cold."

I could have pointed out that she had a thermal insulated carafe and it wouldn't. But when your mom invites you in to have coffee and cake after you've been bagging up mulch for an hour, why say no? "I'll be right in."

Chapter Nine

I was getting ready for an actual date with the man I was actually dating when the first text came in.

Claris: *Darling, I have a job for you, it's unpaid, you'll be brilliant at it.*

The second was from Diego: *Whatever Claris is saying, ignore her.*

Claris: *Diego is a very clever man in many ways, but trust me, this is my area, and you're perfect.*

Diego: *Seriously, whatever you do, do NOT ask her what she's talking about. Pretend you can't hear her.*

Diego (again): *I mean see her. Her texts. Pretend you can't see them.*

Claris: *Don't you want to hear my idea?*

I couldn't help but smile down at my phone. I opened a thread, added both of them, and sent, *Are you two in the same room right now?*

Claris: *Yes, but I'm quicker with my fingers :)*

Diego: *Don't listen to her!*

I was still typing a response when my phone lit up with a call. Claris, of course. I answered, already grinning. "Yes?"

"Darling," she purred into my ear.

"Are you trying to seduce me, Mrs. Robinson?"

She gasped. "Uncalled for! I am barely older than you are. In any case." She resumed her seductive purr. "I have had the most *brilliant* idea."

"Don't let her pressure you into anything!" Diego called from the background.

A fumble with the phone and then I was on speaker. Claris continued, her tone teasing, and I could tell she was addressing Diego. "As if I'd have to stoop to pressure, silly boy. Mason, my dear, wouldn't you just love an opportunity to take part in a truly inspiring revolutionary movement in fashion?"

Diego's voice moved closer. "To be clear, I agree you'd be really good, it's just—"

"Hush, husband, you're acting like it would be a burden, and it would very much be a privilege."

I was still smiling. "If you guys are trying to recruit me to join your espionage organization, you're really not doing a great job. You haven't even told me about all the great parties I'll need to infiltrate and microchips I'll need to steal."

Diego groaned. "It's TikTok. This is all TikTok's fault."

"Okay, that's…definitely not where I thought you were going. I have no idea how to infiltrate TikTok."

Claris laughed. "I have the utmost faith in your ability to adapt. Plus, it's supporting an excellent cause."

"Which is?"

"All proceeds are going to the NAACP Legal Defense Fund."

"Oh. It really is a good cause. But proceeds for what?"

"I want you for Gentlemen's Fashion Week social media, darling. I have determined that you're the man for the job."

Which was also not what I'd been expecting. Count on these two to be full of surprises. "And what does that…mean, exactly?"

"Mainly Instagram and Twitter, and, as Diego says, we're trying out TikTok, at which you would be fantastic."

I considered TikTok a younger queer's game, but that's not to say I hadn't been tempted. "What exactly are you looking for in terms of content?"

"Whatever you want to post. We're going with hashtag-gents-fashion-week, though if you can think of anything shorter, that would be better. These character limits are so challenging to work with, you know."

I nodded, like this was a thing I'd given serious thought to (which I hadn't) and like they could see me (which they couldn't). "I…could learn how to TikTok."

Diego moved closer again. "Are you sure you want to do this? You don't have to decide right this second. I know Claris makes it seem like you don't have a choice, but I promise you do."

Which I knew, though I appreciated the pause. But I actually loved Instagram, and my Reels game was fierce. That skillset should transfer over to TikTok. Probably. "No, I'm into it. I like the brief. So how does this work?"

"Fantastic!" Claris said. "That's social media taken care of. I'll add you to the company Slack, Mason. At your personal email, obviously. That way you can check your calendar and see which bits of things you can attend in order to take photos. And videos, I suppose? Not my area. I'll also introduce you to Perri, my assistant, and she'll get you all the logins and whatever else it is you'll need. So glad we could take care of this today, my dears. Now I'm off to get ready for my evening, but I'll leave you two alone."

"Bye, Claris," I said. "I can't decide if I should thank you or not."

"You are *so* welcome." A kiss noise that might have been directed at me, but also might have been an actual kiss for Diego. "Goodbye!"

A few seconds later: "Um. We're alone now. I mean. Actually, I'll take you off speaker." Fumbling. Breathing. "Hi."

I couldn't help the smile on my face. "Hi."

"So I…had an idea. A way to redeem myself for our last date."

"I reject the premise that our date requires redemption, but I'm up for hearing your idea."

Another breath sound. "God, I really enjoy you. Er, anyway, so, do you want to come over? For a way better date this time? Not today! I mean, I have to get ready for it. Not that I'm planning to greet you at the door in a sexy new negligee or something, I am definitely not, but I have some prep work to do first. So maybe tomorrow?"

Still smiling. The man just made my face do that. "I'm free tomorrow."

"Good! Excellent! Ahem. I look forward to seeing you, sir. Would noon suit?"

"Noon suits me very well," I said formally.

"Quite good, quite good. I suppose I will…see you tomorrow."

"Indeed you will."

"Excellent."

"Fantastic."

"I will…" He paused. "I will take my leave, then."

"That does make sense."

"All right."

"Quite."

Another pause. "I have no idea how to get out of this loop of pretending to be historically British."

I laughed. "I think we just have to hang up."

"I do have things to do. To get ready for tomorrow."

And technically I had things to do to get ready for tonight, though going to lunch at Diego's tomorrow felt so much more real than going out to dinner with Tim tonight. "Okay, I'm going to do it. I'm going to hang up. Because both of us have things to do. And that's the responsible move."

"Yes. You're very responsible, Mason. It's something I admire about you. Such responsibleness."

"Are you trolling me?"

This time he laughed. "We have to get off the phone. If for no other reason than Claris is going to want it back and I should probably plug it in since it's at twenty percent."

"Fine. For Claris, then."

"For Claris. I'll see you tomorrow, kind sir."

"I anticipate it with great impatience," I said, and since I didn't think I could top that, I forced myself to hang up.

But it took at least ten minutes for me to stop smiling and remember that I had to get ready to go out with Tim.

We met up at a wine bar about halfway between our apartments. Tim lived in a collaborative household in Berkeley full of professionals saving for down payments and building up their credit to take advantage of the lowest-interest-rate home loans. Which I thought was clever, but also made me slightly embarrassed by my "one bedroom because I was getting married then I didn't but stupidly kept living in a place I couldn't really afford until years later" housing situation. Not that he seemed bothered by it, and anyway, sex in my one bedroom was preferable to sex in his rented room in a shared house.

"Hey, you," Tim said, kissing my cheek. "I feel like we haven't seen each other in forever."

"Same." It had been over a month. I didn't want him to know I knew exactly how long, so I didn't mention it. And then we stood there with the slightest bit of awkwardness, as if we didn't remember how to talk to each other.

"I've put my name in for—"

The door opened and a server stuck her head out. "Weston?"

He offered a relieved smile. "That's us."

I followed him inside, thinking about Diego's oddly attractive way of performing chivalry and how I'd never known how much I enjoyed being escorted places until that moment he ushered me into the coffee shop. Of course, that was a very minor thing, and Tim would have no way of knowing it since even I was just figuring it out. Plus, it isn't like I escorted *him* anywhere. We didn't have that kind of dynamic.

"How's work been?" he asked as we settled in and began looking at our menus.

"The usual. Customers, accounts, sales, promotions. And you?"

He smiled. Tim was one of those very healthy blond men who look like they should be modeling toothpaste or something, perfect white teeth all in a row, easy smile. "The usual. Expectant parents, babies, health care. But my sister has gotten a job for next fall at Kansas State, so that should be interesting."

"Super interesting. I didn't know she was looking to move."

"Not so much looking to move as she is looking for stability, which is hard to get in academia until you have tenure. She told me she was thinking about applying places, but I didn't realize it had progressed this far. I don't envy the move, though..."

We kept talking, and all of it was fine. Good, even. I did *like* Tim. A lot, really. He was thoughtful about the world, open to hearing about other people's experiences, smart but not a bulldozer with it. Every other time we'd been together I'd spent a fair amount of it reflecting that he was basically everything I'd been looking for in a partner since always. He was very controlled in the way he moved, which made sense, since his body had a serious job to do when he was called upon to deliver a baby. Even the way he held a wineglass seemed very deliberate. You'd have to be, to get through med school, and residencies, and all the other details that went into becoming a doctor. I found all that so attractive: the planning, the intentionality of it, the follow-through. Watching him talk at dinner, I realized that all of those qualities were also the things that made it difficult to picture incorporating him into the parts of my life that I ultimately wanted to share with people. Tim wasn't inflexible—quite the opposite, in fact *non-creepy wink*—but his innate sense of certainty suddenly seemed almost...not limited exactly. But not expansive either.

What was I thinking? Did I really want to go back to dating people whose future planning was summed up with "Hey, should we smoke a joint after this?" Because no. Of course I didn't.

So why was I distracted when I should have been paying attention to whatever Tim was talking about right now?

"But I know you're not as addicted to ridiculous reality shows as I am," he said, smiling a bit ruefully. "How have you been spending your off-hours?"

I'd had no idea he was addicted to ridiculous reality shows. How had I not known that? Possibly because we'd gone out to dinner, and to movies, and had sex in my bed—all of the normal date things—but we hadn't actually spent that kind of time together.

"Oh, working on this world in 7 *Days to Die* that I've been building with my friend Oscar for ages. We've basically got half of Elsa's ice palace done at this point."

"Is that like *Minecraft*? I remember when everyone was playing *Minecraft* all the time."

"Sort of," I said. "There are some differences, but the building is similar. Hey, what are you thinking about for dessert? That fresh fruit thing looked pretty good."

"I'm considering that, but the indulgent part of me wants the cheesecake."

"You should indulge yourself." I felt weirdly caught-out when he looked over at me, meeting my eyes.

"If you think so, then that's what I will get." His gaze shifted from mine and he gestured for a server.

And in its absence I felt relief. Oh god. What was *wrong* with me all of a sudden?

We didn't go back to my place after. He had a morning breakfast meeting and honestly? I was kind of relieved about that as well. My first thought when he told me was, *Oh, good. I want to be rested before my date with Diego*, which seemed lousy. But…maybe it wasn't. I was allowed to casually date two people. Even on sequential days. Wasn't I?

I sent Dec a text when I got to my car and asked him if I was being the bad kind of slutty.

Dec: *There's no such thing. As you already know. What's the real issue?*

It was such a good question. And it was one to which I had no answer.

Chapter Ten

"Um." I was standing at Diego's backyard gate. He'd left a note on the front door directing me to the side of the house. There I found a sign that read *Please ring bell for service*. With a bell. On a string. Slowly, like this was the mundane, unthreatening lead-in to a jump scare, I reached out and took hold of it.

It made a sound. Because: bell.

Ahem. Footsteps approached, which was good, because Diego and Claris lived in the suburbs and I wasn't big into the idea of being a Black man loitering outside a nice suburban home, not even in the East Bay.

"Hey," he said as he pulled the gate inward. "Um. So. Welcome to my garden."

"See, I really want to make that dirty—ohh. Damn." It was like stepping into an oasis, all lush and green and overgrown with trailing vines. "Oh my god," I murmured, taking it all in. A trellis curved overhead and little white flowers dotted amidst the leaves.

"You like it?" His smile was the brand of justifiable smugness that doesn't actually make you want to punch someone. The garden was magnificent, and he damn well knew it.

"You did this?"

"For real." He led me down the path (large stepping-stones in a bed of soft-looking moss) and into the larger yard, which exceeded expectations, seeming to roll out in front of me in layers of texture and color. "When we first bought the house we were trying to be grown-ups, so I hired someone to come in and do the yards. And to be fair, she did a great job. The front is still exactly as she designed it. But the back had been this sort of...neat, acceptable backyard. Here's the seating area around the fire pit, here's the barbecue. Fountain in the corner making just the right volume of trickling water noises."

I raised my eyebrows. "Sounds nice."

"It was! It was...nice. Great for entertaining, which we do, though mostly we don't leave the deck."

The deck, which ran half the length of the house and was draped with more vines, was pretty badass. "I could spend an entire day on this deck, to be fair."

"I *have* done that, and it's worth every moment. But I wanted something more. I wanted...a secret garden, a place to get lost in. A rational man would have called his designer, who knew what she was doing, and explained what he needed."

"Let me guess: you were not that rational man."

"I was a fool. Come on." He took my hand as easily as if we were children, just as he had at the gallery, pulling me deeper into the garden through some combination of enthusiasm and tugging. "I thought, you know, *I'm* a designer, right? I have an artistic eye, I know what I want. I can design a yard just as well as the next person!"

I laughed. Both because it felt appropriate to the story and also because being pulled through curving pathways under a never-ending canopy of vines was delightful. "How'd that work out for you?"

"Everything died. Literally everything I planted died. If I'd planted a garden merely to watch it die I could not have done a better job. And this is after I spent maybe four days wandering around nurseries, buying, and planting. Oh, and I ordered a few raised bed kits online and put those together, which you can never tell anyone took me nine hours and two calls to customer service. And all of it died, Mason. I waited for a couple of weeks thinking maybe the roots were in shock or something and the plants would perk up, but no. Eventually Claris sat me down and told me it was time to have a ceremonial bonfire, pull everything out again, and start fresh."

I felt a slight pang. Yeah, that was a good partner move. I admired it. Sometimes the people you love can't see a thing for themselves so you nudge them in that direction. And/or light things on fire. Of course Claris would be just that kind of partner.

"So then I called the designer I'd worked with before—apologetically—and asked her what I'd done wrong. Which turned out to be almost everything. The soil wasn't right for this, the drainage wasn't right for that. I'd tried to plant things where they could get the sun they needed, but I hadn't really taken into consideration the different exposures around the yard. And I hadn't provided the shade fully half my plants apparently required—when they say 'full sun' they mean 'a lot of sun,' not 'unrelenting sun.' Which was a nuance I hadn't understood before."

"Complicated stuff," I said.

"You have no idea. Or maybe you have some idea. We haven't talked about gardening."

"No idea, can confirm. My mother aspires to having a garden, but we haven't quite gotten there yet. I can bag up mulch like you wouldn't believe, though."

"Oooh, you can? Wait, do you have a lead on a mulch supplier? Because we've been using this really wonderful nursery but everyone in California has discovered them and now it's impossible to get enough mulch for all my beds." He blushed. "I can't believe I'm this guy right now, whining about organic mulch scarcity. And I promised myself that after Manicure-gate I'd be the perfect date."

I shook my head and brushed a little flower off his shirt. He was in dark green, a casual V-neck tee that hugged his biceps and the curve of his belly. He looked fucking *edible*. "Diego, you've just invited me into your secret garden." I paused just long enough for both of us to imagine a few different meanings for that line. "And oh my god, what am I smelling? It's amazing."

He beamed. "Isn't it? That's the honeysuckle, which is blooming a little early this year. And of course the whole place looks different-slash-better when more things are flowering. Are you sure it's okay? The date, I mean?"

"More than sure."

He took a deep breath. "Okay. Just. Tell me if it…stops being okay." He turned and began to walk along the path again.

I followed his steps and inhaled as much of the honeysuckle scent as I could, trying to store it in my memory. "Why wouldn't it be okay? This is gorgeous. I can't believe you—" I broke off as he stepped aside and revealed the little corner we'd come to, a small clearing of soft moss with a blanket over it and a legit picnic basket. "Scratch that, it's a *fantastic* date. Are we having a picnic?"

"I couldn't decide if that was the most preposterous date idea ever, or if it was actually genius. I'm hoping for genius?"

"My good sir," I said formally, "I can only commend your grasp of the perilous second date."

"I rather think of this as our *fourth* date, if I'm being honest."

Gallery, coffee, manicures… "In that case, I can only commend your grasp of the perilous *fourth* date."

He pressed my hands between his. "I am delighted you think so. Just *delighted*."

And then we were two men, standing under a canopy of flowers, holding hands. My heart beat faster and I was aware of everything—a bee's drone nearby, the sweetness of the flowers, dappled sunlight and shadows on the blanket he'd laid out, a slight shift in air currents against my skin.

And Diego. The heat of his palms, the curve of his lips, the way his hair brushed the top of his eyebrows before feathering longer around his face.

I wanted to kiss him. Almost desperately. We were buffeted by warm air and intoxicating honeysuckle and I really wanted to lean forward and… "Are we allowed to kiss?" I said softly.

"Definitely and completely and yes, please. Please, Mason. Kiss me."

So I did. Gently, not allowing my feelings of need (or maybe greed) to take over, pressing my lips against his and keeping the rest of me out of it. You'd think that would end up being a very chaste kiss, but it wasn't. We kissed and after a moment he leaned his face against mine. I expected him to speak, even wondered what he'd say.

Instead we just stood there, in dappled sunlight, our breaths whispering against each other's skin.

He squeezed my hands. "That was so lovely. Thank you."

I didn't think I'd ever been thanked for a kiss before. If I had been, it didn't feel like this. "My pleasure."

We moved apart but took our seats side by side, close enough to brush knees. "I wasn't exactly sure what was called for, so I just pulled a variety of things together. Actually, I *bought* a variety of things. But I did put them in nicer bowls and plates because I wanted our picnic to be fancy."

Cut fruits and vegetables and hummus. Meats and cheeses to roll up together. A bottle of champagne and two glasses, which fit into the lid of the picnic basket. "It's the basket that seals it," I said. "We can't be more than thirty feet from your back door, but having a picnic basket makes all the difference."

"We're actually closer than that, but my magnificent land-scape design has fooled you into thinking this is a bigger space than it is." He waggled his eyebrows, though the move didn't quite mask the vulnerability still lingering in his eyes. "I'm pretty magnificent, FYI."

"No argument here." We picked at different foods for a while, talking about nothing in particular. There was this... soft-around-the-edges sweetness to it after that kiss. Like we'd wandered into fairyland and nothing in the world existed except us, sitting on this bed of moss, sharing food and conversation.

And champagne.

"The thing is," Diego said as if continuing a discussion we hadn't actually been having, "you kind of need champagne for a picnic. Even though I was a little worried it might be too much too soon." His eyes found mine. "Is it? Too much too soon?"

Maybe? I wasn't sure. "I don't know what else you bring on a picnic. Beer's a little rough. Wine seems like you wanted to bring champagne but wimped out. Cocktails would work if they weren't too elaborate, but for dinner, not lunch."

"Exactly the issue. Wine coolers are absurd. Soda seems childlike, though maybe a Sprite-and-grapefruit-juice sort of mocktail would work. And in any case..." He seemed to hesitate. "I don't know. I wanted to get champagne. You dodged the question, don't think I didn't notice: is it too much?"

Sometimes I think I've made a habit of dating self-absorbed people so I would never have to answer questions like that one, in one of those self-protective self-sabotage moves that end up being frustrating even as it does exactly what it's meant to do.

I'd rarely been asked questions like *Is this too much?* And no one had ever asked me after I deflected the first time.

"Too much is…hard to gauge. Was kissing too much?"

"Not at all. Kissing was brilliant. Kissing *you* was brilliant."

It's just never a bad thing to hear, that someone likes kissing you. "I think the champagne had the potential to be too much, but isn't. If that makes sense."

"Yes. It does. And good." He reached for the bottle and settled it between his legs to uncork it.

And boy, I should not have been thinking of our picnic area as a *bed* because now I was thinking about a soft bed, and dappled sunlight, and champagne, and kissing, and…

"Ha. Got it. I messed up opening one bottle of champagne ever and I swear every time I touch one I'm paranoid it's going to happen again. Here." He handed me a glass and lifted his own. "To kissing."

"And picnics," I added, toasting.

"Kissing and picnics could be my whole life and I would not complain."

"Wouldn't you miss your work? I guess I figured it wasn't like a regular job and you'd want to do it even if you didn't have to."

He smiled, looking even more kissable. That or the bubbly was already going to my head. "Oh, I'd never stop designing. The feeling of it, the high when I'm stepping back in the final stages of creating a new design and it's looking just how I pictured it—god, it's a rush. There's nothing else like it. And I love dressing models, seeing clothing come to life, watching people get a taste of it for the first time."

It was impossible not to be drawn in by Diego when he was talking about his work. I leaned back on one arm and stretched my legs, sort of tucking them behind him. "Tell me more?"

"Are you sure? I don't want to bore you."

"I wouldn't ask if I was bored."

"Okay. But stop me if I forget to breathe. Or the sun goes down. Whichever comes first." He settled back against my legs a bit, not leaning, but occupying the same space. "I think maybe it goes back to when I was a kid. This…sense that art was the only way out of my head. I didn't have a super-troubled childhood or anything, probably about the same as most people, but I wanted to…do something. Be something. In a way my parents didn't really understand. When I went to college and studied design they thought I was throwing away my education, which to them was this magical gift."

"They didn't go to college?"

"My dad went to night school, and my mom took community college classes here and there, but neither of them went away to school the way I did. Which is exactly what they wanted me to do, but then I didn't major in business or computer programming or law or medicine. None of the things they recognized as having A FUTURE. In capital letters."

I nodded. "I got a degree in business mostly because my mom wanted me to and I'm not so sure it was the best way to go. Don't get me wrong, she didn't force me, or even guilt me into it. I didn't have any better plan. But now I feel locked into this…idea of what success looks like that I didn't fully think through."

"And I lucked into success on a level I couldn't have imagined mostly because I met the right people at the right time. And Claris. She's got a remarkable ability to see the most advantageous angle of any event." He frowned. "That makes her seem opportunistic. Which she isn't. Well, okay, maybe she can be, but not as a rule. She just can cut through emotions and get to the…meat of a particular situation. I *always* get bogged down in emotions."

"That makes sense. At least, it's one of the things that makes her an effective fundraiser. She takes emotion and turns it into action. 'Oh, you want to feel good about yourself by helping the poor? Let me show you how.'"

"Yes! Exactly."

"How did you meet? I don't think she's ever mentioned it." She definitely hadn't, I'd remember.

"Oh, it was an accident, we weren't even supposed to be—" He broke off. "You don't have to ask about us if you don't want to. I won't hide that I'm married or avoid ever mentioning my best friend, who is also my wife, but that doesn't mean we have to talk about her if my marriage... I was going to say 'makes you uncomfortable,' but that feels a little off. It shouldn't make you uncomfortable. And if it does, that's... that might be an issue. For both of us."

I couldn't decide if that felt fair or unfair or reasonable or messed up. I put down the champagne glass and lay back so I could stare up at the trellis above us, the way the vines shifted in the breeze, changing the light. "I'm not sure it makes me uncomfortable. That's not the right word for it. I guess it just feels like I'm the last man on earth who wants to fall in love with one person and hold their hand in public and not even want anyone else." The loneliness of it smacked me in the face and I had to focus on the shifting vines so I wouldn't get more emotional than a second-slash-fourth date really had space for.

But this was Diego and I should have known that he wouldn't leave me stranded out on the vulnerability limb by myself. He settled down beside me, his arm pressed against mine. "That sounds hard. Is that why you wanted to get married so badly?"

"Yes? I think? I mean, everyone was doing it, and we loved each other, and I wanted to be part of this thing that was so much bigger, you know? Bigger than me and Dec, bigger than marriage itself. Finally we *could* get married, and I

wanted that right. I wanted it to be real, and recognized. I...
It seems so dumb, but I wanted people to see us and know
we were together."

"That's not dumb at all. No part of that seems dumb to
me, Mason." He didn't say anything for a long moment. Was
that...a thinking silence? A *you should say more* silence? A *welp,
I guess this is the end of the line* silence? "We almost didn't get
married. Claris argued hard for a civil union because at the
time there was no marriage equality and it felt wrong to...
take advantage of this thing through some fluke of our gen-
ders happening to make us eligible for it. I wore a dress to the
courthouse and she wore a suit."

I looked over. "Did you design it?"

He smiled. "Of course. I designed my dress too."

"Did you not have a ceremony? Or did you do both that
and the courthouse?"

"Actually, we didn't tell anyone. It was pretty spur-of-the-
moment. The timing, not the marrying. You could ask her to
tell you the story, she'll say I'm a bad influence on her. That's
always how she starts, by blaming me."

I turned onto my side. "But you guys are so happy. I mean.
She must be joking when she says that."

His eyes roamed, maybe seeing the trellis, the vines, the tiny
flowers, or maybe he was looking at the blue sky beyond that.
"We are happy, and she's never regretted it, but the thing was
my idea. And then, a few years in, I was also the one who realized that I'm not actually monogamous. I don't think Claris
really blames me for any of it, she's teasing, but sometimes I
blame myself a little."

"But she's...polyamorous too."

"She doesn't think so. Her connections with people aren't
romantic, but she'll go out and seduce someone on a Friday
night just for fun. Where if I went out I'd be looking for a

deep connection." He laughed softly. "I've definitely envied her sometimes. That way seems…less complicated."

It sure did. I propped my head on my arm and reached across his body to pick up my champagne. Maybe I needed a drink, or maybe it was just something to do while I put together this new information. "I didn't realize that. I mean. I assumed. I just figured it was the same for both of you."

"Oh god, no. Claris isn't all that comfortable having feelings for *me*. If she had to contend with being in love with more than one person she'd explode." He pulled my hand to rest the glass on his chest. "It's not always easy to balance everything, but we have so many years of practice now I like to think we're pretty good at it. And I…have had feelings for people in the past, but it's never worked out for longer than a few weeks, maybe a month here or there."

I had no idea if I was allowed to ask questions, but I could feel his breaths, the heat of his fingers still lightly resting on mine. "Why?" My voice was almost a whisper and I wasn't sure if he'd heard it until he answered.

"Who knows? Maybe I'm too much for people, always bouncing from one thing to the other, or doing weird things like pretending to be a spy."

"Hey, I like pretending to be a spy."

"Or dropping into Regency romance banter." His eyes slid to mine. "I'm not sure I'm an easy person to be with. Full disclosure. If being with me was a thing you were still contemplating after hearing how I begged a woman to marry me and then later confessed I had romantic feelings for other people."

I made an *eek* face without meaning to. "That sounds pretty bad. Not gonna lie."

"It was horrible. I never ever cheated on her, to be clear, I just had these feelings I didn't know how to deal with. We went to therapy for years. It saved our relationship, and I mean that in the broadest sense of the word."

"And she forgave you."

"She did."

"So you can see how I'd forgive Dec for leaving me at the altar," I said teasingly, but he didn't smile.

"I think it might be kind of the opposite? In that, no offense to your friend Dec, but what he did seems pretty indefensible to me. I definitely didn't do everything right, but I tried to... be worthy of Claris's trust. Which meant telling her when I was in over my head. And I would have never put her in the position you were in, where you were kind of...expected to move on from what sounds like a pretty awful thing."

"Hey now, it wasn't that bad," I said automatically.

He didn't say anything, but he also didn't look away.

I was the one who looked away. "It wasn't good. Obviously. But it wasn't... It all worked out."

"Sorry. I didn't mean to say all that. It's not my place. But it sounds like what you really want is stability, and whatever that ends up looking like, I want it for you, Mason. I want you to have everything you need." He raised his head off the ground just a little, but it was enough. I lowered mine and kissed him. "It's terrifying, isn't it?" he murmured against my lips. "Falling for someone when you have no idea if they can return it. But I'm willing to risk it if you are. So? Are you with me?"

I swallowed, unprepared for such a direct challenge. "Is this a double-dog dare?"

"No, just a regular dare."

"How do you figure that?"

"Okay, maybe it's a double dare. But I don't think it rises to the level of double-*dog* dare unless you might break a bone."

"Hmm." I pushed myself up to sitting and set the glass aside again. "I accept your double dare, Diego. Mostly because I want to kiss you more. I hope that doesn't make me seem loose."

He smiled up at me, looking so…sun-kissed and golden and glowing. "I've always had a thing for loose people."

"Prove it."

He hooked a hand around my neck and pulled himself up enough to kiss me. I shifted a leg behind his back and couldn't help inhaling the scent of Diego and honeysuckle, my pulse racing.

A risk. Yeah. Not of broken bones, but of broken hearts. I curled my hand around his neck and opened my eyes to find his, clear and sparkling, looking back.

Chapter Eleven

I'd always thought I was a good planner, an organized person. Among my friends I was arguably the biggest planner, though Mia and I had exchanged productivity app high fives more than once over the years. But all that was before I met Claris. Before I started working with her. Or in the case of Gentlemen's Fashion Week, working *for* her.

Not that she'd put it that way. Not at all. She was...not exactly egalitarian, but not dictatorial either. Her plan seemed to be *Surround yourself with highly competent people and then let them get on with it*, and to her credit, it was working. The GFW Slack was hopping and bopping all day long as folks reported in on contacts they'd made and "positions" they'd "cemented," making me feel like there was a bit of the mob about the whole thing.

Claris had laid out very specific task lists and timelines for venues, catering, decorating, lights, tech, load-in, load-out, promotions, volunteers (by section), and a bunch of other things I'd lost sight of because the overwhelm of information was so complete. Six months seemed like a lot of time to me, but when I saw all the things that needed to happen between now and September, I was slightly intimidated by the complicated moving parts.

By contrast my assignment was pretty nebulous, leading even more to the feeling it was a sort of sop to my role in

Diego's (their?) life. "Oh, and everyone, this is Mason. He'll be posting to a few of the social accounts. Always remember to sign your posts!" I wasn't the only one who had the login and passwords, but most of the rest of them were posting as themselves to their personal accounts in order to spread the #gentsfashweek (less clarity, more brevity) hashtag around and boost followers for the official account.

My first opportunity to do my *cough cough* job came about a month later when Claris tagged me to a channel about a "general check-in" at "the studio." Followed by an explanatory email with directions to the place (way out in "is this even still the Bay Area because I'm really not convinced" territory). Apparently they had rented a vacant retail space to be used by the designers. Which seemed like a really cool thing, since I doubted a lot of young, small-scale clothing designers had studios.

When I finally got to the place, I was impressed. It wasn't huge or anything, but it was big enough. In some previous lifetime it might have been a boutique pet store, one of those joints with a lot of stuff that looked pretty but not functional, at least judging by the chipping and fading mural across the front windows of frolicking (but clearly trendy and perfectly groomed) puppies and kittens. Some raggedy-looking folding shades were being used to roughly divide the room in quarters.

"Mason! Glad you could make it!" Claris kissed my cheek. "Let me introduce you to our stars. You've met them digitally, of course, but there's really no substitute for face-to-face, is there?"

As usual, she didn't wait for an answer before continuing, though I was actually grateful for the opportunity to look around. While my first impression had been more "abandoned retail store" than "hotbed of fashion," once we started walking around I could see that each of the designers had a clearly delineated style of their own and their spot in the studio reflected that.

We passed a cluttered table at the front and entered the first designer space, which was awash in different shades of black and gray fabrics, some stiff, some draping, some almost transparent.

"This is Moe! He's the babycakes of the bunch, and he specializes in waistcoats, neckcloths, and original suspenders. Moe, please meet Mason. He'll be doing a lot of our Instagram and TikTok posts."

Which reminded me. I shook hands and exchanged hellos with Moe before pulling out my phone and tweaking the settings to get the highest resolution, still half-listening to their conversation.

"I'm no babycakes, mama." Moe patted his belly. "Testosterone has given me many gifts, including a place to rest my beer."

"It suits you, darling. How's progress coming on the skirt?"

"I'm not made for the skirt life, but Bren said she'd help me out, so hopefully I can get it to make sense. I just think guys look hot in skirts."

"You're preaching to the choir here. Mase, love, what do you think of a man in a skirt?"

"Anyone wearing something they feel good in catches my eye," I said. "Do you mind if I take a few pictures, Moe? I might shoot some video too. I haven't actually figured out what to do with TikTok, but it'll help to have some footage to mess around with."

"Sure! I don't think anything is in, like, hashtag-spoilers state yet, but make sure you only get fragments instead of whole pictures, if that's okay."

It hadn't even occurred to me that fashion shows would have spoilers, but in retrospect it was obvious, and I'd need to edit the shots I'd already taken. Though maybe that could be the whole theme: teasing people with little hints clearly cropped from bigger pictures. "Got it," I told him, and began wandering around his area while Claris caught up with his progress (or lack of progress) since the last time they'd checked in. Could I also tease the designers themselves? I knew there were three who were less well known than Diego, and if we made the designers mysterious they'd be more intriguing to viewers. Especially younger viewers. Hmm.

Claris had a gift for reining people in and I began to think, listening to her, that she was genuinely perfect for Diego. Or perfect for any creative-type person prone to going off on some tangent about mail-order lace and shipping delays and problems with vegetable dyes being used on high-percentage synthetic fabrics. She smoothly guided Moe back onto what-ever track she wanted him to be on (yes, she was sympathetic about the shipping delays, of course, and exactly how was this going to impact his progress and previously set target dead-lines?), never seeming to lose her patience as I might have.

It was admirable. She was admirable.

I caught a picture of her looking contemplatively at some sample Moe was holding out for her, a few loose strands of hair dark against her pale skin, and opened a text to Diego. *NGL, your wife is kinda hot.*

Then I stared at it. Did I dare send something like that? Was it overstepping? Would he think I was proposing a threesome?

Had he ever given me the impression he had a one-track mind before? Not really. And I knew they both had a sense of humor. So like. I mean.

I hit send. And quickly went back to pictures of whatever I saw that seemed visually interesting: a gray metal rivet on a black velvet background, beaded trim on a sleeve, a necktie of woven ribbon.

Claris brought me to meet Brenda, a delightfully dyke-forward lesbian, which I didn't feel guilty for thinking because she was wearing a baseball cap that read DYKE. "Like your cap," I said, grinning as we shook hands.

"I have one in every color," she replied. "Gotta coordinate with my combat boots, y'know." She was probably in her early forties and I'd made the apparently erroneous assumption that everyone involved in the show would be young. Obviously not. It wouldn't really make sense given you could get into fashion design at any age, and it wasn't as if you aged out of it, like your best sewing years were behind you once you hit thirty.

Her style was entirely different than Moe's. A lot of straight lines and boxy shapes, squared shoulders and curve-minimizing silhouettes. Her sketches, also unlike Moe's, were all of gentlemanly fashions on women, so that was super cool. I clicked away as Claris conducted a very different catch-up, still seeming to come around to the same bullet points, keeping the timeline in focus no matter what she was asking about.

The last member of the design team was a man named Harold whose age could have been anywhere from twenty-seven to forty-five. His hair was silver at the sides but his face seemed youthful and his bearing was that deliciously soft-spoken type that exemplified the phrase "still waters run deep," making you wonder what exactly was going on behind that unruffled yet slightly vulnerable exterior. I mean, I already had my hands full, but Harold would have been my type if I hadn't.

"Everything is progressing according to plan," he said to Claris in his low, steady voice. He switched apps on the iPad on the table in front of him and showed her something.

"I adore you, Harold. You've even color-coded your calendar."

"Of course I have. How else would I be able to visually assess where I am in the project?"

"It makes perfect sense, dear." She gestured toward me. "Mason is one of us as well. The man likes a kanban board."

He smiled at me, displaying perfect teeth. "Oh, me too. Always so satisfying to move items over to Done."

"It really is," I agreed.

We might have talked more but Claris was, of course, forever on task. "I'm glad to hear things are going as expected. No unfortunate shipping disasters?"

"Not as yet, but knock on wood."

She rapped the tabletop. "Every day until the show if need be."

They moved on to topics I couldn't follow except that they were both speaking a variant of High Productivity and Organization with a GTD emphasis and it amused me listening to their voices grow more excited as Claris pulled up her phone to show Harold her promo flow chart.

Not that I needed it, but now I kind of wanted to see the promo flow chart too. I was technically in promotions, right? Aside from the fact that my role was a sinecure. Sort of. I mean. I was actually doing things. Even if she'd basically given me the job to keep me around.

Speaking of my role—what if I did mini interviews with the designers? That would be a fun way to introduce them to the world. Or at least to TikTok. After our tour I went around and bothered them all for a few more minutes, asking how they got into designing clothes and what their earliest memories were of recognizing the power of fashion.

Good sound bites were had and intriguing stories were told, go GFW promotions.

Harold was just wrapping up a meandering story about an aunt who'd made all her own clothes and how captivated he'd been by her ability to express herself with what she wore better than anyone else he knew when the door opened and—Diego walked in.

Naturally I did not stop recording immediately and run up to him. For one: that'd be rude. For two: I didn't know what the rules were and if we were free to greet each other like other-than-friends. For three: he had legit stuff to do and didn't need me to come pouncing on him like a puppy wanting attention.

Though for the record he was in a pair of tight leather trousers and a loose T-shirt and I basically wanted to blow him right there in the dusty front window of what used to be a pet store. Would blow, ten out of ten.

Still, I maintained focus, smiled and nodded at Harold, made understanding noises, and finished the recording with thanks before putting away my phone and slowly moving back up to Moe's section, where Diego was leaning against the edge of the table, head slightly to the side, listening intently to whatever Moe was telling him.

God, he was hot when he was concentrating really hard on something.

He caught my eye and his smile widened, but he didn't lose the thread of his conversation. I veered right and wandered into the only area we hadn't already toured, which after about a minute I realized must be Diego's.

I'd known that fashion designers all had their own styles, their own languages, their own hallmarks. But it was one thing to be able to tell an Armani from a Michael Kors. It was something else to see the different paths each of the designers in the show were taking to get there, the way their own personalized approaches were informed by their sense of style, which thus informed the designs they were currently bringing to life.

Diego made his way to me after checking in with everyone. I was in deep consideration over the effect of a mesh window in the middle of a top hat—as if the hat had been cut in half horizontally and lengthened, leaving only a two-inch ring of mesh around the middle, seeming both like it was holding up the top half of the hat and also like it couldn't possibly support the weight.

"What do you think?"

"I can't decide. It's cool. But how does it look from a distance?"

He leaned in to kiss me lightly. "An excellent question, my dear sir."

So that addressed one of my concerns; this wasn't a total secret.

"And the answer is I'm not sure." He placed the hat on my head and backed away toward the door, eyes on the hat as he went. "Bren? Will you look at this?"

Brenda put down what she was doing with a sigh that didn't feel at all pointed at Diego and said, "Gladly. If I ever manage to figure out how to keep this jacket from looking like a damn refrigerator box I've lopped head and arm holes in, I'll be glad. What's your issue?"

"The hat." A hand-flick in my direction. Was this what it felt like to be a model? Now both of them were looking at me but neither was actually looking *at* me.

"Needs to be higher," she said after a bare couple of seconds.

"You exist to make things more difficult," he told her, smiling.

She blew him a kiss and went back to her area. "Go big or go home, buckaroo."

This time he held his hand out to me and drew me to sit before plucking the hat off my head and smoothing the surely imaginary wrinkles across my shoulders. "Thank you for modeling the look. She's right, of course. I had an inkling and didn't want to accept it, but if you're going to put something up on the catwalk, it's gotta make an impact or there's no point. This would have people squinting the way you were squinting, trying to figure out what they thought."

"Better than hating it, though."

He shook his head. "Oh, no. Not at all. In a straight-up choice between someone hating a look with the fire of a thousand suns or feeling 'meh' about it, I'll pick the thousand suns any day."

The idea of being hated with the fire of a thousand suns didn't seem ideal to me at all. "But wouldn't it be…awful? If people hated you?"

"It's not me, it's a hat. Which I say now, but when it comes down to the line I'm as sensitive as any other artist. But no, it's just, the enemy of engagement is apathy. If someone *hates* your work, really hates it, has a hot coal of pure loathing deep inside them because of something you've done—assuming you aren't being racist or homophobic or anything that objectively earns you that response—then you've made them feel, and that's engagement. If all they do is blink at it and turn away, well, you've done nothing at all."

It seemed like a relatively harsh grading curve to me, but I was no artist. "I envy it a little," I admitted. "The passion, the drive to create something, the ability to make people feel."

"This is where I definitely do not say anything about your ability to make me feel." He coughed. "But I know what you mean. It doesn't have to be art, you know. Claris does it with spreadsheets."

Brenda, a few feet away on the other side of a folding shade, guffawed. "She should have that on a license plate holder. 'Project managers do it with spreadsheets.'"

"Do I hear my name being taken in vain?" Claris called.

"I think Bren's suggesting that you use spreadsheets as part of sex acts!" Diego called back.

"Sorry, darling," she said to Moe, "clearly I need to go defend my good name." When he laughed she only pointed her finger and said, "Shush!"

"Not saying it's a bad thing." Brenda appeared around the shade just in time for Claris to wrap an arm around her. "Just saying it's a thing."

"I do not have sex with spreadsheets."

"I didn't say you did. But I bet you get off on them."

Claris's lips turned up in an unmistakable smirk. "Well. No comment there. Ahem. Though I'm not sure why my relationship to spreadsheets has anything to do with fashion."

Diego patted my thigh like it was nothing, just a casually intimate touch in a small group setting. "Mason was just saying he envied art-related passion. I think Bren was making the point that passion can have many applications."

"And so it can!" Claris ruffled Brenda's cutely spiked fade, making her duck away to protect her hair. "Spreadsheets being only one of them. Mase, love, you have plenty of passion."

I'd nearly forgotten where we'd started this conversation after the twists and turns it had taken. "Sure, you know. It's just I once loved my job and now I don't, so I think I'm jealous of anyone who has a thing in their life that inspires them the way everyone here is inspired."

"If you're looking to find that in a job, pup, you'll probably be disappointed." With an extravagant bow, Brenda added, "I'm a cashier in a discount clothes store, I know of what I speak. The idea is not to marry your job. Don't look to it for all the emotional support you'd look for in a partner, you know? Go there, do it, leave, and don't think about it again until the next time you're there. In the rest of your life, do shit you love." She shot a sour look over her shoulder. "Speaking of, I should be wrestling with this stupid idea I had in the middle of the night and thought was genius and now I hate it and it's too late to back out. Oh, the joys of doing what you love."

Claris tweaked her ear. "Good girl. Back to work!"

"Demon."

"Sweetpea."

They grinned at each other. Brenda retreated and Claris came to sit down beside me on what appeared to be a plastic storage bin full of feathers. "While I am not quite as jaded as some, I do think you might look outside your job for a sense of meaning at this point in your life. Maybe it will enable you to be happier where you are. Maybe it will open doors so you can move into a different position. But either way I suspect you need to feel like you're *doing something*, and that will help immeasurably."

"Now that you say it," Diego mused, "the two of you *are* a lot alike. Before Claris went freelance she was so disheartened with the daily grind I thought she might quit her job and open a cupcake shop."

"Oh, no, that was never a real thing. That was just something I said to mock the straight white ladies on reality shows." She leaned in and lowered her voice. "I'll tell you what I was super tempted to actually do, though. There's a whole strange underground market for well-worn and unwashed lingerie, and I think I could make a *killing* at that. Don't you, darling?"

I laughed. "See, that's not at all where I thought you were going with that."

"Where did you think I was going with it?"

"Oh, I don't know—save the whales, move to a jungle somewhere, buy a houseboat and live on the delta for the rest of your days. But selling dirty panties, nope, did not go there."

She sighed. "I still think that would be a good idea. It's something one already has, which one already uses, and all one has to do is pop it in the mail. Hardly a large commit-ment for a side hustle."

Diego pulled her hand to his lips and kissed the back of it. "I'd buy them. If I didn't, um, have access to them already. But I think you're forgetting that you'd have to keep buying new ones to replace the old ones and you don't even like the frilly sort, so."

"True. I suppose I'd have to do research to find out which types were in high demand. Anything with lace lining the thigh elastic is right out."

"You could cross-promote," I suggested. "Diego could de-sign, you could sell, put a tag and include a business card with every purchase."

Both of them laughed. What is it about making people laugh that's so damn satisfying? I couldn't help smiling at them.

"Alas, I'm afraid the demographics aren't exactly the same. Diego designs for men and while my hypothetical clientele would be men, I doubt they'd be shopping for the same things in both contexts."

"So sorry," Harold said, apologetically approaching us. "Diego, is there any way you could take another look at what I'm working on? I think it's nearly there, but…"

"Of course! That's why we do this. Excuse me, you two, and try not to come up with any new plots while I'm gone."

"There goes our fun!" Claris teased as he walked away.

"Is Diego something of a…mentor?" I asked. "I'm trying to work out how this all goes."

She bent her head forward. "Not to speak ill of the de-parted, but this show is the brainchild of a guy who was quite a bit more well-known than Diego or any of the others—which is why he'll work himself to the bone to make sure it goes off without a hitch, but that's neither here nor there. When Diego was merely one of the designers, largely chosen because they *didn't* present a threat, he took on a support role for the others. Now that he's nominally in charge, he's actually built in peer critiques to the workplace environment." She glanced fondly toward the back of the room. "He's really something else, that man."

I nodded, envying her slightly possessive pride. "No argument here."

"The lovely Brenda's right, you know. About you, I mean. Find something to do with yourself, darling. Something that has nothing to do with work. Maybe something that has nothing to do with your ordinary life."

"Aren't I doing that?" I motioned to the studio.

"Hardly. Unless you're telling me Diego has nothing to do with your life."

"He certainly makes it feel a lot less ordinary."

"Touché, but my point stands. Volunteer somewhere for a while. Maybe a couple of somewheres. You have a fire in you to help people—I've known that since we met. Give vent to that, Mase. You deserve to have a sense of fulfillment, even if it's not from your job."

Volunteering hadn't actually occurred to me—aside from Gentlemen's Fashion Week. I had volunteered at an animal shelter in high school because I'd taken an elective in community service, but not since then. "You think?"

"Why not? Put yourself out there and you may be surprised what finds you. Not in a 'law of attraction' way, in a very straightforward 'if you go about life with an open net you can't predict what you catch' way. And it can't hurt to try."

"That's true."

Claris nodded as if we'd decided something. "Good, that's settled. Let me know if you need any help, I have contacts all over the place. Now will you show me what you're thinking about for TikTok? I confess, I have really no idea what peo-

ple like about that platform, but I do think we should embrace it..."

We spent the rest of a productive evening mapping out some
ideas for promotional social media engagement and occasionally being called upon to offer our thoughts on this or that
design element. It didn't feel like work. It didn't feel wholly
social. It felt good, though. Like I was part of something. Like
Gentlemen's Fashion Week had value and even in a small way
I was contributing to that.

Man, though, sometimes Claris was just spooky with the
insights. She was right. I needed this. I walked back to my
car whistling and spent the rest of the night culling the pictures I'd taken and cropping things to look more mysterious.
Maybe it had been a fake job given to me as an excuse to have
me around, but what the hell. Might as well do it right.

Chapter Twelve

For a while after that I mostly saw Diego at GFW events, some in person, some on video calls where he and Claris would be sitting at the counter in their kitchen in the same shot and the rest of us would be little boxes in our various houses and apartments. It took me about half an hour of trying different backgrounds in my place before I came up with one that didn't feature the futon of Butt Divot fame, my disorganized bookshelves, or the uninspired stretch of wall behind the futon. I settled on standing up at my own kitchen counter so at least everything in the distance was blurred.

It might be weird—and I'm not saying seeing him on video was a great substitute for in person—but I relished watching him in his element like that. He talked like Claris ran everything, and she did always start the meetings, but once they got going Diego would more often than not pull the agenda toward himself and keep it running. And I might be wrong, but I swore each time he did it Claris smirked very slightly, like that had been her plan all along. She'd gently nudge him back to the topic if he went off on one of those designer tangents about fabric availability, but even that was less about Diego and more about Claris facilitating and nudging all of us back on track. (I may have at one point talked for two minutes about all the research I'd been doing on TikTok demographics until she said she'd be happy to add an agenda item to the next meeting if I felt it was helpful for everyone to have that information. It might have made me feel silly except Diego was just *looking* at me through the camera's lens as if I was the sexiest rambling maniac he'd ever seen, so I said that wouldn't be necessary and yielded the meeting back to her. And blushed. I may have blushed. Clearly he wasn't the only one who was a little too much at times, and hell, didn't that mean "too much" as a concept was absurd?)

And we texted. We texted all the time. We texted about GFW, about what we were having for dinner, about what we were reading. We sent links to YouTube videos and Spotify tracks, shared podcasts, and mutually became obsessed with *Snap Judgment*, keeping each other up at night talking about the stories. When I woke up in the morning, I checked to see if he'd sent me anything, and when he had my heart did a little joyful flip thing. We always said goodnight before going to sleep.

When I informed Dec that I had no idea what I was doing with this amazing man, he stuck his tongue out (in a snap) and told me to enjoy it. My friends notably did not ask about Tim. And Tim? Was busy. So was I. I hadn't texted. He'd texted like once in the last who-knew-how-long. It was just…one of those things. Where two people get busy and sort of…drift. That's all. Not a big deal in the long run, I told myself. Happened to everyone.

It had been a whole week since I'd managed to see Diego face-to-face, which is probably why when Claris told me he was doing a student art show at the same coffee shop where we'd first met up I readily assembled a very casual (and flattering AF) T-shirt-and-jeans combo, topped it with a dark red fedora, and walked over. I donated my five bucks at the door (optional, but made me feel good) and grabbed my complimentary latte, ready to be not-judgy about bad high school art.

Far from being the drudgery I expected, the student work was *hot*. Not in a sexy way, in a *pay attention and be impressed* way. There were some amateurish pieces, sure, but a lot of it was well beyond anything I could have imagined doing as a teenager. Or ever.

I was studying a portrait of a lizard, which had captured the lizard skin texture amazingly well, when a voice slightly behind me said, "Incredible little bastards, aren't they? I'd be consumed with envy except I'm far too clever for that. Darling, how are you?"

"Enjoying the show." I kissed Claris's cheek and gave her dress an appreciative nod. "You're full-on Maleficent today."

"But no horns! Though I am swooping from place to place without any responsibilities to speak of, in true Maleficent style. Poor Diego is stuck talking to every parent who ever put a crayon drawing on a refrigerator. He would have been over to say hello immediately but he's embroiled in a deep conversation about artistic ethics with a very earnest sixteen-year-old, you know how that goes."

I didn't, but I could imagine. "So you're Diego's agent in this case?"

"I'm his agent in most cases. Now. Tell me everything."

"Um. Everything?"

She held out her arm after we'd released hands. "May I escort you around? Diego will be a few minutes yet. Though I really can't undersell how much he wishes he was speaking to you right now."

What do you do when the wife of the man you're dating asks to escort you? Offer her your arm, of course (so different than linking arms with Mia; Mia's energy was lemon yellow where Claris's was claret red). We began walking around, slowly, stopping before each piece. "It's hard for me to believe kids did this work," I admitted.

"Rather remarkable, I agree. Though if you can get him to show you his youthful sketchbooks you might look at even the, shall we say, less obviously of merit work differently. Don't get me wrong, my husband is a genius. But it's also valuable to see that every line he's ever drawn has not been perfect." We moved on to a sculpture in a pool of light. "It's one of the things that makes him such a valuable mentor."

"That doesn't surprise me at all."

"No, I'm sure. You being quite perceptive yourself. But you know what we've never spoken of? Art. What do you create, Mason?"

"Um." I wracked my brain for a decent answer to that question, feeling wholly inadequate. "I...don't create? I don't think."

Her eyebrows rose in delicate disbelief. "How is that possible? You don't make crafts out of grocery bags or concoct multi-layer desserts? What about doodling? Surely you express yourself in some creative way."

I tried to mentally scan my apartment, searching for some good answer to Claris's insistent question. "I'm not sure I do. Do you count making worlds in video games?"

She smiled. "I knew there had to be something! A man who dresses the way you dress must have other outlets. So then you like designing in space, that makes perfect sense."

Before I could ask her exactly what that meant, the bright bubble of Diego's laughter reached us from across the room and I couldn't help turning my head to glance in his direction, flushing when I realized how obvious I'd been.

"Nearly time now," she said cryptically, guiding us to a mixed media piece that appeared to be an effort to push the exact lines of just how many booze coasters could be covertly collaged and turned into art. "Now, this one's just cheeky. How fun."

We spent a couple of minutes debating whether anyone school-related had noticed the fact that this particular student had made art out of alcohol ads before she leaned in closer to me and lowered her voice. "It's time to rescue Diego. He's been cornered by An Authority Figure With A Mission. That's never good because he cannot say no to people. If we leave him he'll agree to do nothing but teach high school art pro bono for the next three years."

"Will he?"

She *mmm*'d. "He just might. Of course, it wouldn't be so bad except he won't say no to anyone else either. By the end of those three years he'll have collected a dozen other similar commitments and won't be able to finish any of them while also making time to eat and sleep."

Not that I needed a precis on a guy I'd kissed in a garden of dappled sunlight, but then again, she said it all without any hint of true criticism. In fact, it almost felt like she was…sharing something about him with me. Which was almost a form of intimacy, to be honest. Still, I had to remain…like, neutral or something. "Eating and sleeping are pretty important."

"They are, darling! They are."

We approached from the side and Claris detached from my arm when we were still some distance away. "Divide and conquer," she murmured. "Principal Zimmerman! How good to see you. Tell me all about the way you're distributing the proceeds from this event. I know it's going to a nonprofit, but I'm not familiar with the group. And do the students receive paperwork of any kind? Presumably they can count the work as donations to charity?" She kissed Diego on the cheek, said something I didn't catch, then led away the principal, who seemed a bit flustered by being forcibly carried off.

Diego beamed at me. Was already beaming at me by the time I turned away from Claris. "You made it. I'm so pleased."

"I'm glad I did. The student work is amazing."

"Isn't it? I was so inspired working with this group. Claris says I tell her that every time, but it's always true!" He licked his lips, which was distracting as hell, but I tried to stay focused on his words. "I'm so glad you're here."

For an extended moment we just…looked at each other. I had the sensation of that movie effect where a character stands in place and the world moves in fast-forward around them, except it was both of us sharing this bubble of stillness amid all the chaos.

Which was broken when a glass shattered. I blinked, coming back to myself. "Claris is really bringing the Maleficent realness tonight. She showed me around a little."

"I saw. And was jealous. She has a lot more freedom at these events than I do. With good reason, but still, I would have liked to be the one to escort you."

"I do like the sound of that." I smiled. "My dear sir, I'm sure we can find time to walk around together presently."

That got me a smile, and damned if he didn't look good in a pair of jeans with a button-down shirt. "Just promise me you won't give away all your favors."

"How could I?" I laughed—at the absurdity of our conversation, at the paradox of feeling so close to someone while surrounded by strangers. "Also you look amazing. I'd say more but it would be inappropriate in this environment."

"Oh, same, Mason. Same. Is there any way you can stay a little longer? I see Concerned Persons bearing down on me, but I should be able to extricate myself shortly."

I followed his gaze and saw what appeared to be two parents towing a reluctant teenager. "That does look urgent. I can stick around for a bit."

"Wonderful! Thank you."

The couple was closing in, the dad-type clearing his throat

in that blustery Vernon Dursley way that always makes me want to roll my eyes. "Mr. Flores, we're Starla's parents, and we just wanted to ask you a few questions about what criteria you used to choose which pieces would be in the show..."

Yikes. I slipped past them, but not before noting that Starla, assuming that was the reluctant teenager being dragged in their wake, looked mortified, her skin stained a blotchy red. Did she not have anything in the show? Since I had nothing better to do, I went around again, this time paying attention to the names on the artwork.

It didn't take long to find Starla's piece, which was...wood. Uh. There was more to it than that. Tiny lines were carved into it in four columns, clearly representing writing, but parts of it were burned, other parts gouged out, some stained with dark colors. It took reading the title for me to figure it out. *The Twenty-Seven Amendments* by Starla Friedman. As in the Ten Commandments, but more American. A commentary on the frailty of rhetoric, maybe.

It was propped on a stand made of cardboard with artistic weathering so that it looked as if it was about to collapse. In all, the piece seemed pretty clearly to be a critique of the default American narrative, and as such, I was for it. *Well done, Starla. Don't listen to your parents.*

I was in the middle of reminding myself that I'd just made up a whole story that might not even be true when Claris appeared at my elbow once more. "I told you he can't say no. Here." She pushed two glasses of sparkling non-alcoholic-something into my hands. "Take him in the back for a brief break. He realistically only has a few minutes, but it should be enough to say hello."

"We did. I mean. Before."

She rolled her eyes. "Yes, well, say hello again. Assuming you're interested in having a few minutes alone with my husband."

"I—I mean—" I sputtered to a stop, taken too by surprise to play along. "I wouldn't have said it like that…"

"Darling, don't be so easy, you'll attract predators like me. Come now."

I followed Claris not unlike Starla following her parents, though I trusted that I was a lot happier about talking to Diego than she had been. This time Claris barely made a nod to politeness before grabbing his arm and excusing them to "important business" in the back. Diego nodded to me, inclining his head in that direction, so I…followed again.

Never really thought of myself as a follower, just gonna put that out there. But when there was the possibility of talking to Diego, suddenly I could follow all day long.

I found them in the back of the cafe, a small storage room with shelves lining the walls, smelling of stale coffee and cardboard dust.

"Enjoy your cider, I'll hold down the fort, and then we can wrap the show." She kissed him on the cheek, murmured something in his ear, and went back out to the front.

After a slight hesitation I offered one of the glasses. "I like Starla's *Amendments* piece."

If there was a right thing to say, that had been it. The tension eased from his face. "Isn't it great? She has such a fun grasp of context and symbolism."

"Her folks weren't into it?"

"They were careful not to say that exactly. But they did ask why her painting of a woodpecker wasn't more *appropriate* to the event."

"A woodpecker?" Skepticism laced my tone. Or, okay, dripped from it. "They wanted to replace a well-executed commentary piece with a woodpecker."

"Because it was more appropriate."

"Right. Heaven forbid a teenager display critical thinking skills."

He grinned. "Exactly. Starla excelled in my workshop and caught every point I made, but her parents are just the sort of people who wouldn't have even let her enroll in it if it was actually called Critical Thought and Artistic Commentary or something like that."

"To be fair, that would be a terrible name for a workshop."

"Hey! But yes." His eyes caught mine and held. "May I kiss you? Just, um, to say hello and I'm glad you're here and goodnight and all the other things I don't actually have time to say?"

I whistled. "Sounds like this kiss has a big damn job to do, Diego."

"Mmm. Say my name again."

"Diego," I said, watching him watch my lips.

He stepped forward. "Again."

"Die—"

The kiss was desperate, his lips attacking mine with force, his tongue darting forward, then withdrawing, his fingers suddenly clutching the back of my neck. Then, before I could fully commit myself, he pulled back. Pulled his lips off mine, though his grip kept me in place. "God, I needed that. Thank you. I've been playing a responsible adult for hours and I so wish I could fall to pieces for you right now. Also I cannot believe I just said that, please don't hold it against me."

I blinked. "How could I possibly hold that against you?"

Now he stepped away, turning his face slightly, dropping his eyes. "It's too much. It's too soon for that kind of talk, and I know it, I just…was a little overcome. Forgive me, Mason."

I touched his jaw, coaxing him to look at me. "So we can revisit this when you feel like it's not too soon, then."

He bit his lip for a second before releasing it. "I'm sorry Claris is forcing you to be my mandatory rest period, but I'm really glad you're here."

"Is that what I am?" I teased. "A mandatory rest period?"

"Oh gosh, would that offend you?" His tone was much lighter.

I pretended to think about it. "Maybe I'm a pit stop."

"Maybe you're a summer cottage in upstate New York, with a lake view and a private beach."

"Maybe I'm a spa weekend."

"Maybe you're a house in Bath I'm renting so I can take in the waters."

I laughed. "Okay, you're really bringing the Georgette Heyer now."

"I could have sex with you for knowing that reference."

"Oh yeah?" I tossed a glance toward the coffee shop. "That could be arranged, friend. Though unfortunately not right now."

The curtain to the storage room fluttered and Maleficent was back. "Brilliant idea. Shouldn't Mason come over for dinner, darling? We can't do this weekend, but what about next Saturday?"

Diego shook his head at her. "How can I tell you to stop butting in when you butting in benefits me?"

She beamed. "I am *the worst*. You two sort it out, and then I'm afraid I need you out front." With kisses blown at both of us, she fluttered away again.

"She is the worst," I mused. "So, Saturday?"

He giggled. "We should change the day just to show her who's boss."

"We could, but don't you think she'd realize we'd only done it for that reason and it would make her feel even *more* powerful?"

"You might be right. Saturday works for you?"

At this point I didn't care. I'd *make* it work for me. "Definitely." I hesitated. I couldn't help but hesitate. He'd kissed me, though. Desperately. Surely that made it all right that I leaned in and kissed him now. "I look forward to seeing you, my dear sir."

"As do I. I mean seeing you. Not seeing me. Obviously. Ahem. Anyway." One more quick kiss and both of us backed away. "I should—"

"And I should let you." I tipped an imaginary hat to him. "Good day, sir."

He returned it and added a bow. "Good day to you, sir."

I waved to Claris as I left. And then, with the pleasant memory of Diego's lips on mine and his fingernails digging slightly into my skin, I drove home.

Chapter Thirteen

Eating with them in their cozy dining room was, in a word, delightful. Claris was wearing what she called her going-out togs, which consisted of a curves-hugging dress and a scarf wrapped around her hair, managing to be both practical and somehow flirty, an effect she was clearly going for if all the eyelash-batting was anything to judge by.

"She's warming up, pay no mind," Diego explained.

"I'm not as young as I used to be! The muscles one uses to seduce the youth must be exercised, you know." More batting, more eyelashes. "Is it working?"

I put my hand over my heart. "If I were not spoken for tonight, I would be all aflutter, I promise."

"Good!" She poked Diego. "You see? I can still make people *aflutter.*"

"Don't I count? You make me aflutter on a regular basis. Also, I'm not sure we're using that right, it feels like we're missing a verb. 'Go' aflutter? 'Feel' aflutter?"

"Maybe technically, but as long as we know what we're saying I don't think it's a problem." She leaned in a bit, as if speaking only to me. "See if he gets a bit verbally flustered tonight. It's an adorable tic of his when he's especially—"

"Okay, okay, that's enough out of you, madam! Don't you have youth to corrupt or something?"

She turned a radiant smile on him. "I do! I do have youth to corrupt! I'll be too tired to corrupt the youth soon. I remember the days when I was never too tired to corrupt the youth."

"Heaven forbid."

"Oh, hush. You love it when I'm corrupting people. And I've enticed Perri to come out with me, which should be marvelous."

His face relaxed slightly. "I do love to hear about your conquests. Have fun tonight."

"You know we will. Now." Claris took in both of us before speaking again as if she was imparting Very Important Information, possibly state secrets. She arched one eyebrow. "You two should take advantage of this time as well. The next few months will be a whirlwind, so don't waste this moment before everything intensifies."

"We're not *wasting* it, even if we don't have marathon sex, you know." He sounded almost grumpy, as if they'd had this conversation before. "Not everyone needs to fill an empty evening with multiple orgasms in order to feel like they've used their time wisely."

"I have no idea why everyone doesn't choose to have multiple orgasms whenever the opportunity arises, but I'll accept that it must be true. However, that's not what I meant." She held out her hands, one to each of us.

Diego, whatever his grumpiness about the topic, took her hand immediately. I hesitated, unsure exactly what was happening, or how I felt about it. Then she wiggled her fingers at me and, what the hell, I took her hand too.

"Spend the whole night on one delicious kiss if you want to, that's not the point, but this event will start ramping up soon and I don't want all of this potential to go to waste because of the timing. So be good to each other." She squeezed and then released my hand, turning to Diego. "Should I distract your date so you can set up the boudoir, or...?"

"Oh, hush."

"I was serious! This is me offering my support." The smirk, though. Claris could smirk with the best of them, managing to look both smug and somehow adorable with it. "See how supportive I am?"

"Go seduce someone, woman! Mason and I will decide what we do with our time."

She sighed heavily. "As you wish. But if you only let me plan it! I'd do such a good job."

He maintained the severe expression for a moment before it crumpled. "To be fair, Mason does love a Gantt chart, he told me himself."

Claris clapped. "Yes! Gantt charts are necessary when one is managing a number of simultaneous—"

He shoved at her arm. "Yes, yes, tasks, dependencies, blah blah blah, go away now so I can have my date."

"But now I want to stay and talk about project management with Mason."

"Veto!"

She grinned and kissed him. "I suppose the youth require corrupting. And we can discuss Gantt charts some other time. Have a lovely evening, gentlemen." Claris rose from the table and winked at us before leaving the room. "Don't wait up."

The moment she was beyond the doorway the energy changed, didn't deflate exactly, but settled. I looked at Diego, wondering what he was thinking. "I don't have to stay for long," I offered, wondering if Claris was pressuring him into more than he was comfortable with.

"Oh, um, I mean—I thought you might stay—even spend the night if you—but of course if you *want* to leave you should do that. But only if that's what you want?" His voice rose hopefully on the last word.

There are times when one should ask permission, when it's

hotter to ask permission than to take without asking. Then again, there are also times when you kiss the flushed, bashful man in front of you because you can and you know on some fundamental level that he wants you to.

This was the latter.

My lips closed in on Diego's, my hand cupping the back of his neck. His hands came to my sides and held me there, or held himself there, against me but not too insistently, our bodies close but not clashing against each other, our lips the only forceful point of contact. My toes curled as his tongue grazed mine, just for a second, a split second, a tease more than anything else, but it was perfect.

"I need you," he murmured when there was enough room between us to speak. "Say you'll stay?"

"I'll stay. For however long you want me." And the starkness of it—how much I meant it—made me pull away. I fumbled, desperately trying to cover my words with action, picking up my water glass and nearly sloshing it over the sides before I managed to drink any of it, but of course I only inhaled some of my water and ended up bent over coughing, with the man I desired pounding on my back to help me breathe.

I straightened, rubbing my teary eyes. "I actually feel out of shape after that coughing fit, like I'll be sore tomorrow. I'm getting old."

"Are you?" He lifted a hand to my cheek and brushed away the moisture there. "If this is you old, I'm absolutely in favor of it. Especially if it comes with kissing like that."

"Maybe I've learned a few things." I held his gaze, trying to stay serious, then both of us kind of laughed. "I sound like I'm seventy-five trying to sell myself to a twenty-year-old, 'Oh, well, but I've learned a lot in my years, I can teach you about pleasure you've never imagined...'"

"I'd go for that, honestly. But since I'm actually slightly

older than you, I think I get to be the wise older gentleman."
He cleared his throat. "My dear Mason, I wish to formally
invite you to enjoy the hospitality of my household, my bedroom, and most importantly, my bed. If it would please you."

I nodded seriously. "It would please me very much. I grate-
fully accept."

He paused. "Unless you are a spy. In which case I will still
have sex with you but I think it only fair to let you know ahead
of time that I will not trade classified intel for sexual favors."

I lowered my voice and leaned in, our lips almost brushing.
"Are you...certain about that?"

"I... I was..."

With agonizing slowness I closed the gap between us and
kissed him, in this unhurried, delicious way, allowing my eyes
to shut, resisting the urge to pull him against me, just allowing the kiss to progress gently until he moaned. "It only gets
better from here," I said softly, in character. Or not in character. The lines were blurring.

"I'm willing to negotiate." Kiss. "For more." Kiss.

"In that case..."

We made out sitting in their formal dining room, hands
beginning to roam over shirts, knees knocking against each
other. He pulled away and cleared his throat again. "Ahem.
Shall we go through to the, ah, boudoir?"

"Indeed, sir. I think that would be appropriate."

I followed him through the living room and up a flight of
stairs to the second floor. The house wasn't big, but, much
like the yard, the way the space was used kept it from feeling
cramped. Four doors upstairs. We went into the room to the
left and I could tell immediately that this was Diego's space.
Not only because there was a dress form in a corner heaped
with fabrics and a desk piled high with magazines and vari-

ous sewing things, but also it just…smelled like him. Deep and rich and woody.

He groaned. "I pictured this so much better. Clean, for one thing. With candles lighting every surface. Sexy music playing. Bed turned down invitingly. Ah, it's tragic."

I grabbed him and cupped both of his cheeks. "Is it really that tragic? Nothing saying we can't do that some other time."

"Yes, but this is the *first*, and it should be special. I feel… I feel special. That you are special. I wanted to show you how much."

"I guess you'll have to show me some other way." I leaned in slowly, pressing my lips to his, watching his eyes flutter. "You're a creative man. I'm sure if you put your mind to it…"

"I'll put my everything to it." His hands curled around me, sliding up my back, resting on my shoulders as he stepped even closer, his feet between mine, our bodies in contact in a new way, making me flush. "I just pictured flickering light and shadows and my skin glowing for you."

I kissed a path to his ear. "If you want me to close my eyes and not peek while you get things ready, I can do that."

"Oh, would you? Or—was that a joke? Because if you're serious—"

"I'm serious."

He pulled away for a moment, eyes locked like magnets on mine. "Am I being foolish?"

"How does foolish come into it? Listen, you are an artist, you design things, you picture them clearly, right?"

"I try. They don't always come out that way, but I try to imagine what they'll be."

"So this is that, isn't it? Why would we do something different than how you've pictured it if we could just pause for a second and give you the chance to make it the way you'd imagined it?"

"Mason, you are…" He kissed me urgently, then pushed me away. "Okay, close your eyes, tight, absolutely no peeking or I'll have to do something terrible to you."

I closed my eyes. "Slap my face with a glove and demand satisfaction?"

"Exactly. Because you will have betrayed my trust."

"The trust of no peeking."

"It is a solemn trust, sir!"

"Indeed it is."

I could hear him rustling around me, the sounds of fabric (clothes being moved? the bed being made?), occasional jostling of glass or metal, the air shifting around me as Diego moved through the room, out of it, back less than a minute later, his footsteps soft on the deep pile carpet that covered only the upstairs, in contrast to the hardwood and flagstones downstairs.

The sand-scrape of a match, the smell of sulfur followed by smoke followed by wax melting.

"Almost there," he murmured.

"Take your time. I'll just stand here thinking of how good you're gonna look when I'm kissing you until you beg for more."

Stillness, as if he'd stopped moving, maybe stopped breathing. "Is that what you think? That *I'll* be the one begging?"

"You never know."

"You don't!" he agreed enthusiastically. "That's why I wanted everything I could control to be perfect, because first times are fraught with the unknown. What if it's awkward? What if it's off for some reason?"

"Those things don't scare me. You just keep going."

"Oooo. What does scare you, then?"

I answered almost without thinking. "Oh, that's easy. What if it's perfect and then it ends and you can never get that back?"

It was far too raw a thing to say in this moment, waiting for him, my eyes shut, my world dark. I wanted to take it back but before I could do, or say, anything else, his arms came around me and he pressed himself against my back. "Same solution, though," he said, lips on my neck, kissing before he finished the thought. "Should I keep going?"

I didn't want to open my eyes, not yet. "Yes," I whispered. "Please."

"With absolute pleasure." His hands shifted down over my chest as he nuzzled my neck, not quite kissing, just dragging his lips along my skin. "You smell so good." He inhaled deeply and in any other circumstance it might have seemed like a cheesy line but standing there with my eyes closed and his hands tugging up on my shirt made me feel too present to doubt his sincerity.

I allowed him to pull off my shirt, feeling naked in the darkness behind my eyes more than in my shirtlessness. His arms came around me again, his lips drawing in my earlobe for a moment before he said, "I've imagined undressing you like this, thank you so much for letting me."

There was nothing to say to that, I had no words to equal it. I reached back to pull him against me and in doing so I could feel how hard he was already, how much even just this—candlelight and promise—aroused him. "How do you want me? How did you imagine it?"

A puff of breath against skin damp from his lips. "In every possible way. May I lay you back and explore you? It's what I want more than anything else. I know it's a cliché, but to be given permission to touch and taste and…and leave my mark on someone as their grace leaves its mark on me…it's my favorite thing."

My hands ran down over his back, his butt, keeping him close. "Of course. That's…that sounds amazing."

"I intend it to be amazing. For both of us." One of his hands rested on my chest while the other drifted lower. "Oh, Mason, oh god. I can't believe you're here with me." He rubbed my cock lightly through my jeans, gentle pressure I couldn't help but arch into.

"Please," I murmured. The position was so…exposing. Standing there, my arms back to hold his body, my chest bare, my eyes closed. The firm pressure of him behind me, the containment of his hand on my chest, the sweet teasing of his fingers.

"I probably should have mentioned sooner that I'm a master at delayed gratification. Claris says it's my darkest sin."

I withheld a moan, pushing my ass back against him. "If this is sinning, I'm for it. Though if she means you're a tease, I agree."

He laughed. "Sorrynotsorry. I need to kiss you now, face-to-face."

"Here for that too." I didn't open my eyes until he'd come around in front of me, our positions changed, my hands now resting on his waist, his arms around my shoulders. And then—candlelight. Candles shining from the dresser, the bedside table, a small table by the window beside the little two-seater couch. Candles glowing through a doorway into what I assumed must be a bathroom. "Oh, Diego."

He kissed me, pulling my focus from everything else. "Say my name again. God, I love hearing you say my name in that voice. Can we just stay in this moment forever? Say it again, please say it again."

I pulled his face to mine and looked into his eyes, dark in the shadows. "This is so beautiful, Diego. Is this how you pictured it? How you pictured us?"

"Better. It's so much better. I couldn't have imagined how good it would be to have you in front of me for real." Hands trailed down my back, then up again. "How your skin would feel under my fingertips, how you'd smell."

"You imagined how I'd smell?"

He caught his lower lip between his teeth. "Is that exceptionally strange? Forgive me."

"I may find it in me to forgive you," I said gravely. "But only if you kiss me."

He leaned in and then we lost what distance we'd had, what silliness we'd donned, hands everywhere, lips everywhere, his breaths and my breaths coming in fast. I was pulling his hair to control him, his fingers were digging into my hips, everything lost in this stretch of frenzied kissing and tasting and gasping.

"Please," he whispered urgently, "please, please."

"Please what?" I teased him, pulling his head back so he couldn't kiss me. "You haven't asked for anything."

"Please everything, please right now, please give me yourself as much as you can, it's what I love, what I need."

I couldn't stop looking into his eyes, all that need writ plain, the vulnerability of asking for it almost shocking me. "Yes. Take me, Diego. Please take me."

He made some sound, some savage low groan, and pushed me backwards until my legs hit the bed, his hands scrabbling at the fly of my jeans. "You're so gorgeous and so strong and so fucking hot. I mean—I mean—" He finally looked down to better undress me, leaving me to watch him, to run my thumbs up either side of his neck as he focused on his task, to notice the way his eyelashes were highlighted by the candles, the way his skin glowed with a thin sheen of sweat. "I mean, um, your appearance pleases me greatly, good sir. I cannot wait to, ah, to take your member into myself, to serve your desires with my body."

"Oh fuck yeah." I kissed him, ignoring his protest as he

tried to finish undressing me and only managed to shove my jeans down to my thighs before getting distracted.

Though not for long. I sucked in a breath when his fingers made contact with my cock, sliding over it, lightly stroking up to the head and then down again. "Not gonna be much for you to explore if you keep doing that. I'm like a teenager right now." I couldn't possibly admit how much the foreplay had turned me on, how hot it was that we were taking forever just to get our clothes off, how much I'd liked standing there with my eyes closed while he took his time with me.

"There's a lot more of you to explore than your penis, my good man."

I cracked a smile. "My member, you mean?"

"Your member, yes. Though don't get me wrong." He executed a smooth twist that made me come up on my toes, seeking greater stimulation. "Your member does hold my interest."

"Oh?"

"Yes."

I ducked forward to kiss him again and pressed my hands against his chest, over the buttons on his shirt. "When do I get to see you? Any objections to me returning the favor?"

"In fact, I would like that very much."

"As would I." Slowly, slowly, I began with the top button and went one by one as he continued touching me, stroking me, never with any intention but to draw out my pleasure, only stopping so I could pull the shirt off his arms. "Diego," I murmured with reverence as I revealed his skin, the curve of his belly, the soft, dark hairs on his navel, the smooth plane of his pecs.

"I'm not as fit as you, I know—"

"You are so sexy." I kissed the top of each shoulder, like I was anointing him as the object of my desire. "So beautiful." My hands ran down over his nipples, brushing lower, coming to rest at the top of his much looser jeans, hooking my thumbs just under the waistline. "What happens after this? After we share our skin, our bodies?" I was looking down, at the shadows between us, the way the candles made his skin golden.

He leaned his cheek against mine and I closed my eyes again, willing him to say something that would make me brave. Brave enough to open them. Brave enough to believe in this. In us.

"That's easy," he whispered, the words practically caressing my skin. "After this we sit down quite seriously, with a spreadsheet, and make a Gantt chart of all the tasks and subtasks that need to be completed in order for two people to fall in love, including a timeline of deliverables and relevant benchmarks."

"You bastard." I smiled helplessly and bit his ear lightly in punishment. "I'm having a moment of insecurity and you joke about Gantt charts."

"I did mean it as a joke, but I think it could be done. We'd define this as the beginning of the beta-testing period, maybe include a soft launch date, design a metric for assessing the success of the—"

I grabbed him and kissed him, hard, gripping the back of his neck, hooking one of my legs around him so that when I inevitably fell backwards, he fell on top of me. And I just kept kissing him. I could have stopped but I didn't want to, I wanted the awkward leg-twining, the panting for breath, the *oof* as we came down and the giggling as we jostled for position.

The feel of his weight on my body as he meticulously kept himself away from my more, ahem, vulnerable bits, even when I used my leg to pull myself against him.

I tried to get more, but he refused to let me. "We should have sex now," I hinted. Broadly.

"Mmm. You shouldn't let on how badly you want me. It'll only make me want to tease you longer."

"You're a monster."

He kissed my forehead, my cheeks, my lips, smiling down at me. "At your service, darling. Now. Lie there and let me have my fun."

We shed our pants and he crawled over me, making me the subject of intense study in a way I've never been for anyone before, rubbing the stubble on his chin against my inner arm until I squirmed, licking a line from one nipple to the other, then a second line down my sternum, bisecting the first. He deployed his teeth to nip at my ear, to tug lightly at my navel. He batted his eyelashes against my inner thighs and rested his face against my chest, as if listening for my heart. And after all that he laid himself down over me and said, "May I mount you, Mason?"

To which there was only one possible answer. "By all means, my good fellow. By all means. Ride like the wind." I bucked up at him to make him laugh.

And laugh he did, the sound warm and sweet and buoyant, making me feel lighter than air.

Chapter Fourteen

I spent the night. Of course I spent the night. I fell asleep listening to Diego's breaths with the sweat still drying on my skin, feeling sated and tired in all the best ways. There would be time to think about it all later, after the candles had guttered out and the dusting of magic over the evening had faded with the stars.

Morning arose gradually in my awareness with the sound of low voices and an absence in the bed beside me.

"Trust me." Claris's voice, lightly amused.

"I...but don't you think..."

Her laughter, muffled immediately. "I can't believe you're arguing with me over this after lighting every candle we had in the house last night."

"Keep your voice down! And I know. Was it too much?"

"It appears to have worked like a charm. Just take the tray, husband, and romance your gentleman, would you please?"

"You're insufferable."

"I am delightful. And now I'm leaving. Goodnight! And my darling, you deserve the very best, you deserve to get back absolutely everything you offer others."

"Oh, just give me that and go."

The door closed on her laughter.

I pretended to be just waking up, lifting my head and squinting. "Was that Claris?"

"Ignore her. Um." Diego was standing, apparently frozen in the act of setting a tray down. "She brought us...things. I'm not sure she's been to sleep yet, to be honest. She's hardly ever up this early. Is this too early? It's probably too early, I'm sorry, we can go back to sleep."

But I was eyeing the tray. "Is that coffee?"

"Yes? With cream and sugar in a little serving set I don't think we've ever used before. Also iced cinnamon buns she must have bought, with some cookies and sliced fruit." A line deepened in his forehead. "She must have gone to the store for this. I can't believe..." He looked up.

And caught me openmouthed, staring at the tray. "I said to her once. To Claris. I told her—I don't remember why—we were talking about what we looked for in people. I said I just wanted someone I could drink coffee in bed with on Sunday mornings. But how could she remember that? It was at least a year ago, probably more."

"You'd be shocked at the things she remembers." He picked up the tray again and brought it toward me. "Shall I pour?"

"I... I guess so." It was one thing to be set up by a man's wife to date him. Was it another to be brought coffee and breakfast in bed by her? Seemed like it should be, but I was finding it hard to be critical at the moment.

He handed me my coffee and slipped into bed beside me, only the tray between us. "This is so nice."

"Yes. It's. Um." I took a sip to save me from finishing my thought. Except I wasn't sure I wanted to hold it in. "This is how I imagined it. When I told Claris that. Just, I imagined sitting with someone, smelling coffee, still being naked from the night before." A blush heated my cheeks. "Granted, I didn't imagine his wife bringing in the coffee, but—"

"If I'd known this is what you wanted, I would have set it all up, I promise."

Which was sweet, Diego was sweet, and I knew he meant it. "It never even occurred to me. I mean, it's just a thing I say. I never thought…it would happen. I was telling Claris because she was married and I knew—or assumed, anyway—that meant nothing would happen between us." I'd certainly never mentioned it to Tim, who left with militaristic efficiency within twenty minutes of waking up in the morning if he spent the night before.

Diego raised an eyebrow. "So how does that work? You only tell people you *can't* date what you want in someone you *could* date?"

"I didn't actually plan to tell her, it just sort of happened. I don't tell anyone that. Usually."

"See, I foresee the same problem." He leaned his head back on the pillow, smiling at me, the curve of his lips soft in the morning light. "If you don't say what you want, how can you get it?"

"I…" …didn't want to think about it. Not right now.

"Which reminds me, you know. I did promise you we could talk about…futures. In the plural. Futures of different flavors, if you will." There was a sweetness to him lying there, so relaxed, none of my own tension reflecting back at me. "There are so many options, Mase. If you want to hear about them."

And I did. I really did want to hear about them. But not right now, my skin so thin already, as if I was *thisclose* to being exposed. "We should definitely talk about futures at some point, though pre-caffeine may not be the best time. This coffee is delicious."

"Isn't it?" he asked, going along with my change in subject. "We have an amazing coffeepot. It's the only appliance we truly couldn't live without." He picked up a strawberry and held it out to me. "These can't possibly be in season, but they look delicious."

Feeling naughty and flirty and a bit soft around the edges myself, I leaned in to take the fruit from his fingers, holding his gaze the whole time.

"Oh dear me," he breathed.

I chewed slowly, aware of his gaze. "Delicious."

"You're delicious."

"See, that should be a cheap line but it's not."

"I'm glad it's not. I definitely don't mean it to be." This time he held a cinnamon roll to my lips. "Would you like a bite?"

"Why thank you." It wasn't a thing I'd do with just anyone, on just any day. If you'd asked me about feeding each other food in bed I would have probably cringed and said it sounded messy, while some small part of me secretly yearned to not care about how messy it was as long as it was romantic.

And it was. Both a bit messy and a bit romantic. Diego solved the issue of my sticky fingertips by slowly sucking the sugar from them and I, for my part, blushed and kissed him and, well, suffice to say we set the tray aside and did other things in the bed, other messy, romantic, amazing things.

I hadn't been *super* worried about encountering Claris, but it had a bit been on my mind. Obviously the two of them had it all worked out and weren't really bothered by their arrangement, but I still felt...not awkward exactly, but *aware* of it. Aware that running into Claris in the hallway wasn't exactly the same as running into a date's random roommate.

When it happened, though, I didn't have too much time to worry before she'd grabbed my arm and, uh, forcibly escorted me downstairs. "Darling, I need you, come with me."

"Um..." Not that her *Darling, I need you* was anything less than charming. She'd said the same thing to me once at a "#SportsNite" event the bank had sponsored, which I'd mostly gone to because I was in competition for a promotion and it was my first time seeing a sponsorship through.

Mind you, it's not all bad, being escorted by a beautiful woman in a bathrobe and not much else. And it didn't feel at all like A Thing. However attractive Claris was, and she didn't think I was exactly a toad either as far as I could tell, we'd never had sexual chemistry, so it didn't feel suggestive that she was in a state of undress as she half-dragged me to the kitchen. Which was good, because I was pretty tired out. Ahem. From prior events. Upstairs.

Sex. We'd had sex. Really good sex. In a number of physically taxing positions. Some of which I had not tried before, but would definitely be trying again. It wasn't often I felt outmatched, but Diego was a designer, of clothing, of candlelight, of sexual adventure. I'm just saying.

Cough, cough.

She pushed me into a stool. "How did you like your coffee in bed?"

"Oh, hey now, that's not fair. I told you that in—in—well, not in the context of you actually doing it."

"You're welcome! I assumed you wouldn't have mentioned that to Diego, of course. Sometimes you two are peas in a pod." She began pulling things out of the refrigerator. "Lunch will be whatever you can piece together from the fridge. I'm sure my husband will be scandalized but I can't be bothered to make anything and I have less need to impress you. Now me, I *always* tell people what I want, and I usually get it."

"I do all right without your help, lady," I said, though the part of me desperate to know all about what Diego wanted was definitely at war with the part of me that had boundaries.

"Do you, though?" She flicked an eyebrow in my direction but thankfully continued instead of forcing me to answer. She pushed a plate across the breakfast bar at me and gestured at the food she'd laid out with a flourish. "Macaroni salad, a variety of olives, cold cuts and cheese, clementines, grapes, kimchi, French bread."

"When I have leftovers at my place it's usually pizza with the edges curling up or Chinese food I'm not sure is still good."

"This is not *leftovers*, it's—ah—first-run food playing a new venue."

I laughed. "Fair."

"And anyway, I find it incongruent that you're so well put together but can't cook. Surely you haven't always had people to do that for you?"

"Well, Declan mostly. And I can do basics. I can cook mediocre eggs and make toast." I ticked them off on my fingers. "Mac and cheese out of a box, which my mom tells me is not actually mac and cheese at all. Uh. Frozen lasagna? Anyway, mostly I eat some protein with some veggies and call it good."

"Ah, so you can cook meat?"

"I can put a chicken breast in the oven for half an hour, anyway."

She sighed. "You fascinate me. Do you remember the first thing we worked on together?"

"I remember Min Chou introducing you as 'watch out for this one or she'll have you donating your real money, not the bank's.'" Not that Min had been immune to Claris's charms either; she'd gone pink when Claris teased back that she couldn't resist a pretty face.

"Now, now, that was only the one time, and I was just giving her an excuse to do what she already wanted to do!"

"That'll be the title of your memoir," Diego said, coming in without warning. Carpeted stairs, man. I hadn't heard him at all. He smiled at me—his hair adorably tousled, pillowcase creases on his cheek—before looking at Claris. "*I Was Only*

Giving Them an Excuse to Do What They Already Wanted to Do: The Claris Russell Story."

"In most cases I *am* doing that." She seemed untroubled by the idea. "Can you really argue I'm not?"

"Wouldn't dream of it." He kissed my cheek. "We should be feeding you real food, not random things we have in the kitchen."

"It looks real enough to me." I took the opportunity to eat an olive. "Yep. Real food. Can confirm. Anyway, Claris, didn't you *need* me for something?"

"Yes!" She spun from where she'd turned to the coffee maker and the bathrobe parted in a way that—well, let's just say I was right when I figured she didn't have much on underneath it. She flushed, but when she spoke her voice was the same brand of heedless playfulness as usual. "Apologies, my dears. I was so eager to share my idea with Mason that I hardly paused to dress. I'll be back."

"That was embarrassing," he murmured as she went upstairs. "Not that she's modest—she isn't—but we do like to solicit consent in this house before exposing ourselves. She'll actually worry about that later."

"She shouldn't. I mean, yes, I agree, consent, but also I'm not friends with real modest folks so I've seen more than that at Sunday lunch before."

"Still, we both apologize." He picked up an olive and held it to my lips. "Are you having a good morning? Or...day? I have no idea what time it is."

"Are you kidding? Woke up in bed with a gorgeous man, was swept away to feast on leftovers by a beautiful woman. Not really sure how many better ways there are to spend a morning. Or day."

"Good. I'm so glad." He licked his fingertips, leaving his lips shiny with oil from the olives.

We couldn't let that opportunity slide. I kissed him, slowly, taking my time, my non-olive hand sliding into his hair. He moaned softly into the kiss and I studied the delicate network of veins in his eyelids, the way he seemed to have a cowlick in his eyebrow, a few of the hairs growing in opposite the others.

"Glad to see my, ah, hostess faux pas has not done any lasting damage," Claris said lightly, sailing back into the kitchen.

I couldn't help pulling away. "No problem."

"You might have at least waited until we were done kissing," he grumbled at her.

"What, and stood in the hall tapping my foot? Unlikely." She pulled a notebook toward herself and ate a forkful of kimchi straight from the jar as she wrote something down.

"Did you just…you're not gonna put that on anything?" I looked at Diego. "Dude. Did she just?"

He shrugged. "She also orders Marmite off Amazon. Don't ask me where she gets her odd food foibles."

"Marmite on toast is delicious, and kimchi on anything, including a fork, is also delicious. Speaking of food, eat up! Someone should do something with this macaroni salad before it dies a horrible death in the back of the refrigerator."

"We could just throw it away before it starts growing things?"

"But how do we know for sure we won't eat it later?"

I enjoyed listening to their domestic banter. It was a lot like being around my friends: people who'd known each other a long time and had invested years in having the same sorts of conversations in the same sorts of ways. I did wonder if there was…room for me. Room for anyone. I was contemplating their closeness and obvious love for each other when a door shut loudly upstairs.

Claris smiled. "I knew she wouldn't be able to hold out long if she thought she was missing something." She glanced toward the doorway and raised her voice. "Can I interest you in macaroni salad for breakfast, darling?"

The woman who emerged (after thumping down the stairs unseen) was Perri, which I knew because I'd seen her on countless Zoom meetings, though we'd never met in person. She was short, dark-haired, brown-skinned, and looked completely put together, not at all as if she'd just rolled out of bed. Her long hair was in a twisted plait pinned to her head, she had on a tunic-style shirt over linen trousers, and boots with a heel.

I immediately tucked my borrowed bathrobe tighter around myself and straightened up.

Claris pulled her slightly resisting form close and said, "Love, Mason spent the night, isn't that nice? Mason, you already know Perri, and don't be intimidated by her strange habit of getting fully dressed to have a cup of coffee."

"I reject the idea it's a strange habit to get dressed, Claribel." The woman held out her hand to me. "Good to meet you finally."

I cringed and wiped mine off on a napkin before shaking. "You too."

"Did she keep you up all night again?" Diego asked, passing Perri a fresh mug of coffee.

"Naturally. You'd think she was looking to adopt a stray the way she goes after them. 'What about this one? She has a nice rear. Oh, or this one, he's quite tall.'" Perri shot a look of mingled fondness and exasperation at Claris. "Really."

"Now, that's not fair. We did find a good one." Claris leaned toward me. "Tall and thick and strong and delightful. I never tire of the way a man sounds when—"

At the same time both Diego and Perri began to speak, their actual words lost in the volume of their interruptions.

Claris, of course, laughed. "What? I was only saying—"

"Do not finish that sentence." Perri narrowed her eyes. "Do not."

"Oh, fine. You two are no fun sometimes. Anyway, sweetheart—"

I couldn't be certain, but judging from the storm darkening Perri's face I thought *sweetheart* might be intended to irritate her.

"—I was just going to tell Mason about our promo plan for the TikTok."

"I know you're just saying it that way to be obnoxious."

"Who? Me?" Even at her most transparent, Claris made you want to smile.

Or me. Not so much Perri, who ignored her and turned her attention in my direction. "I know you have a library of clips you haven't posted yet. We have fifteen weeks and six days until the event and I think it's time to start phase two, increasing post frequency. Is that something you can do?"

Claris put her hand on my arm. "I have all the faith he can."

"Me too." Diego kissed my cheek.

"I can do it," I said. "I have a lot of material prepped and ready, and more than that to edit down into mysterious clips and hints of pieces without giving away too much. I've got this."

Perri nodded, seeming reassured.

Having settled the thorny matter of TikTok, Claris was moving on. "Now who's up for cheesecake?" She let go of me and went around the counter. "I bought it spontaneously and forgot about it, but I'm sure it's still good. Probably."

I took advantage of the moment and kissed Diego again. "I feel like I've just gotten on a roller coaster and the safety bar's locked in place and I can't get off until Claris lets me."

"Not inaccurate."

"I'm okay with it."

He smiled. "Good."

★ ★ ★

I didn't go home until four, and even then it was only because Diego needed to work. (He claimed he didn't really need to, but I can read between the lines, and he obviously did.) I got back to my apartment in yesterday's clothes, and at some point in my thirties the walk of shame must've become a walk of "hey, I got laid last night, go, me" because I didn't feel anything but happy.

Or maybe that was just...being with Diego. What had Claris meant, that he deserved to receive everything he offered other people? Had he been treated badly in the past? I couldn't imagine treating Diego poorly, or not realizing that he gave over so much of himself. The man was a genius at intimacy.

EPIC DATE, I messaged to Dec.

DETAILS, he sent back.

I replied with an animated zipping-lips gif.

I wasn't ready to talk about it all. Not yet. Not with my friends. But I wasn't going to hide that it was good.

It was good, though. Wasn't it? Yes. Yes, it was. Candles. Kissing. Coffee in the morning. Very, very good.

Chapter Fifteen

Becoming "the voice" of Gentlemen's Fashion Week was an accident. Completely. I'd only stopped by the studio to drop off a couple of potted plants to make that front table seem a little less abandoned. I didn't even pot them myself, bought them that way from Target. No big thing.

But Moe happened to be there, which was good since I didn't have a key and hadn't fully thought the whole thing through—of course the designers mostly had jobs and lives and didn't spend their every waking moment pinning fabric and head-tilting from six feet back to see if they'd gotten the right draping or whatever. So I arranged the three plants in the center of the table and went back to say hello.

I didn't mean for it to become a TikTokortunity (Declan made that up and I don't care how dumb it is, I'm keeping it). I was talking to Moe and he was explaining the role of clothes in his life, the way he'd been able to express himself through his outfits long before he had the words to express himself in other ways, and I just…thought it was profound, so I asked if I could record him saying it.

That first interview? Where I'm in the background awkwardly prompting him and he's in front of the camera awkwardly trying to remember what he said and how he said it? Terrible. In retrospect. But I posted it with a few hashtags and it got some views and some engagement, so I ported it over to Instagram and posted it there too, this time remembering to tag Moe and Diego and add all the GFW hashtags we were using.

That got even more engagement. People liked it and commented about how inspiring it was and even shared it. More than all that, we got a rush of new followers.

I'm not real studied at social media but I know that when something I put up on my Insta gets a bunch of comments and new followers, I should do that thing again. So the next time I had the opportunity to talk to someone I started by asking if I could record, but that was Diego, so he waggled his eyebrows suggestively at me until I told him we were doing serious work.

And, since it was Diego, once he started talking about creativity and art and love and life, well, it all just sort of came together. Not for nothing, but the man could talk. And I didn't mind looking at him either.

Since I couldn't publish twenty minutes of a guy I thought was hot monologuing about Art, I cut it to him saying, "I never dreamed I'd ever be in a position to influence other designers, or even to collaborate with other designers in a meaningful way. Gentlemen's Fashion Week has already changed my life and my perspective on fashion, and we haven't even had the show yet." And then he grinned right into the lens, all hotness and dimple.

I got butterflies just watching it. My Diego interview (I asked *a couple* of questions, anyway) prompted me to petition Claris for a GFW YouTube channel so I could post the whole thing, which she approved and I did, and then, well, then we were off to the races.

It wasn't quite like one of those movie montages where suddenly a ragtag team of outcasts take the world by storm… but I'm not gonna say it *wasn't* that either. We were only a bit ragtag, yes, and we only took a relatively small part of the local fashion community by moderately steady rainfall, but suddenly people who weren't us were hashtagging GFW. Not hundreds of times a day, but enough.

Which is when Perri's emails with instructions started to increase (in her role as Claris's assistant, not her role as Claris's lover). Claris was a freaking kitty cat next to Perri.

Please make sure you use #gentsfashweek in every post; edit posts to fit if necessary.

Please make sure you tag each person in a photo or video, on every platform, and check with me to make certain we have a photo release on file.

Please post no fewer than once a day per platform, ideally at different times, and no more than five times a day until the seven days preceding the event, at which time it will be appropriate to post with increased frequency.

Please ask subjects to stand with some part of the work in view if possible.

It was enough to make a man lose his damn mind. "I do have a job," I mumbled at my phone one night as I was grabbing a salad with Diego before going home.

"Perri again? She's the best and also the worst." He frowned. "No, I take that back. She's not the worst at all, but she does have a very dry email tone."

"If I hadn't actually met her I'd probably think she was a monster."

"Yes, if I didn't know how often Claris ties her up and makes her beg for mercy it would be harder to take."

I did a double take. "Did you just... Claris...ties...begs... Perri...oh my god."

He grinned. "Yep. It's adorable. And perfect. She's definitely the person Claris has played with the longest. You'd think working together would make it impossible—or that doing scenes together would make working impossible—but they manage it."

I was still boggling over the whole thing. "Does Claris just make everyone you guys are banging into employees or what?"

"Everyone? No. And you're a volunteer." He leaned in. "Play your cards right, mister, and maybe you'll get hired on permanently. So to speak." He immediately took it back. "Oh god, no, I didn't mean—that made it sound like—I'm not, like, trading sex for work—not that there's anything wrong with actual sex work but that would be more like some kind of creepy quid pro quo and that wasn't—"

I interrupted the stream of words by kissing him. "I think I understand. And I'm not feeling sexually harassed. Plus, I'm not sure I'd want to work full-time with the person I was dating, to be honest with you."

"No, most people wouldn't. It works for Claris and I because she has so many jobs apart from this project—or any project we do together." His freshly-kissed lips curled. "On one hand the idea of seeing you all day long is *very* appealing. But on the other…there's something a bit romantic about being away from each other, don't you think? That moment you walk into the studio is like a flash of lightning on a dark night to me."

"Yeah, I'm not sure I'd want to give up the anticipation of walking up to the door and knowing I'm about to see your face." I swallowed, hearing the words and realizing just how true they were. "But Claris is a genius. We'd never have a chance to see each other if I wasn't taking pictures and doing interviews."

"You know they're calling you The Voice of Gentlemen's Fashion Week now?"

My jaw dropped. "Are not. *Who?*"

He shrugged. "Who knows? *They.* The general internet

they, you know. Collective pronoun encompassing everyone you haven't personally met but who has interacted with something you've posted."

"Oh, that they," I teased. "*The* they."

"Yes. That they. The they. The usual—" hand wave "—they. *They* are calling you The Voice of GFW because you're never on camera but they can hear you. And because you have such a very good voice."

"Why sir." I raised an eyebrow at him and held it there, watching his dark eyes dart up then back down to mine. "I didn't realize you held an opinion about my voice. An objective one, I'm sure."

"Not at all. No. Quite subjective in fact. Let's see. I like your voice on the videos, when you're asking serious questions but without making them Too Serious. I like your voice when you're just about to laugh, like the feeling is bubbling up but you haven't let it out just yet. I like your voice when—"

"Do I really sound different at all those times?"

He shot me a *don't interrupt* look. "I like your voice when you're thinking deeply about whatever I've just said, like it's so important to you that it deserves a hundred percent of your attention. And of course, I also like your voice when you're so aroused you can barely speak at all, and again, after you've come, when it's low and gentle and you ask me how I feel." He was blushing despite holding my gaze as if in defiance. "So I've made quite the study of your voice and I can say with absolute certainty that I would take no other voice before yours—as The Voice of GFW."

"In that case, I'm glad. Even though I don't really know what that means." I kissed him. "It's amazing, you know? The show. The event. Even if you are calling it a week when it's really like one Friday night."

"There are other things going on! We're having virtual

workshops from each of the designers, and a virtual coffee hour to kick it off that Perri wants to do over Skype or something. I think we're going to raise an awesome amount of money for a cause we actually believe in, which has been a goal of ours—mine and Claris's—since we got married."

"Oh yeah? What's the goal? Be in a position to give to charity?"

"Well, we always did that. Even when we had almost nothing we'd get together once a month and send twenty bucks somewhere. It just sort of made us feel like we were helping, and gave us perspective on, y'know, how grateful we were to have what we had, to be able to give what we could give. But the idea of holding an entire event solely as a fundraiser, and a fundraiser that in itself is representative of our values…" He shook his head. "It's honestly so incredible, Mase. Sometimes I can't even believe this is my life."

I traced a line along his jaw with my thumb. "You're really hot when you're all passionate. Not to bring the tone down or anything."

"Calling me hot is never bringing the tone down. And thank you. I mean. Assuming that was a compliment."

"An observation, anyway." I leaned in to kiss him. "We should eat salad. And probably I should go home. It's nearly ten."

"It is." He scooted his chair closer so our knees touched. "Or we could do something else with our time right now and pack you up the salad to take with you?"

"But if I'm eating it, wouldn't I rather be with you?"

"But if you're with me, wouldn't you rather be doing something else?"

"Fair point." I kissed him.

He kissed me.

We did some more kissing…and forgot about the salad.

★ ★ ★

I'd brought in two more plants, and Brenda had contributed a couple of aloe "newborns," sprigs of new plants that appeared in the pot with her old one, which she'd put in soil and watered, claiming they'd take off on their own.

Then one day I showed up and there were little signs in the pots, tiny paper signs on toothpicks. "Mallow Aloe" and "Edward Elephant Bush" and "Fernando Fern." The bits of paper, about the height of postage stamps but slightly longer, had intricately designed borders and old-timey script. I had no idea who'd done it, but I went out and brought back a small cactus garden with a plot of sand and rocks, which I arranged into a heart.

A few visits later the pots were bedazzled. Sometime after that they were connected to each other by fabric pathways and two tiny creatures were basking on little beach towels laid out over the sand. Then came the hanging lanterns made out of translucent beads with LED lights poked through them.

I started posting pictures of our odd little studio garden with promo—one of the few glossy promo postcards propped in Edward Elephant Bush's succulent leaves. (Claris didn't think GFW should invest in a huge run of postcards, but she'd wanted it to *seem* like we had. "It never hurts when the right people think you're flush, darling.") A family of woolen critters appeared under Edward's branches.

Then one day, as I was checking it the way I did each time I arrived, I noticed something new. A mailbox tucked away at the far corner of the pot. I opened it carefully, trying not to damage the cardboard structure and Popsicle-stick post. As I'd almost expected, a tiny note was tucked inside, with its own tiny envelope and small letters reading FOR MASE.

I grew slightly self-conscious when I was doing all this— Brenda and Moe were working away, Claris was due in any second with something Harold had ordered and shipped to the house because he wasn't at his apartment during the day to receive it there. But amidst all that I felt like I was opening a very small love letter.

The paper inside was actually folded. This dude. I shook my head in appreciation even as I bent forward to make out the tiny words.

M—
Meet me out back at 7 sharp. Civilization is at stake.
—D

I bit down hard on my lip to keep from grinning outright and then realized my back was to everyone and allowed the grin.

The studio had a small back room where Harold and Brenda had racks of pieces they'd finished or scrapped ("Either way I'm done fucking looking at 'em," she'd explained), and there was a door we always kept locked that led to the alley. I wasn't sure if it was technically an alley or not since it backed up to a cyclone fence and an empty lot full of weeds and crumbling foundations. Whatever it was, at seven sharp I casually slipped into the back room and from there I casually—okay, actually feeling covert as hell—unlocked the door and slipped outside.

And gasped. Outright. No other way to put it.

He'd set up a whole damn dinner: table with tablecloth, glowing lamps, two serving dishes with domed lids, actual plates and silverware, even cloth napkins. He was standing beside it all in a suit, smile lighting up his face, eyes glinting at me. In what felt like the far distance, cars honked and traffic continued on its merry way, but here, in this bubble in a back alley with bits of broken asphalt and old bottles underfoot, Diego had made an oasis.

He'd strung lights and streamers over the chain-link fence, making it feel even more like we were in our own private bubble. The man thought of everything.

"Sir," he said, and ushered me to a folding chair, which he pulled out. He bent low, his lips brushing the top of my ear. "Thank you for agreeing to this rendezvous. I feel certain we are unremarked."

I bit back a giggle. Two men having a fancy dinner in an alleyway in full sight of anyone driving past were not exactly top secret. Then again, I kind of liked it. We were at the far side of the strip mall, four storefronts down from the cross street where traffic zoomed by on their way to somewhere else. We'd be a colorful blur in the distance, a question mark passing through the mind of any driver aware enough to see us.

"We must remember this location for future meetings," I said in a low voice.

One side of his mouth quirked up. "You wouldn't say that if you knew how many trips it took from the car to get it all set up. I've been here for an hour and a half."

"Um, excuse me, you've been here for an hour and a half and didn't even say hi? Rude bastard."

"I will not excuse you, I was busy. Obviously." He fluttered his eyes and took a deep breath, returning his face to Spy Neutrality. "I hope you don't mind that I've ordered for you. I got us both the entrée du jour."

"Mmm, and what's that?"

He lifted the first lid with a flourish. "Gourmet sandwiches on fluffy bread."

I bit down on my lip again but harder. Arrayed on the fancy silver dish were two Subway six-inches. "Ah, yes, a…delicacy."

"Indeed. Here, allow me to serve you." He delivered my sandwich with the help of a silver pie server, carefully placing it in the center of my plate.

"This looks exceptional," I said with gravity.

"The occasion seemed to merit something a bit special," he agreed.

"The occasion of saving civilization."

"Exactly." He served himself the second sandwich and replaced the lid before sitting down.

"And what's in the other serving dish?"

He sent me a coy look. "Dessert."

I felt a pleasant sort of shiver make its way through me. "I see. Or I don't see. I'll see later." I lifted myself off the folding chair enough to kiss him. "This is all so lovely. Thank you, Diego."

His fingers slid behind my neck to hold me in place, a wordless *you're welcome* that led to more kissing. Thankfully the sandwiches were still good a few minutes later when we were ready to eat. As far as I could tell, the delay had not led to the destruction of the world as we knew it. We took our time eating. And kissing. And eating. And…you get the idea.

Dessert turned out to be two naked half-rounds of cake and a tub of grocery store frosting. Which I surveyed in a state of, okay, total confusion.

"This…seemed like a better idea in my head." He was also surveying it. "I couldn't find a heart-shaped cake tin. It made more sense when it was heart-shaped. The idea was, you know, you have two halves of the heart and then you put them together and frost them as one? Not that I actually buy into the idea that people are two halves of a whole, just that I thought it was a super-fun way of saying, um, that I…"

He was still looking down at the cakes on their platter, his hands kind of fidgeting over the offset spatula he'd picked up. I coaxed him into another kiss so he'd look at me. "Saying what?"

"Um." He set the spatula down and reached out, his fingers barely brushing against mine. "Mason, my dear man, I would like to, um, frost our cakes together. For the foreseeable future." His eyes dropped. "Oh god, that sounds dirty. I meant for it to sound romantic."

"It sounds both." I kissed him and kept kissing him. "I would love to frost our cakes together. That's hot."

He leaned his head against mine. "I made us courtship cake."

And that—that word—did something to me. Something light and bubbly inside my body, something that made me feel like floating. "We should frost it. And eat it. We still get to court even if we don't eat the whole thing, right? Because I am full of sandwich."

"Definitely. We can freeze the rest for later."

I almost said "Just like wedding cake," but I caught myself in time.

Even as we laughed and frosted and had a minor competition about who could most seductively lick frosting from an offset spatula (we tied), I could feel myself falling deeper. I fed him a bite of courtship cake with the forbidden words *I love you* on the tip of my tongue. I held back.

Be careful, I told myself, as if I hadn't already gone and fallen in love with him.

Chapter Sixteen

In the middle of the design phase for GFW, someone who knew someone who was a friend of someone's reached out to Diego to ask him if he wanted to show a few of his pieces at a benefit for Black Lives Matter. So-and-so had backed out, leaving a gap in the program, and yes it was last minute, but did he think he could maybe…

Of course he immediately said yes, and even Claris couldn't fault him for it, though it was being held during a week when she wouldn't be able to go. She'd had a trip booked for Tuesday through Friday of that week for months. "Always go Tuesday-Friday so you're leaving just as most people are arriving," she explained to me while shoving a few dishes into the dishwasher after they'd hosted a GFW planning-sesh-slash-lunch.

"Sounds ideal. You taking company with you?" I waggled my eyebrows in case the inference wasn't clear enough.

She laughed. "Darling, I take a trip to get away from everyone I know." She paused for a second before adding, "There may be one or two prospective play partners in the general vicinity if I get bored. Naturally. But they know better than to make demands."

"You're a harsh mistress, Claris."

"Oh, you have no idea." She shut the dishwasher with an air of satisfaction and turned fully to me. "And you'll need to ensure Diego doesn't exhaust himself too much at the benefit. He'll want to, but he'll need you to reel him in."

"Yeah? Shouldn't he be the one telling me that?"

"Ask him! He'll tell you the same. If he runs around all night without taking the occasional break he won't be able to sleep later, and if he can't sleep he'll lose work the following day, and if he loses work—well, it will make him more stressed out than he would be if he'd just reined in his urge to devote himself to A Cause, no matter how worthy."

I didn't want to argue with Claris over what seemed to me to be her more micromanaging tendencies. Obviously their dynamic worked for them, but that didn't mean I wanted to repeat it. So instead I went with, "Oh, I get it now. I'm The Black Friend, right? This is about optics!"

She smacked my arm. "Yes, I recruited you two years ago to be my contact at the bank all for this moment, having foreseen not only that my husband would fall for you, but also that with very little lead time he'd be asked to fill in at an event raising money for a movement at which you would be, as you say, good *optics*. Because I am a psychic evil genius like that. Now be serious—what are you wearing?"

"I…" But no. No way. I wasn't skating over that little admission. "Did you just say he—"

"I what?" Diego kissed my neck as he came to sit beside me and leaned across to kiss Claris. "What am I?"

She beamed at him. "Nothing at all, my dear. I was just getting ready to vet Mason's sartorial choices for the benefit."

"Since his sartorial choices for everything are spot-on, I'm not sure what you're worried about." He raised his eyebrow at me. "Well? Go on. Describe what you'll be wearing, I want to picture it."

"Black dress pants, burnt umber shirt, midnight blue tie, black jacket. Probably." Not that I hadn't thought about it. I had. And maybe done a video chat with Dec to make sure I'd look serious and also, as he said, *seriously hot*.

"I approve." Claris glanced at Diego. "Do you think—"

"I could wrangle something for a pocket square in burnt umber? Definitely. I can't wait to see you all gussied up, Mase. I'll just stare at you all night long waiting until I can ravish you."

The thing—one of the things—about being me is that people don't usually say shit like that. In my entire sexually active life no one had ever casually mentioned they couldn't wait to ravish me. And you know? That was a damn shame, because the promise of ravishing turned out to be pretty freaking sexy.

"Looking forward to it," I managed.

"I do believe the gentleman is blushing," Claris said. "What a lovely time you'll both have, I want pictures, and now I need to run." She waved and made off toward the rest of the house, her heels tapping on the wooden floor. I'd grown so used to Claris's way of moving, her energy, the sound of her going from place to place in her own home, I thought it would be a bit strange to be there without her.

Diego might have been considering along the same lines. "You know, you're free to stay here during the week when Claris is on holiday. You're free to stay anytime, obviously, but especially then."

"You afraid you'll be lonely without your lady?" I teased.

"I do get a little lonely. But more I was thinking you might be more comfortable staying here longer if it's just the two of us. Or not! No pressure. Um. At all."

The truth was—while ugly or sad or pathetic of me—he was right. I really liked Claris and I thought I'd gotten a lot more comfortable with the entire arrangement, but I was always thinking about the fact that we weren't the only ones home. I tended to stay in Diego's room when I might have otherwise gone to the kitchen for more coffee because there remained a lingering sense of awkwardness, like on some level I was trespassing on someone else's domain.

It was all kinds of heteronormative and problematic and I was frustrated with myself for thinking it, but I did.

"Now I feel like I've just said something completely out of turn," he said into the great aching silence during which I said nothing at all. "I apologize for overstepping."

I grabbed his hand, trying to put my feelings into words. "You didn't. I appreciate it. I'd like to stay with you if you'll have me."

"Have you? I'd be thrilled. I *am* thrilled. And it really does go for any time. I think you know by now that Claris is not at all possessive."

"No, I can see she isn't." But maybe I was. A little. A thought that did not sit well with me, so I pushed it away. "She was telling me it's my job to keep you from over-exhausting yourself at the event."

He shook his head and squeezed my hand before releasing it. "It's really not. It's not her job either, but I've given up on fighting about it. And honestly, it isn't like it hasn't been helpful in the past, but it's one of those things I'm trying to work on."

"Not over-tiring yourself?"

"Not trying to give everything to everyone, I think? More specifically. Especially with events like this one, where I'm sort of representing. I'm one of two non-Black people of color and every other designer there, appropriately, will be Black. Which is spectacular—we have enough clout now in the local fashion community to fill an entire show with people of color, you know? But I'm also aware it's a big responsibility."

"It feels like pressure?"

"Yes. On the other hand." He shrugged. "It's always pressure. We'll raise a ton of money. We've got a ton of rich white charitable types coming and they're always good for more than the ticket price. Anyway, you don't have to babysit me at the show. I swear."

"Claris really didn't say that. Or mean it, I don't think. But maybe we should have, I don't know, a secret code." I leaned in and lowered my voice. "A secret spy code. You in?"

He leaned in and lowered his. "You know I'm in. What exactly is our secret code in the service of? King and country?"

"A good night's sleep."

"Ah, far more valuable than king and country."

"Don't let the queen hear you."

He smiled. "You know, you're quite the catch, my dear fellow."

"So are you. How about if you feel your, um, alias as a secret agent is about to be compromised you can scratch the back of your neck, like this—" Instead of scratching my neck, I reached out to his, letting my fingers trail provocatively under his hair, sliding below the neckline of his shirt, nails dragging back up into his hair and scratching there. I let my thumb anchor the whole motion by rubbing circles on his neck.

He made a sort of purring sound. "Never, ever do that to me in public. Oh my god, now we have to have sex again."

"Tsk tsk, not yet. You haven't agreed to the terms of our secret code."

"I agree, I agree, and I have a lot to do, so we're going to have to make this a quickie—" He pulled my hand from where I was still seducing him via his skin. "Let's go, mister."

"See, you're saying that like it's a punishment…"

He growled and pulled me along toward the stairs. Not that I was going to complain. "Is this part of your secret agent contract, though? Are you a honeypot? Are you only having sex with me to extract information that will put the world at risk?" I was really enjoying this now. "Will me having sex with you literally jeopardize the safety of the planet?"

His eyes went wide as he pushed me through the doorway. "Yes! I was hired by my secret organization to infiltrate the top level of your secret organization by whatever means necessary, but I had no idea I'd like you this much, so now I'm violating my vow of loyalty to my country in order to, y'know, to—to—"

"Have extraordinarily hot sex with me?"

He groaned. "Yes, and oh god, it has to be fast, I'm so busy, *promise* me, Agent."

I put my hand over my heart. "I solemnly swear that I will not hold you at the brink of orgasm for an extended period of time just because I can and also possibly because I have a crack team of saboteurs breaking into your top-secret organization's network as we speak but you'll never know because when you were blissed out on endorphins earlier I stole the SIM card out of your phone and now no one can reach you."

He pulled me into him until both of us careened into the bed. "Thank god for that. Kiss me, secret agent man."

So I did. Because, y'know, national security. And stuff.

Chapter Seventeen

I was getting addicted to coffee in bed with Diego on Sunday mornings. We'd had to finagle some things to make it work—he'd be working late on a Saturday, or I'd be heading to church with my mom—but I'd just get there at ten or leave at seven; either way, we'd make time.

And even that, the seemingly effortless way he carved room in his world for me...felt special. Felt new. Oscar told me once that I might have better luck dating people who "weren't infants" (he meant in a maturity way, not a creepy age way). I hadn't really thought I'd been doing that, dating people incapable of being grown in the context of a relationship, but maybe I had.

Diego, anyway, was an adult man with adult responsibilities and a corresponding ability to assess his priorities in order to find time to bring me coffee in bed on Sunday mornings, and I gotta say, it was *nice*. After that first week, when Claris brought us breakfast, it was all Diego. Fancy mugs, chocolate-dipped cookies that melted into buttery deliciousness in my mouth, crescent rolls fresh out of the oven. The man was inspired.

And that on top of all the other things he was doing.

"Your romance game is fierce," I said as he came back to bed the Sunday before the BLM benefit.

"Is that right?" He offered me a slice of papaya, which I

ate from his fingers. Strange how things seem ridiculous in theory, but intensely sexy in reality.

"Indeed. Where did you learn such tricks, sir?"

"Oh, here and there." He kissed me, his tongue stealing the hint of fruit from my lips. "Mostly I just do the things I'd find romantic if someone did them for me."

"Then I'll have to bring you breakfast one of these Sundays."

"No. Sunday is your day." Another sweet kiss. "And anyway that's not what I mean. It's not an even one-to-one, I'd like breakfast in bed so I bring you breakfast in bed. That's where the so-called golden rule screws things up for people."

"Does it?" I snuggled down, holding open my arm for him. And he came, gracefully, as he did everything, his weight welcome against my skin.

"Well, if you only treat people the way you'd want to be treated, then you're making a flawed assumption that other people *want* to be treated the way you want to be treated."

"Don't you think it's more general than that, though? Like. 'Treat people with dignity and respect' seems pretty inarguably good for everyone."

"That would be an excellent golden rule. But it's not the actual golden rule. Think of all the things that people take for granted. Just to be kind of silly about it, when Claris and I got married we asked for no gifts. We'd moved in together already, had a small place, and neither one of us really wanted other people to decide what we were filling it with. But nearly everyone, acting with the misguided idea that since they would want gifts we also wanted gifts, got us stuff anyway. Some of it was *terrible*." He shuddered to illustrate the point.

"That's what registries are for! Dec and I had more fun filling out our wedding registry than we did almost anything else having to do with our ill-fated almost-marriage."

He smiled, but gently, tilting his head to gaze at me. "You talk about that like it's no big deal."

You couldn't really shrug with a guy in your arms, but I did a one-shoulder-shruggish movement. "It's not now. It was at the time, though. Really fucked up my head for a while. Like a breakup, but a thousand times worse."

"It's amazing you're still friends."

"*Best* friends," I corrected. "Dec's like…not that he's childish. He's not. But sometimes he can be naive, maybe. Or, just, he can hide from himself when he wants to. Later—a long time later—during one of his many exhaustive pleas for absolution, he described it as if until that moment, when he was getting out of the limo, it all hadn't been real. And I think that was true. Hard to be pissed at a guy who's so good at denial he literally doesn't believe he's getting married until it's actually happening."

"Maybe." He began to run his hand slowly up and down my body, from the center of my chest to my belly and back up again, raising the hairs there, making me feel tingly. "It must have been devastating, though. When it happened."

"The worst. The literal worst. I know no one died or anything but at the time I couldn't conceive of living through it. I went home and holed up at my mom's place for like three weeks, nearly lost my job, refused to speak to any of my friends because for a while I thought they'd all been in on it from the start, which of course they hadn't, but it was hard to, like, *breathe*. That's how bad it was."

"And then what?"

"I don't know. My mom was wonderful. She started out understanding and loving and comforting and by the end of three weeks she was like, 'I love you, but you need to get your butt out of bed and go to work.' Which I guess is what I needed to hear. Though I kept going home every night for a while because everything at my apartment reminded me of how I thought we had this big future together. I'd gotten another dresser for Dec. My roommate had moved out, so I had to borrow money for rent until I could find another one. Dec tried to help me pay but I wouldn't talk to him." I brushed my fingers in Diego's hair, feeling soothed by the motion, as soothed as I was by his hand on my skin.

"Sounds almost impossibly hard, to be honest."

"No one died, though. And really the hardest part wasn't forgiving him. I knew I was going to end up forgiving him when I couldn't stand the radio silence and asked my friends how he was doing. The hardest part was admitting that he'd been right, in a way. Wrong in almost all the ways, but right in the way that counted most: we weren't ready. Us being married would have been a disaster. So. You know. Here we are."

"Not quite. You never fell in love again?"

Early morning sounds filled the silence after his question. Birds chirping happily outside, an insistent meowing from the back porch next door that indicated we weren't the only ones up and ready for breakfast. But in the room it was just us, breathing, the movement of his fingertips, the soft shift of the fabric as I brushed his hair out over the pillowcase.

"No." My voice was lower than I'd intended it to be. I didn't want to treat this as if it was some off-limits subject, and I didn't want to let on just how lonely I'd been, how hard I'd looked for love, like it was sunken treasure and I was combing the entire ocean floor inch by inch. "I dated a lot of people. Did the apps, went on blind dates, let my mom set me up one time with the daughter of a work friend. But when there was chemistry there wasn't cohesion, when there was common ground, there wasn't a spark. I've made friends in that time, and gotten laid, but falling in love has remained mostly elusive." I couldn't help looking down at him, my heartbeat rising as I specifically didn't say it.

You know. *It.* The thing you shouldn't say unless you know the other person means it in the same way you do. The thing you might not say even then because saying it is like jumping out of an airplane and not knowing if your parachute will work.

Diego pressed a kiss to my chest, then another, then one directly over my heart. "Only mostly? So it hasn't eluded you entirely?"

I brushed the hair back from his face, where it had fallen when he began his kissing campaign across my skin. "I thought it had. I was beginning to think it might elude me forever and I was going to need to accept that...that it was time to settle down with someone who was good, even if I never felt like I was flying when I kissed them, you know? I thought maybe I was a one-trick pony and I'd wasted my trick."

His lips curled up but he didn't look at me. He dragged his tongue up my sternum, ending with another, wetter kiss. "But now you feel less like you wasted your trick?"

"Or at least I've got another one in me." I pulled him up to me and he came, willingly, eagerly, throwing a leg over mine, his body aligning perfectly over me. "Just recently, though," I murmured. "So I'm having trouble believing it's real."

"It's real. So real. Mase. Look at me."

Which should be hot, not terrifying, but for me it was both. Like I could lose myself in his eyes and never find myself again, but also like I couldn't live without them. "I don't want to screw this up."

"How can you? Plus, you can always blame me."

"No, I can't. You have a successful relationship. Obviously if this fails it'll be my fault."

"Excuse me, I can screw things up as well as anyone, and

I'll thank you for not underestimating my ability to fail." He kissed me, lingering, lips a light pressure on mine.

My eyes fluttered shut, giving myself this moment, allowing myself to feel the thing I was too afraid to say, even though I was sure he felt it.

"It's real," he whispered. "It's so real. It's real to me. I'm glad it's real to you too."

"It's real." I reached up, pulling him in closer, harder, kissing him almost frantically.

"Oh god, Mason…"

We hadn't gone at each other with so much fire, so much abandon, as if both of us were no longer being polite. I pulled his hair, he bit at my nipples, we gasped and moaned and left scratches on each other's skin in a desperate coupling, a need to be close, to be inside and outside, to leave marks to show that it *was* real, it was very fucking real, and in this moment the only thing that mattered was our bodies colliding in space, our lips meeting, our hearts beating, our rasping breaths and sighs and murmured laughs in the inevitable moments of awkwardness, of a leg coming down wrong, or a kiss landing not quite where intended.

I'd never imagined being able to laugh like this with someone I was in love with, someone I thought about all the time, someone I wanted to see every day. Never imagined a shocked moment of dead air after an ill-timed fart, followed by mad giggles and more kissing. We lay together after like animals in heat, still panting, sweat-slick bodies hot against each other.

"Upon reflection," I said slowly, "I believe you are correct. All signs do point to this being, in fact, A Thing."

The huff of his laugh cooled the skin of my chest where he'd rested his head. "I concur entirely."

And in that spirit of mutual agreement we dozed the rest of the morning.

Chapter Eighteen

The Black Lives Matter benefit was at a swanky hotel in downtown San Francisco, which meant navigating not just the traffic but also parking. Since Diego was getting there while I was still at work I decided to ride along with Jack and Oscar, who'd bought tickets before I even knew I was going. It was the opposite of anything I'd ever thought Oscar would do, but Jack was exactly the sort of white progressive with disposable income who could be relied upon to buy tickets to fundraisers.

It was a little weird that Diego was meeting Oscar (and Jack) before, say, Dec—as Dec had pointed out to me in a series of snaps earlier—but on the other hand it was also less stressful. At least I knew Oscar wouldn't be giving my mom a precis of the event.

"I hate literally everything on earth," Jack grumbled as he attempted to parallel park in a spot on a hill while driving a stick shift. "Please tell me Diego's fashion show will not be in San Francisco."

"Berkeley," I said. "Still no parking, but fewer hills."

"Thank god."

"Hey, I was all for staying home but no, you wanted to save the world." Oscar rested his head back and closed his eyes. "Go go gadget beta blockers."

Jack glanced over. "Are they helping?"

"Maybe. Or maybe it's the placebo effect."

"They're blood pressure meds. It's probably not the placebo effect."

"I don't care if it is, they're working."

"Maybe I can help," I mused. "Should I give you a little shoulder massage or something, Oscar? You know. Relax you?"

His shoulders climbed almost to his ears. "Oh my god, *do not* touch me. Do not. I will scream like a little girl."

Jack and I exchanged smirks. He shook his head. "The man is fucking with you. Obviously."

I leaned forward so my head was between their seats. "Hell yeah, I am. Sure you don't want a snuggle?"

Oscar shuddered. "Shut up. Both of you shut up."

"And, at last, we have parked." Jack killed the engine and pulled out his phone. "Of course we saw the place twenty minutes ago so who knows how many miles we're gonna have to walk to get there..."

"I'll wait in the car. Bring me back something from those fancy trays they pass around. Deviled eggs. Or a what d'you call it, amuse bouche." Oscar hadn't opened his eyes yet.

I snorted. "You want us to smuggle you out deviled eggs? What, in our pockets?"

"Shut up."

Jack closed whatever he'd been looking at on his phone with a triumphant sort of flourish. "We're not even that far away, we must have doubled back at some point in the knot of one-way streets. Buck up, Oscar. Time to go." He patted Oscar's leg in this way no one had ever touched Oscar, not in the time I'd known him. Almost perfunctorily. Like he was so used to touching Oscar, he didn't even think about it.

And Oscar didn't flinch. Sometimes you have no idea what your friends really need until they find it.

Another few assorted moans and groans later, we were on our way to the 'do.

The fashion show part of the evening happened once everyone had gotten a glass of champagne and a few refreshments (deviled eggs not among them, to Oscar's disappointment). I shot a slightly giddy TikTok for GFW gushing about how important it was to support the local scene, and how exciting it was to be on the "front line of fashion"—yes, I actually said that, and yes, I almost immediately regretted it. Still, I wanted a chance to link to the benefit's site, and, well, I was genuinely giddy. I hadn't seen Diego since early that morning and I was eager to, uh, hear how the show had gone backstage. Sure. That. Not at all that I wanted to run up to him and kiss him for putting out such brilliant work on such a short timeframe. Or working to raise money for an important cause. Or just generally being freaking amazing.

"Ugh," Oscar muttered as I scanned the crowd. "You're all lovesick and disgusting."

"Don't be jealous," I shot back.

"Really not. I've already got my—my—" He faltered hard on what exactly Jack was and broke off in confusion.

I grinned. "You're adorable."

"Shut the fuck up."

Jack patted his arm. "There there, snookums, it's okay with me if Mason knows our pet names for each other."

Oscar glared at him. "You ever call me that again and I swear I might not be able to control myself."

"And I'll come home from work one day to find you've reorganized all of my suits in backwards order and *then* where will I be?"

I could not help giggling. "That was mean."

"I'm a mean man," Jack said solemnly.

"Both of you can shut up. Plus, isn't that Diego over there?"

It was a sure sign of my desperation that I fell for it. I knew the second I turned that Diego would not, in fact, be "over there." But I looked just in case.

"Wow, Mase, you really do have it bad. I've seen the dude's picture on Google once, as if I'd be able to spot him in a room full of people. If you walk six feet away I won't even be able to see you anymore, you'll just become part of the panic-hued blur that—"

"There he is," Jack said, cutting across the ramble and nodding to my left.

Oscar spun on him and demanded to know how he could recognize someone he'd only seen on the internet, but I was gone before I could hear the answer.

My path was blocked by a lot of beautiful people in glamorous clothing, and you had to love a room full of so many people of color tricked out in their finest. I was having some warm, fuzzy feels by the time I got to Diego, who spotted me before I managed to navigate the bodies to get to him.

I saw his lips form the words *Excuse me* and then he was striding (or, okay, ambling nimbly) through bodies to get to me. We kissed before anything else, all fire and energy and delight.

"You were amazing," I said breathlessly. "The models were amazing. It was all amazing."

"Thank you, god, it's been such a rush, everyone is so nice and helpful, they even got my name and bio on the program with the GFW links—"

"—I saw! It's so good—"

Then we were kissing again, taking advantage of the crowd to share a moment together in a way we couldn't have done if there were fewer people.

"And look at this place!" I micro-gestured. "I can't believe it's this full."

"The tickets sold out last week. Did you see scalpers? We heard a rumor there were scalpers."

"Oh my god, fundraiser scalpers, that's wild! Everyone in the show was great. Some of those designs were so beautiful." I hadn't been able to gush—not in the company of Oscar and Jack—but now it all came out of me. "The headdress with the snake!"

"I know! And it's a very nice snake, they let me pet it. What about the suit with the tails that morphed into a bridal train?"

"Right? You have to talk to whoever that is for GFW next year!"

He laughed and because I was so damn happy I laughed too, as if the energy of the day demanded it.

I took his arm more formally—after a few more kisses—and said, "Okay, we're supposed to mingle. I have my orders. Mingle, but not too much, make sure you stay hydrated...oh, have you eaten anything?"

"When? We've been working forever."

"Let's start there and grab you some water as well. And then: mingling."

He inhaled long and then exhaled, leaning his head briefly against mine. "God, you're the best. Okay. And if I scratch the back of my neck?"

"I'll rescue you, obviously. Because state secrets."

"King and country," he agreed.

"Exactly."

For the next couple of hours we wandered from group to group, sometimes joining for a while, sometimes stopping just long enough to network and for everyone to lavish praise on Diego's "looks." An older white lady congratulated him on "bringing ethnicity into his clothes—but not in an *overbearing* way, you know," at which point I choked on a sip of wine and he scratched the back of his neck so we got out of there as fast as we could. For the most part, though, everyone was lovely and not at all racist.

Claris only checked in once, demanding a selfie of both of us together, then sending one of herself in a bubble bath. "Down, boy," I said to Diego, who was focusing on the message to a singular degree.

"Um. Right. Where…what were we saying?"

I laughed without even a tinge of jealousy. Maybe he was hot for his (truly hot) wife, but he was here with me, and I knew without asking that it's where he wanted to be. "Who the hell knows what we were saying? Claris derailed it by being naked. Anyway, they just brought the snake out, I demand you introduce me."

"That could go…so many different ways."

"Come on!"

We spent some time with the snake and its super-cute young handler, who gave off basically all the queer vibes, between their rainbow-dyed hair, eyebrow piercing (I didn't know the youth still did that), and the word QUEER tattooed across their fingers. Not a lot of mistaking that. So we stayed to chat a bit and they told Diego his flowery suit shirt was their favorite piece in the show.

"That means so much to me!" he said, and meant it, because he was genuine and sincere and just so *Diego*. My smile muscles hurt from laughing so much, from beaming every time he opened his mouth. By the time we were saying goodbye to Oscar and Jack my face was actually sore.

"It was wonderful," Jack said, shaking Diego's hand. "I'm glad you had the opportunity to participate."

"Me too. Next to this my own show will be a lot more low-key."

"I look forward to that one too."

"So do I," Oscar said, giving me a quick, tight hug. "But

right now I look forward to going home. Bye, Mase." Brief wave. "Diego. We—"

He was interrupted by a man exclaiming, "Can I shake your hand?" and grabbing Diego's hand without waiting for a response.

White guy. In case it needed to be said.

"Your pieces were just fabulous, I loved all three of them, shame you had to follow the snake though, wasn't it? I couldn't believe that! Not that I'm against it, just that it was unexpected, you know what I mean? And you're married!" He turned to me and held out his hand.

His grip was clammy and I extracted myself as quickly as possible.

"I had no idea you were—I mean, I knew you were married, but I had no idea—well, you know." He smiled brightly. "How long have you two been together?"

I froze. My face went perfectly still and I must have stopped breathing because no part of me could move in the harshness of that too-personal and yet totally casual question.

Oscar, somewhere far away, whispered, "*Shit.*"

"We've been together awhile," Diego said smoothly, taking my hand. "I'm so glad you liked the show. Thanks for coming and I hope you have a wonderful night." The pressure of his grip increased and I followed/was led away, with Jack and Oscar trailing in our wake. "Just keep going until we've made the point we don't want to talk to him," Diego murmured. "Sometimes they pursue, but mostly they get the picture."

I heard all that, but only beneath a loud buzzing in my ears, a rush-of-blood sort of sound, like I'd just come off the free fall of a roller coaster and could only hear the wind. A casual question. The sort of personal question strangers feel compelled to ask all the time. The sort of assumption strangers

make all the time. *You're obviously together, you must be married.*
And we weren't. We'd never be.

Which I knew. Had always known. Had thought I'd gotten over.

"That sucked," Oscar said from behind me.

"People are intrusive and have zero boundaries," Jack added.

It had sucked and people did have zero boundaries. So why
was I suddenly so angry? Not at the guy—though wow, I seriously hoped someone eventually decked him—but at myself. I would never be That Guy. The married one. The one
who could tell a story about how I'd met my one true love.

As long as I was with Diego, that could never exist.

"You okay?" he asked after leading all of us out into the
lobby for a little breathing room. He kissed me lightly but I
barely felt it. "Mase?"

"Yeah. I don't know." Except I did know. I just didn't want
to feel it.

"We'll take some time and when we go back in he'll have
gone off to bother other people, okay?"

I was staring at the pocket square. Burnt umber. He'd worn
it to match my shirt and offered me one to match his string tie.

"Mason?"

Shit. I had to get it together. I looked up—at Diego, and
past him, at Oscar, who was meeting my eyes with something
hard glittering in his. "You know. I think. I'm a little." Sentences. I needed sentences. "I'm a little tired."

Diego frowned and took both of my hands in his. "That
was awful, but I swear, it gets easier to deal with the misun-
derstanding. If you think about it, it's just a sign that we look
right together, you know? He assumed we'd been together
for years. That's kind of…kind of cool, isn't it?"

"Is it?" I couldn't stand how much he wanted me to en-
gage, to feel better, to make *him* feel better. I shook my head.

"Sorry, I'm just…" I could say I was too tired. I could say I needed to get home so I could get to work in the morning. I could make up any excuse in the book.

Or I could not.

"I need a little bit of time," I said, keeping my voice very low and very measured. "I know that you've had to deal with this for a while, but it's new to me, and I…just need some time to think about it. I'll call you tomorrow."

He swallowed hard, like he was gulping back unspoken words, and nodded. "Okay. All right. Thank you…thank you for coming. It's meant everything to me."

Because Claris couldn't be here and I'm the backup plan, yeah, I know. I didn't say that, though. There's a difference between being in a lousy mood and being a prick. I squeezed his hands and let go. "You did so well tonight. It was extraordinary. It was so….so amazing. Watching you. Your show. Your designs up there." Suddenly there was a very real chance I might lose it right here in the lobby of a glamorous hotel. "Goodnight."

I backed up a few steps and then made for the door and waited outside for Oscar and Jack to catch up.

No one spoke until we were back at the car and after we'd pulled into traffic. Then Oscar said, "Welp. You're gonna regret the shit out of that later."

I stared out the window and let the lights blur into streams of color. "Go to hell, Oscar."

"I'm just saying."

Jack sighed. "As an idea, snookums, and I know this is hard for you, but you might consider *not* saying. For once."

"Hey, he was an asshole to me when I fucked things up with you. I can't return the favor?"

"Maybe you want to give it a few days before you point out all the ways Mason's going to feel bad? Just a thought."

"Fine. But he will feel bad. And this time he won't have Dec to blame for it."

And that—*that*—hit home. "Seriously, Oscar, shut the fuck up." Except instead of sounding strong and pissed it sounded watery and miserable.

But at least this time he shut the fuck up.

Chapter Nineteen

I could have kicked myself for saying I'd call tomorrow. "Tomorrow" is one of those concepts that leaves no wiggle room. Couldn't claim it meant tomorrow-next-week, or that it was too vague to be assigned a real meaning. It was what it was. And it came way too fast.

I should have felt sad and heartsick and all those things, but I didn't. I felt angry at myself and annoyed with Diego. I knew intellectually it wasn't his fault, but on the other hand, wasn't it? Why did he have to be so happily married to such a wonderful woman? And why did he have to be so hot and sensitive and smart and romantic? Why did he have to exist in the first place? Was that really necessary?

Beneath the anger was nothing. Just a thick wall of nothing where I didn't have feelings at all. Between anger and numbness, I wasn't in a great state when I finally dialed Diego's number, each ring adding to my general feelings of ugliness.

"Hey, I'm so glad to hear from you!"

That. That was how he answered.

Before I could speak he said, "I was thinking, you know, it's the last night Claris is gone, maybe we should go out. Do something just for us. Or we could order in and light candles? Also, do you want to bring some stuff over here? I don't want to pressure you, but I'd love for you to spend the night whenever you feel comfortable, and that would probably be easier if you had a change of clothes and a toothbrush here, don't you think?"

Oh. Oh god. No. "I…"

"You don't have to, but I wanted you to know it's an option. I cleared out half a drawer for you. And you've seen my closet, so no worries there." He laughed, but it was a forced, high laugh. A laugh like he knew things weren't quite right between us.

I closed my eyes and rested my head against my kitchen counter, where I was standing, like this was a call to the credit card company to question a fraudulent charge or something. "Look," I began my rehearsed speech. "This has been nice, but it's not what I want."

"By 'this' do you mean…please tell me you mean working for GFW. Or…or going with me to events. Because that's fine! You don't have to help with the show at all. Or even go. Or…or anything."

He wasn't playing by the script. "That's not what I meant. This. This…between us. Isn't working. I'm sorry." *I'm sorry* was the kind of thing you said, wasn't it? I was pretty sure I'd said it before to make someone go away, but those two words had never burned my chest like they did now.

"But…everything has been…maybe this week was too much. I would understand that. I know I'm a lot to take on a regular week, and then this last-minute thing happened, and you were over more than usual, which I loved, but I can understand if being around me that much was…was too much. I just. I mean."

Oh god. He was…crying? Oh god, oh fuck. I squeezed my eyes shut harder. "You're not too much, Diego. You're not. I loved spending time with you."

"I loved it too. I don't understand what changed from, like, both of us loving that to right now, when you're saying…you're saying…please don't be saying it's over. Please?"

My heart might be breaking right there listening to his voice on the phone. "I'm sorry. This is my fault. I thought I could do it. I thought I could be okay with not…having the things I wanted."

"But… I thought what you wanted was…romance? And stability. And…and coffee on Sunday mornings? We have those things! We have candlelight and snuggling in bed and silly games that we only played together. I don't… I've never had that with anyone else."

"Me neither." Oh god, why was this so hard? Shouldn't it be easier than this?

"Mase, I…listen, I know this isn't how you pictured it, but…there are so many ways to do things…to do this…"

I swallowed the very real desire to cry myself. "It's not… it's not how anyone pictures it. I want to hold someone's hand and know that when people ask how long we've been together they're asking the right person."

"Wait. This is about last night? This is about some entitled asshole at a show who asked a question he had no right to ask? You're breaking up with me because of *him*?"

"It's not just him. It'll be all kinds of people." The defiance in his tone gave me strength—or maybe it was bravado—and I straightened up as if to fight with him more effectively. "People ask questions about other people's marriages all the time. You think that's not going to happen again?"

"I think I don't care what some jerk says and I'm not sure why you do."

"He asked about me as if I was your husband when I'm only your piece on the side!"

"My *piece on the side*? Is that what you think? Is that how this looks to you?" Shuffling against the speaker as if he was moving, pacing even, his voice unevenly coming through the line. "I don't have *pieces on the side*, but if I did, I wouldn't invite them to spend a week with me. I wouldn't bring them breakfast in bed or throw picnics for them in my garden. Is that really what you think? That I could be so—so—*dismissive* of you? Is that what I am to you, a piece on the side while you're out shopping around for something better?"

I thought of Tim, of easy smiles and fancy restaurants and the security of being with someone who had a 401(k) and a ten-year plan. Then I remembered lying beside Diego in the sun and wanted to stop thinking altogether. "I wish that's all you were to me," I snapped. "Then this would be easy. I'd say I was done and that would be the end of it. But you—you gave me this illusion of something that can never be, this thing that's completely impossible."

"I *gave* you an illusion? What, the illusion that you get to be in love? That you get to be doted on and cared for? Is that the illusion you're talking about?"

"I want more than that! I want to be the person someone else chooses."

"You are! How are you not the person I'm choosing? Just because I've also chosen other people doesn't take something away from you, Mason, that's not how love works, and it's definitely not how *I* work, which I was beginning to actually think you realized. I thought maybe you were seeing *me*, not a symbol for some relationship that's not quite good enough."

"All I see here is that I'll never be number one with you. I'll never have a family, and that's what I want."

A choking sound on the line. "You could *have that*. We were building it! That kind of thing doesn't happen in a day and we've only been dating for a few months."

"And how long did you date Claris before you got married? Less than a year, right? It was that fast."

"We were stupid and we got lucky it worked out at all, and leave Claris out of this, she'd be irritated with this whole conversation."

"Easy for her to be 'irritated' when I'm the one who's going to get hurt."

I knew—in the silence that followed—I'd missed something. Overlooked something. Failed completely to understand something fundamental. Because all I could hear was Diego breathing.

"Is that what you think?" His voice was soft. Angry? Sad? "You think you're the only one who will be hurt? You think Claris won't be? Or me? You think you aren't right now crushing me into dust?"

"More. I'll be hurt *more*. Because you have each other."

"That's not how this game is played. A broken heart is a broken heart."

"Not if you're happily married with a broken heart," I countered. "Then it's a broken heart and a happy marriage."

"You might give this some thought later." He was even quieter, as if he was fading away. "Maybe the problem isn't me, Mason. Maybe you need to look at yourself. When I look at you I see a man I want a future with, but I think you can't see past the imaginary future you thought you'd have to the very real future we could have together." Before I could say anything to that, he added, "I love you and wish you only the best things in life. You deserve everything you want, whenever you figure out what that is. Goodbye."

And then he hung up.

Hung up.

The man hung up on me.

Said all that and then—poof—just gone. The line buzzing in my ear until I hit end. Which I did. Like a grown man who had just closed a door. Not like a lovesick teenager who'd just lost their one and only. Which I wasn't and hadn't. Obviously.

I leaned my head down against the counter and closed my eyes again.

Yeah, well, that was the end of that. I should feel relieved. I would feel relieved soon. In a few days. It wasn't like it had been with Dec, it's not like I'd spent years building my life around the guy. Only months. And not *around* him. I would never make that mistake again. Just sort of near him. In the vicinity. I'd allowed my life to brush the edges of his.

And this was why. This was exactly why you didn't get close to people. Because they were impossible. Relationships were impossible. Sure, my friends had all somehow managed to partner up in non-gross ways, even Oscar, but for the most part relationships are the worst. As seen on TV.

Maybe I should get a YouTube channel. *Mason Ertz-Scott Presents: Relationships are the Worst.* Dec could be my first guest. Except I'd have to reel him in because he'd just want to talk about how awesome Sidney was. Okay, fine, Oscar could be my guest, because he'd never talk about how awesome Jack was, thank god. Though he was a lot less grouchy than he used to be. Not *happier*, exactly—he didn't have a personality transplant—just less grouchy.

Mia and Ronnie couldn't come on the show at all, though. They were pro-relationships.

Oh god. Oh fuck. Diego had hung up on me after saying "Goodbye" in that soft, terrible tone. Like it was forever. It didn't matter that I'd called him to say the same thing. I could have taken it back.

I wouldn't have taken it back.

That moment he saw me—was it really only last night?— and his eyes lit up and he smiled and he barely paused for politeness before he was coming toward me and we kissed like we were the only people on earth and—

The memory choked me and I pushed it down. This was better. Inevitable even. Also oh, ow, fuck, it hurt.

There was only one thing to do. Which wasn't *dissolve into a puddle of weeping.*

I texted Dec, *I'm coming over.* And I didn't wait for a reply.

Sometimes your best friend just has to drop everything to make you feel better, particularly if that friend once left you at the altar.

"You broke me forever," I said when he answered the door.

"Oh my god, what happened?" He covered his mouth with both hands and said, muffled, "You look awful."

"I look good, you bastard. I always look good."

"Um, of course, yeah, good." He pulled me into a hug. "What happened?"

"I broke up with Diego. Or he broke up with me. Or we broke up with each other. Or…" I leaned my head against Dec's and inhaled. "Everything's fucked up and I'm pretty sure it's your fault."

"Yes! Yes. I am too. Let's blame me. Come on, sit, do you want coffee? Tea? Wine cooler?"

My face contorted. "Seriously? A man shows up in my state and you offer him a *wine cooler?*"

"That's fair, but it's the only booze I have and you looked like you might be in need. Are you? I could run out for something."

I flopped onto his couch. Or his landlord's couch. The couch in the main house where Dec dogsat while the owners were away. It was a great couch. A perfect flopping couch, not like my old futon, which if you executed a flop would get you right in the spine with its metal slats.

I sensed him sit down on the coffee table next to me. "Mase?"

"It's over."

"I'm sorry."

"Why? It was so obviously a bad idea." I cracked one eye open. "You should have told me it was a bad idea from the start. That's part of the reason it's your fault."

"In my defense, I didn't think it *was* a bad idea, so I couldn't have told you that. Scooch over."

"Dec, we're like two grown—"

"I said, scooch over." He pressed himself against me and teetered there on the edge of falling until I scooched over. He wrapped an arm around my chest, threw a leg over mine, and stared down into my face like he was trying to see inside my brain. "What happened?"

"Nothing. It's just over. I'm done. He's done. The end."

"We messaged when you were in the car on the way to the thing last night and you sounded really happy."

"Well, that was stupid of me and I learned my lesson."

"Mase."

"Dec."

He sighed. "Fine, you don't want to talk about it, whatever."

"It's not that I don't want to talk about it, it's that it couldn't have worked out with me and him any more than it could have worked out with me and you."

His forehead creased in deep lines. "Uh. That makes...no sense. It couldn't have worked out with you and me because we were too young and also didn't actually want to be married to each other forever. But you and Diego—"

"—can never get married in the first place so why didn't you stop me?" I looked away. "You should have told me how stupid I was being."

"But you weren't. You were…happy. Happier than you have been in a long time. Mase, what happened? I don't get it."

"What happened is I came to my senses and realized that the married guy who's married can never marry me."

"Is that… I mean." He paused. "I guess I didn't realize it was the, like, the actual wedding part of getting married that mattered to you? I thought it was more the…relationship."

"No, that's what matters to *you*. And Sid. And probably Oscar. But I want to throw a big party and invite everyone and stand there with a person. And be chosen by them."

His face crumpled. "Oh, Mase, I'm so sorry. I fucked that up so badly."

"It's not about you, sunshine."

"Yeah, but…"

I set my expression into something I hoped gave off real serious *not in the mood to argue* vibes and he faltered.

"I'm really sorry it didn't work out. That sucks. Do we hate him now or what?"

"God, I wish. No. We don't hate him. We just have to say goodbye to him." Which reminded me so much of his voice, Diego's voice, soft and tragic as he said the word. I looked away. "It's fine. I'll get over it."

"You were really brave for trying, though," he offered. "Maybe this is a transitional love. On the way to someone else."

I didn't want to be on the way to someone else. I wanted to feel the warmth of Diego's skin under my palm as I kissed him. *Oh god, stop.* "I shouldn't have started it. I had a perfectly fine thing going with Tim and then this happened and I'm just pissed at myself for even bothering."

"I mean, define 'perfectly fine thing.'"

I gave him a look. "As I said: I had a *perfectly fine thing* with

Tim and I'm pissed I dropped that in favor of—whatever this was supposed to be."

"Suuuuuper helpful, being pissed at yourself. Well done."

"Shut it."

"Make me."

"You realize if I tickle you right now you're gonna go over the edge and land on your ass, right?"

"You realize I will totally take you with me, right?"

So I didn't tickle him and he didn't pull both of us onto the floor. He put his head down next to mine on the arm of the couch. "I have ice cream."

"How much, though?"

"Partials of at least three flavors. I had kind of a week at work."

"Aw, tell me about it over ice cream buffet?"

He blinked at me for a long moment, and I felt this wave of gratitude that we never lost touch, that after all the shit we'd put each other through we could still do this, *be* this, for each other. "You sure you don't want to talk about your thing?"

"No. I mean yes. I'm sure. Bring me your ice cream, young man, and we shall feast."

His smile quirked to one side. "Sir, yes, sir."

Diego would have picked up the thread, would have taken it further, played along, invented a character, maybe, or a storyline. He was so good at that. So good at making me not feel foolish.

So good at reading me. Even better than Dec sometimes.

Oh god. "I need ice cream like *right now.*"

Dec jumped up. "On it! Bowls or just spoons?"

"Spoons. And we're eating all of it."

"Totally agree."

Chapter Twenty

I woke up the next morning feeling free and fresh and like I had an entirely new outlook on life.

Okay, maybe not exactly.

I woke up the next morning knowing I'd had way too much ice cream, not enough actual food, and I was too old to combine dairy and sugar in those quantities. My only consolation was Dec sending me a snap of him looking miserable with a little bird flying around his head like in an old cartoon.

We need to lay off the ice cream, babe, I sent back.

He sent back vomiting emojis, which, yeah, fair.

I was not, however, going to give in to the doldrums. Screw that static. I showered and shaved and wore one of my favorite ties to work. When I caught a moment with my supervisor I told her that I was wondering if there was anything I should be doing if I wanted to pursue growing in my role.

She seemed…genuinely delighted? Not in a fake "Oh, um, yes, of course, well…" way, but she got smiley and sounded happy and talked to me for half an hour about different paths she could see for me. Did I want to go more into sales and marketing? I could become a product specialist. Or maybe I wanted to focus more on community relations, in which case I might end up on the more corporate side of things, but given what I'd demonstrated with my work supporting local organizations, maybe that was a direction I'd be interested in taking my career?

And like—I had a career? Apparently? I mean, I knew that, sorta. But part of me had always expected to move on to something else eventually. The bank was the first job I'd had out of college and it was meant to be temporary. But maybe…it wasn't.

Anyway, that was an ego boost, which was good, because whenever a minute or two passed with nothing specifically happening I remembered Diego's voice in my ear and almost started to feel something, which I did not have the energy or time to deal with. The name of the game was: never stop moving, never start feeling. So I didn't. Though I did manage to shoot an email to Perri explaining that something unavoidable had come up and I wouldn't be able to continue on with the GFW socials, but all the passwords were the same as they had been and all the raw videos I'd recorded and clips I'd edited were in the shared drive. I also offered to help out until they could find someone to take over my job. The event was still two months away, but I didn't want to leave them in the lurch. Within three minutes she'd sent back one word: *Understood*. No request for any additional help.

Which, okay. That was that. I was…done. With all of it. *Understood*.

Since it was Saturday I got off work earlier than usual and headed to Ikea, texting the Motherfuckers thread from a stoplight. Ikea's basically like Disneyland but with home furnishings and before I knew it Ronnie and Mia and Dec and Sidney were there, sitting on different couches, contemplating different bookshelves. Ronnie and Mia volunteered to test out all the beds for quality control purposes.

Finally we all settled into a living room we liked and pooled our ideas for my apartment.

"I've got it." Mia pointed at a couch. "That sectional, that chair over there, this coffee table, two of those bookcases along the wall between your windows. Rearrange so the sectional faces the far window, then you can get that cute little bistro dining set and you'll have a dining room."

Dec nodded but Ronnie didn't look convinced. "I don't know. Wouldn't that make it feel like you were kind of making part of the living room into a hallway if the back of the couch was to it?"

"Hadn't thought of that. You would be kind of walking right into the back of the couch. But over that you'd see a cute little living room!"

"True."

"Unless you maybe emphasize that?" Sidney suggested. "Instead of making it incidental, make it intentional. That could be your entryway."

"The *foyer*," Dec said. "Yes! Classy."

I tried to picture it and couldn't. "How, though?"

They closed their eyes for a moment. "You walk in and you've got the back of the sectional. So you could add a little cabinet or even just a coatrack and a small table or something—a place to take off your shoes and put your keys. That plus the back of the couch would make it feel very entryway, but without being too crowded or losing the openness. Maybe a mirror on the wall."

Dec clapped and kissed them. "You're super hot, FYI."

They went pink. "Quiet."

"Shan't."

"I love that," Mia said. "Also I was spending money like you're rich, but you can do the same stuff with your current furniture and just add a few smaller pieces. Though I really love that sectional. And you really *could* use more space to sit that isn't the floor."

I'd checked all of my accounts and my budget. I couldn't afford a ten-thousand-dollar apartment remodel, but what the hell, I could treat myself to some home decor. "Everything I've got now is stuff we found on the street or was passed down from other people when they upgraded. And anyway, I like building flat-pack furniture. Let's go crazy. And then you're all going to have to come back to my place for load-in because I won't be able to fit everything into the car."

In the end, we did get the armchair, but not the sectional, to Mia's sadness. (By the time we'd made it to the cashier she'd already gone online and bought a slipcover for the futon I currently had to make herself feel better. "If you're going to keep that thing but change everything else, it should at least look decent!") We did pick up the bookcases, a longer coffee table than the one she'd originally found, a legit kitchen island, a couple of stools, and all the things I'd need to give myself a fake entryway.

And, okay, a huge rug, some kitchen stuff Dec claimed I needed, new towels, new sheets, a bedside table that matched the one I had so I could feel like an adult with one on each side, and a few other odds and ends. It didn't come to ten grand (or realistically anywhere close), but let's just say it was more than I'd planned to spend.

Since we only needed two cars for the stuff I'd gotten, and since Ronnie and Mia had gone on a mini spending spree of their own, we loaded all the stuff into my and Dec's cars. He dropped Sid at their place so they could get some work done while the rest of us went back to my apartment and unloaded all my goodies.

"Still think you should have gone with the bistro set," Mia said after we'd rearranged everything that didn't need to be built to her satisfaction.

"But now you have *an island*." Dec caressed the box. "I've

always wanted an island. With butcher block on top. And stools! Look how cute your stools are, Mase!"

"Agree." Ronnie righted the one she'd just finished building and sat down. "And comfy. So. Now that we've thoroughly cluttered the place, I think Mia and I will go home."

I gestured to the boxes we'd piled everywhere. "What, take me shopping, instigate my purchases, and leave me with all the boxes? What kind of friends are you?"

Mia kissed my cheek. "The very best. We have some boxes too, you know."

Dec sighed longingly, still fondling my not-yet-built island. "I think I'll take off too. I like lurking creepily nearby while Sid edits videos. Unless—" He glanced at me. "Do you want me to stay? I mean—"

"No," I said firmly. "I'm not fragile, I'm fine, go ahead. Thanks for Ikea-ing with me."

Mia shot a look at Dec. "Wait, why would you stay?"

"No reason." I did *shoo* motions with my hands. "Go on, get out."

"No, but—"

"Everyone can leave now," I said loudly over Dec whispering, "I'll tell you later." With friends like these. "Oh my god, fine, I broke up with Diego. Or he—we—broke up. It's really not a big deal, I'm not sad, I'm not fragile, everything is fine. Now go so I can get building."

Mia's eyes widened. "Oh, no, Mase, I'm so—"

"*Don't.* It's completely okay."

Ronnie got up from the stool and gave me a hug. "Now this all makes sense. I hope the retail therapy and building help, Mase."

I gritted my teeth. "There's nothing to help, it wasn't retail therapy, I've been meaning to do this for a long time, and now I have, so everybody wins."

"Right, yeah." But she tossed A Look at Mia and Dec.

"I'm really fine," I insisted, only it was one of those times where you heard yourself say something and the pitch of your own voice made it sound like a lie. I forced myself to take a deep breath and said to my dearest friends (minus Oscar), who were all shooting me Sympathetic Faces, "It was fun, now it's over. No need to worry about me. I have a lot to do. I'm going to make a sandwich and get to work."

"Do you want me to bring some dinner over—"

"*No.* I really just want you all to stop looking at me like I've been diagnosed with something. Everything is *fine*." How many times had I said the word *fine* in the last five minutes? Ten? How many more times would I have to say it to make it true? Maybe a thousand.

But no, *don't think about that.* I herded them to the door and sighed with relief when I finally closed it behind them.

Then I turned back to the Ikea-flavored apocalypse that was my apartment. Time to get to work.

I built furniture until two in the morning. I had Sunday off and nowhere to be, so furniture building it was. The armchair went fairly easily, the coffee table took more finagling than I'd expected, and the bookcases took half of forever. I forced myself through putting together the bedside table, by which point I was so tired my vision was blurring.

Still, I wanted to wake up and see pretty things, so I kept going. I'd leave the kitchen and entryway for the morning, but I added the new bathmat to the bathroom, and put up the new towels. I also changed the sheets and duvet cover, fluffing everything and repositioning the bed to account for the second nightstand, which looked damn good.

I always slept on one side of my bed, the side toward the door. As if it mattered. As if anyone spent the night long enough to have the other side. So tonight I decided to sleep right across the middle, diagonally, taking up all the space.

If I was going to be alone, I might as well enjoy it, right?

I'd also picked up a little runner rug for beside the bed, which looked even better than I'd thought it would with the new duvet. After all that I took a shower, said goodnight to my refreshed-looking bathroom, wiggled my toes on the new rug, and climbed into new sheets, stretching my feet all the way to the far corner and flopping around a little until I could find a comfortable spot.

I should have slept hard after all that. The long day. Ikea. Building. Decorating. I should have hit the pillow and slept like a damn rock.

But I didn't.

The moment I closed my eyes it all hit me, all of these emotions, all of this loss, all of this…this fear. That I'd never be happy. That I'd always be lonely.

I tried curling into a tight ball and ordering myself to go to sleep. When that didn't work, and it was nearly four a.m., I got back up.

Ikea instructions should come with a warning to never build when tired. By the time I had that dumbass island finished I'd probably fucked up and had to redo eighty percent of the steps. Also I low-key hated the thing. But that was just an association from the drama of building it. Right?

I made coffee and drank it while standing at my new kitchen island, which wasn't as wobbly as I was worried it would be, surveying my domain. Mia had been on target; I needed a new couch. A real couch. A non-futon couch. Especially with the bigger coffee table I'd bought mostly because I knew a bistro table wouldn't be someplace my friends could eat, so we actually did need a bigger table in the living room. But now the table threw the balance off wildly unless I wanted to keep both armchairs and sort of position them at the short ends…

No. No way. For one, it would look terrible. And for two, Mia would probably haul the old one out when I wasn't looking and leave it on the curb with a FREE sign.

Still. Now I really wish I'd picked up the sectional. What's another seven hundred bucks?

I stomped, folded, and haphazardly stacked the boxes to take down to recycling. It was easy enough to bag up the trash and leave it in a corner with the armchair. I had the little hanging entryway organizer deal halfway built when my body hit a wall.

Went back to bed. Slept. Got up again. Made more coffee. Wondered what I'd been thinking to buy all this stuff. And also why I hadn't gotten new coffee cups because I'd had the ones I was using since Dec and I got them just after college. Just before our ill-fated wedding.

He'd let me keep everything. Made me keep everything. Out of penance or whatever. As if I wanted to look at that stuff and all the memories it held. These days most of the memories were just endless days like this one, getting up, making coffee, waiting for something to happen. Waiting to start my life.

I worked on the apartment the rest of the day and fielded numerous sympathetic inquiries into my well-being and offers of food, which were really coded requests to drop by and make sure I was *really* okay, not just claiming to be okay. I said no and kept plugging away until I was more or less satisfied with my space.

I did tell Mia to cancel her slipcover order. I was for sure getting a new couch. I did some shopping on the Ikea website to make sure I knew what I wanted and where I'd find it in the warehouse so I wouldn't have to go through the store, then went *back* to Ikea and picked up a sectional. One slightly longer than the original that Mia had pointed out, in dark leather, for a bit more than seven hundred bucks. But you know what? I had the money and I wanted it.

And it looked damn good in my living room. Then, finally, I was done. Two days, a lot of money, two trips to Ikea, and a brand-new apartment. More or less.

Now with entryway. Excuse me, *foyer*.

Chapter Twenty-One

I loved my new apartment. I had this one terrible second with it where I thought *I have to take a picture to send Diego*, but I shut that shit down and distracted myself by applying to volunteer at the queer youth center Claris worked with. It was local and they seemed to be doing cool stuff and anyway, I had time.

A lot of time. More time than I'd realized when I'd just been going to work every day and drinks once a week and nights out with Tim here and there. For a stretch in my mid-twenties I'd gone on dates all the time, or Ronnie and Oscar and I would hit the clubs and see if we wanted to take anyone home (me and Oscar) or vet our friends' one-night stands (Ronnie). I had no idea what I'd replaced all that with. You-Tube? Podcasts? Video games? Probably video games.

When I'd been going around taking pictures and shooting videos for GFW I'd rediscovered entire hours of my life, as if before that everything between leaving work and going to bed had blurred into one long, fuzzy question mark. Now that I was used to Doing Something with that time, I got restless sitting in my (much improved) apartment.

I tried to Konmari my stuff, except I'd just done that like six months ago and there wasn't really anything I could now purge. Go, me?

I tried going to a club I used to hit all the time when I just wanted to get laid, but it made me feel old and by eleven I was ready to go home and listen to a little *Magnus Archives* while getting ready for bed. I'd queued up *Snap Judgment* before realizing that even hearing Glynn Washington's voice made me think of Diego and want to cry. So I quickly backed out of that and filled my ears with something else.

And I didn't actually want to get laid. Being around all those pretty young things smiling and strutting for each other like peacocks waiting to see whose plumage would impress them the most just kind of depressed me. It had been fun back in the day. I remembered the feeling of that smile, closing my eyes and dancing by myself secure in the knowledge that other people were watching and appreciating. I just didn't have the energy for it anymore.

Check that off the list of ways to fill time, anyway.

I extended my pre-work gym time by half an hour and added a yoga class to the mix. I'd been neglecting the gym a bit when I was doing all those other things, so I told myself this was a good excuse to get back to it and push myself. I hadn't done yoga since college. The Motherfuckers had all joined a Saturday morning class held on the quad, but only Mia and I kept going after the rest of them decided sleep was a way better idea.

She worked retail hours, but I dropped her the link to the class I was doing and said she should hit it with me when she could.

The youth center got back to me almost immediately and asked if I wanted to be a "tutor" (in quotes). One of their big pushes was providing afterschool activities and "facilitating space for youth to fulfill their full potential," which the guy who answered the email explained as, "Basically, a lot of our kids either don't have safe places to go after school, or don't have adults around who will help them reach their goals, whether it's college or finding a job or finding a training program. Or anything else! :) So we try to have a couple of 'tutors' on hand in the afternoons to help out with that."

I said that sounded awesome (because it did) and to sign me up. We made an appointment for me to go down the next day for a meeting. I could definitely do that on my week-day off, and the center was open later than I'd realized, so maybe I could go in on days I worked too, if the whole thing seemed legit.

Even with all that I felt antsy. Maybe I needed a project. One of those self-improvement projects, like learning a lan-guage, or taking up watercolors or woodworking. Maybe I needed to get serious with Tim. At least that potentially had a future. I just needed to be patient. Relationships take years to develop, after all.

We were doing drinks at The Hole and I was in the middle of telling my friends I was getting back on the dating horse, which they should have been happy about, when I realized they were all doing that *shooting meaningful looks at each other* thing. "What? You guys think Tim's found someone else al-ready?"

A round-robin of blinks. "Nooo," Ronnie said, but with a dangling cliff on the end of the sentence.

"So what?"

"I don't know, I guess. You know, it's probably good to get out there. And you do know Tim, so that's..." She looked around. "Right, you guys?"

Mia seemed more perplexed than made any sense. "Sure, if that's what you want."

"Of course it's what I want," I said, nettled. "He's totally normal and stable and *single* and has goals and a consistent in-come and yes, that's what I want, okay?"

She visibly pulled back. "All right."

"So he's boring," Oscar said.

"Fuck you, Oscar."

"You guys, come on," Dec said. "Don't fight, okay?"

"I'm not *fighting*," I said through clenched teeth, wary of raising my voice and being The Guy Who Gets Shouty At The Bar. "But you know what? I kind of had an epiphany and decided to make some changes, and if you guys can't be happy for me—" I shrugged, having no way to finish that thought.

"Oh sure, yeah," Oscar said sarcastically. "An epiphany, also known as a breakup."

I could feel myself starting to get pissed like a heater had switched on under my skin, flooding me with anger and warmth, and struggled to keep my voice down. "So what if that triggered it? I shouldn't have bothered with that situation so now I'm going to focus on the things that I *should* bother with. I didn't need to be gaming for forty hours a week, and now I'm not, and it feels good. I've overhauled my lifestyle, lessons were learned, the end."

"It's been literally three weeks," he countered.

"Look, I'm not saying you have to change *your* life, I'm just saying I want to change mine, and it's for the better, so fucking lay off."

He rolled his eyes. "Yeah, okay, Mase. But I know exactly what *running from your feelings* looks like, so you're only lying to yourself."

"Hey, hey, hey." Dec leaned earnestly over the table, almost knocking over his half-empty glass of cola. "Let's not fight. Just. Y'know. If you did want to talk about how you were feeling, Mase, we're totally here for it."

"Excuse me, I *am* talking about how I'm feeling. I'm feeling great. I'm doing yoga, I'm volunteering—or at least I will be—I redid the apartment, and I'm looking at language courses, so I'm actually doing really well, I don't know why you're all looking at me like I'm a ticking time bomb because I'm not."

"We aren't," Dec said. "Not at all. Right, guys? Just, we want you to know we have your back. Whatever you want to do, we have your back—"

"It sure doesn't feel like it. What the hell is everyone's problem with Tim? He's a good guy and none of you wanted anything to do with him, which is such shit after all the losers I've dated. Then I meet this totally unsuitable person and suddenly you're all supportive? What the actual fuck." I had not meant to say all that, but now that I had, I realized I'd been thinking it for a long time.

"It's not that," Mia said. "It's not that we don't support you. It's just that we want you to be happy."

"I *am*."

Oscar laughed harshly. "We've actually seen you happy, dumbass, so we know what it looks like, and that Tim guy wasn't even close, but whatever."

"Come on," Dec said. "I'm sure Tim's great, and if you love him, we'll love him. We'll care about whoever you care about, Mase, and if it's not Diego, that's fine, we just—"

"I'm *not* talking about that." The words cut through the air so sharply his teeth clanged together on whatever else he was about to say. "I know you want me to go pair off so you can stop feeling guilty, but that's not my fault, and I'm not going to hook up with someone just so you can feel better, so get over it, Dec, okay?"

Everyone froze. Except Oscar. Who clapped, slowly, with intention. "Yeah, good show. Mase, pro tip, when you go after your closest friends who are only trying to help, you're the asshole."

"Shut up, Oscar."

"You can't hurt me, but you can hurt Dec, so congratulations on that."

Had I? Fuck. I hadn't meant to. I hadn't meant *not* to, I guess, either, but it wasn't like I felt happy about it.

Dec shook his head. "I'm fine. It's fine. Sorry. I didn't mean… I wasn't trying to say…"

Mia patted his hand and Sidney shifted a little closer to him. A show of support because *I* said something fucked up, when I was usually the first in line to make him feel better.

"Yeah, I think I should take off." I put down some money because I hadn't bought my round yet and scooted my chair back. "Sorry, Dec. Like." I had no idea what to say and I was still pissed, still defensive. "Never mind."

I left. The bar. Drinks. My friends. Jack silent, Oscar smug, Ronnie ponderous, Mia sad, Sidney focused on Dec, and Dec…wasn't actually crying. But I knew what he looked like when he wanted to cry, and that was it.

Oscar being right was the worst feeling, but I was clearly the asshole. I got home, got a beer, sat down to play video games and felt like a hypocrite, so instead of doing that I finally forced myself to do some research into budgeting programs. It had been on my list of Adult Shit To Do for years and I'd never actually sat down to do it.

I spent the rest of the night trying to figure out how to work the thing I'd downloaded, how to organize categories, and how much money needed to be put into them. It required a lot of going back into credit card statements to see how much I spent on gas each month, how much car insurance and maintenance cost, what kind of money I spent on household goods, and what felt like a hundred other things.

Aside from my massive Ikea haul, I apparently didn't spend that much money on big purchases. I was pretty shocked at how those Amazon transactions added up, though. Since I wasn't going out to eat all the time or indulging in a daily Starbucks habit I'd figured I was living on the cheap, but by the time I'd looked at the entire last year I felt like Jeff Bezos should be sending me a thank-you card.

It took one more beer and a huge bottle of water, but by the time I went to bed I had a functional budget I understood how to use, and that felt pretty fucking solid for a night that had started out horribly.

See? I was fine. More than that: I was taking care of business. Being proactive. Being productive. Getting my shit together. These were all life-affirming changes, whatever my friends thought. And what did it matter why I was making them? I was making them, and that was the point. Full stop. The end. I deserved a pat on the back, not a critique.

In case you're ever wondering, *I deserve a pat on the back, not a critique* is actually not a great lullaby.

In the midst of all this adulting and taking care of business and feeling totally fine, I called Tim. Things had dropped off between us, but nothing bad or negative had happened, so I figured I didn't risk much in saying hello and inviting him out to dinner. He seemed happy to hear from me and we made a date for that Friday night. I even made reservations for us at one of the better seafood restaurants.

"So good to see you," he said, kissing my cheek, as he usually did.

"You too." We went to our table, which overlooked the darkness of the bay and the lights of San Francisco in the distance.

After a few minutes of small talk and placing our orders he smiled at me, expression quizzical. "I was a little surprised to hear from you, to be honest. I thought you'd moved on and just not had the grace to tell me."

"Yeah, sorry about that. I got caught up in this whole—in this project I've been working on." As much as I wanted to look away, I didn't. "It was not my intention to ghost you, I should have said I was busy."

"Water under the bridge. Project for the bank?"

And so somehow I found myself explaining Gentlemen's Fashion Week to Tim, who of course made all the right noises and nodded in all the right places. "You sound quite passionate about it," he said when I was done.

I flushed hot and took a sip of water. "Sorry, I guess I got a little carried away. So, um, what have you been doing lately?"

"Mostly the usual things." Pause. "I dated someone for a while. Thought it might be getting serious."

Which was not what I'd been expecting. "Oh. What happened?"

He shrugged. "It didn't. But it hit me harder than those things used to hit me. I must be getting old."

"Right? I just had a mild midlife crisis and bought out Ikea to redo my apartment."

"I'd like to see that one of these days," he said, smiling in that way that meant it was an open invitation for me to ask him back after dinner, that way that implied sex was definitely on offer.

But instead of thinking about sex with Tim on my new sheets, I could only think about how I'd never brought Diego to my place, wondering what he would think of it, imagining the way he'd grin when I told him he was standing in the foyer.

"I'll give you a call when I have everything set up," I finally said, realizing the silence had gone on too long.

Tim seemed to realize it too. "Sure, give me a call sometime. Oh, I think those are our entrées now. I hope I don't regret getting the salmon…"

And that was…it. We caught up on things—the status of his sister's new job, my mom's various house projects—and then we cheek-kissed goodnight outside the restaurant and headed for our separate cars to go to our separate places to sleep alone in our separate beds.

I'd gone from dating one stable (if slightly boring) guy, to falling stupidly in love with a guy who was anything but boring, to having nothing but an empty apartment to look forward to at the end of the day. Well, and a bunch of new furniture. So at least there was that.

Chapter Twenty-Two

I tried to go back to normal. My new normal. My new, productive, kickass normal. A normal in which I met (and genuinely liked) the folks running the youth center. A normal in which I had another discussion with my boss about moving up and she outlined some ideas that went beyond small promotions and went more into different areas of the company—if I didn't mind working in a more corporate environment.

I'd never actually thought about it before, but we had a serious conversation about the "demographic makeup" of the higher-ups. "And they're all really trying to get in line with the bank's goal to create opportunities for underserved communities, but since a lot of them are former frat boys, you know..." I figured I probably did know. And I wasn't sure I wanted to work with that, but then again, I'd decided to keep my options open. So that's what I was doing.

The new normal was good. New-normal-Mason had a serious budget and lived in a better apartment (though he also had a lower savings account balance). He was going places with his life, exploring new roles in his communities, doing all the things people were supposed to do. Also Oscar and I had made up via 7 *Days to Die*, because while I didn't want to go back to the old butt divot days, I'd missed the mental space I occupied when I played games, and we'd almost finished building Elsa's ice palace.

I definitely wasn't compulsively checking in on the Gentlemen's Fashion Week socials to see how things were going. (Fine, they were going fine. Though engagement was down because posting went down after they ran out of my pre-edited clips, and TikTok had all but been abandoned after a couple of halting video attempts by the designers. My guts twisted a little when I realized how old-normal-me had effortlessly fallen into a regular posting schedule and no one had picked up the mantle...but it wasn't my problem. Not really. Not anymore.)

New normal me was actually feeling better at work, whether because I was doing fulfilling things outside of work like Brenda had recommended or because I felt less like I was treading water in my actual job, I didn't know. Or care. I wasn't having to drag myself in every day anymore, and that was a huge improvement. I was moving up in the world. Moving on. Everything felt solid.

Just back from my break, fresh cup of coffee in hand, walking to my desk, and *bam*, a voice, *that* voice. "Oh, there he is! Yes, I'm sure you've been quite helpful but you see my husband banks with Mason and he told me that Mason is the only man for my business, but thank you all the same."

God. No. *Claris.*

I swallowed a sudden lump in my throat and pretended I hadn't heard her. Like a grown-ass man being cornered at work by his ex-boyfriend's wife. Oh god, my ex-boyfriend, I hadn't thought of Diego like that—hadn't allowed myself to think of him as my boyfriend at all—and now that I had, little emotional nerve endings shriveled up in pain.

But no. It wasn't going to be like that. I was a professional and Claris was a consummate professional and this was going to be perfectly professional, dammit, if I had to show her the blandest, most resting-bitch-customer-service face I had.

"Mason!"

I set my coffee down and took her offered hand. "Claris, how good to see you," I lied, lied, lied. *How terrifying to see you* would have been way more accurate.

"I'm sure," she replied dryly. "I'd like to open a savings account for some funds that have abruptly been returned to my portfolio. Will you help me?"

"Of course. I could hardly refuse." Meaning, *It's my job, I literally can't refuse, and you know it.*

Her utterly benign smile reminded me that however good I was at performing politeness, Claris, who took joy in acting, would be better. "I am so glad to hear that. Once you find a man—or anyone else—whom you can trust with your, ah, holdings, it's always such a relief to work with him. Now then." She presented me with a folder identical to the one Diego had used to open his accounts. "This is everything you should need."

I took a look. It was, naturally, everything I would need. "Thank you for being so prepared."

"I'm sure you know that I am *always* prepared."

Good god, if she'd purred like that at me in any other context I would have had to adjust myself. As it was, I just tried to focus, hard, on inputting all the correct information into the correct fields, which apparently Claris took as an invitation to soliloquize.

"Trust is such an important quality in one's partners, don't you think? In business and in life. Take the situation we're facing today. If I give you access to my assets, shall we say, how do I know you will preserve their worth and not squander their value?"

Could the metaphor get any freaking more obvious? I made a vague noise to show I was listening, and the annoying part was that I couldn't help but listen. Claris was exceptionally hard to ignore.

"Money, like people," she continued smoothly, "need not be exclusively committed to one establishment. In fact, one might argue—and I would—that it makes far more sense to carefully manage your assets across a few sensible institutions than it does to invest them with just one person. No offense, of course, darling."

I looked up, meeting her eyes for the first time since she'd sat down. "Some people like the security of knowing they've put all their trust in one person. Or institution."

"And to those people I wish a hearty good luck, though I would consider that security dubious at best and a foolhardy illusion at worst. But when an opportunity arises that offers maximum rewards, wouldn't you advise a client of yours to thoroughly assess their investment strategy?"

"I guess that would depend on the risk."

"But doesn't everything come with risk? I think sometimes there are risks that are so baked into our experience we almost forget to consider them risks. With new ideas one's always so much more sensitive to the potential for negative outcomes. Have you ever found that to be true yourself?"

"Claris, I..." ...had no idea what to say. I went back to my screen, my fields, my forms.

She, with uncharacteristic mercy, didn't push harder.

We completed the regular account opening procedure right up until the end. I thought I'd gotten away with an extended metaphor and a question I couldn't answer the way she wanted me to answer it.

She stood up, holding her things, and I repeated that it was good to see her (less of a lie now that she was leaving). My gaze caught hers and she looked... I don't know how else to describe it...*sad*. Dreadfully sad. "There are few times in our lives when something comes along that has the potential to introduce extraordinary joy into the world. I sincerely hope one of the two of you will come to his senses, sooner rather than later, and realize this is just such a time. Because I have to tell you, it's *infuriating* to watch you fuck it up." Her lips turned up in a cheerful smile that didn't begin to touch her eyes. "Goodbye, darling. See you again soon."

I forgot to say goodbye. She whooshed out, leaving me hollow-feeling and suddenly very alone.

What was she talking about? It was over. Had been for weeks. He hadn't spoken to me. I hadn't spoken to him. I'd moved on. Definition of over.

The thin veneer of control I'd maintained since putting down the phone on his broken *goodbye* abruptly vanished. When I sat back down in my chair I felt deflated, as if Claris had poked a hole in me and all the air had rushed out. I returned to the old normal for the rest of my shift.

Damn Claris.

Across all versions of myself, some things stayed the same, like going to church once a month with my mom. I was rarely tempted to skip church. I'd resented it when I was younger and only gone out of obligation, but at some point I'd noticed that both of us were getting older. Not that my mom *looks* old at all. Just there was this one day I showed up to take her and I saw her like I'd see any woman her age, and thought about her as *an older lady*. Suddenly my brain recognized her as someone who maybe wasn't going to be around forever.

So even when I don't really want to go to church (don't tell her), I always want to spend that time with the woman who kicked my butt when I needed it and cuddled me in the middle of the night when I needed it—and almost always knew the difference.

This phrase Claris had said, about the thing between Diego and me having the potential to bring "extraordinary joy" to the world, stuck in the back of my head and I couldn't shake it loose. It was absurd. Obviously. The world being pretty freaking indifferent to minor love affairs and all. But no one I'd ever been with made me feel more like…hell, I don't know. Like it *mattered*. Not just me, or him, but us. Like *we* mattered. That picnic? If I tried I could still remember the sunlight and shadows on his skin.

Not that I wanted to remember that. At all. Just that it was still in my accessible memory and my brain let me know it.

Even though technically I'd broken up with someone, which for most people was a cuddling situation, I knew my mom would see that it was bothering me. Not just in a *bummed I'd broken up with someone* way. Any cuddling I might have expected for a bad dream when I was five would be a distant possibility compared to the ass-kicking I'd get if she worked out that I'd actually—whisper it now—had very quiet second thoughts.

I wanted to avoid the ass-kicking. But since I wasn't puking or even feverish, I was going to church. So I put on my Sunday best and drove to my mom's place to pick her up.

When I was younger, we had a little two-bedroom apartment (that should be in air quotes; my "bedroom" was just large enough for a bed and a dresser, no closet). Mom went back to school when I was a teenager and became an accountant, which was better money than the low-level admin stuff she was doing before, and obviously not having a young kid helped too. These days she's in the bottom apartment in a cute house owned by the two gay guys upstairs. She's even got full run of the backyard, which she loves.

She was inspecting a rosebush when I pulled up to the curb but she hadn't gotten out her pruning shears, so I figured I wasn't too late. If she'd started pruning it would have been a commentary on how she'd assumed I wasn't coming, so bullet dodged.

"Did you take the scenic route?" she asked after kissing my cheek.

Okay, bullet mostly dodged. "Traffic wasn't terrible, Mama, thank you for asking."

She smirked but kept her face forward like that way I wouldn't know she was amused by my sass. "Small mercies. We'd miss the whole service if it was any worse. How was your week?"

We did this each time I came to church. I told her about the conversation I'd had at work about possibly moving up. I also told her about the youth center and volunteering there.

"You know, you could always find overlap between the two."

"Overlap?"

"Mm hmm." She moved her hands in the air, a quintessential thing my mom did to explain, which always made me smile. "Find a job doing financial or fundraising work for a nonprofit. I'm sure there isn't a ton of money in it, but you might see how it compares to what you're doing now. Naturally if you wanted to stay with the bank your earning potential would be higher, but there's something to be said for following your heart, son. And you sound excited about this youth center."

"I am, but I don't think they're hiring. I'll think about it, though." It was, at least in part, what Claris did. And I knew how devoted she was to the organizations she had contracts with. I doubted I'd be a good independent contractor, though. Wouldn't I always be worried about where the next job was coming from? How did you ever feel a sense of financial security doing that? How on earth had Claris and Diego managed to save money with both of them working in fields that were so intermittently profitable?

Why was I thinking about them right now?

I cleared my throat. "How was your week?"

"Good, good. Can't complain. Your cousin Paula is getting married."

"Oh, good for her. Do we like the guy?"

She shrugged. "One's as good as the other, I guess. He's Middle Eastern, so of course your grandfather is losing his mind over it."

"I hope not to Paula's face."

"Of course not. I get the pleasure of all that. Oh, he doesn't have anything against 'that sort of person,' it's just he doesn't see how such a thing can possibly work out."

"Wow. That's special, Ma."

"It'll be fine. Paula's fiancé seems like a nice young man and he'll win Dad over before the wedding. Let's see, what else has happened since you were here last…"

She was still describing the twins one of her neighbors had just adopted when we pulled up to the church. I let her out in front and drove around trying to find parking. Every now and then I think it'd be cool to live somewhere that wasn't a densely populated urban center. Imagine going places and not having to build in twenty minutes to find parking and another fifteen to walk back to your destination. A boy can dream.

There's something about being in church. It never got ugly for me the way it does for a lot of queer folks, probably because despite being Involved—organizing potlucks and singing in the choir—my mom was never a real fire-and-brimstone parent. She accepted that my sexuality included people who weren't girls with only a minimum of jaw-clenching disapproval, seamlessly moved us to a new church when the old one didn't embrace my developing pansexual self, and never stopped telling me how much she loved me, even if for a while there it was tinged with a bit of "I really hope you settle down with a girl."

All of which dulled the edge of some of the church's more hell-flavored rhetoric. Not that I believe the same way my mom does. But I believe in *something*, and when I stand there with all those people of faith, voices raised to God, I feel that something in the air, same as they do.

I didn't track what the sermon was about. Got distracted and couldn't quite get back into the mode of things. It was easier afterward, smiling, saying hello to people I'd known for years, meeting babies and partners and the usual things. It wasn't until we got back in the car that I realized my mom had noticed my distraction.

"I need some things put up in the attic," she said.

"Aw, I was thinking I'd head back early, get ready for the week—"

"Then I suppose I'll get around to doing it myself at some point." Meaningful pause.

"Yeah, okay, I'll do it before I leave." Not that she couldn't navigate a ladder on her own, but the "attic" was this small, spider-infested, mouse crap-covered crawlspace nestled under the upstairs unit's master bedroom and every time she went up there she had nights of asthma attacks after.

She patted my leg gently. And then sprang her trap. "Something on your mind? You were miles away during the service."

Ah. Right. If it hadn't been the attic it would have been some other excuse to keep me there long enough to interrogate me. "No," I flat-out lied to my mother, which was dangerous, but since both of us knew that she knew I was lying, it wasn't really a lie.

"I'll put some coffee on."

I resigned myself to spending the rest of the day at her house.

An hour later, all attic-bound items had been shifted to the attic, I'd changed a lightbulb I didn't think had been changed since the nineties, the ladder had been stored away at the back of the house, and we'd loaded a few bags of clothes into my car to be taken to Goodwill for donation. "Make sure you get a receipt this time."

"I know, Ma."

"I can write it off."

"I know."

"Here, take your coffee."

So I took my coffee (it was decaf; my mother only had one cup of caffeinated coffee in the morning and then somehow survived the rest of her day on decaf, it was mind-boggling) and went into the living room. I took a look at her bookcase while waiting for her to add sugar and milk to her own coffee, but she hadn't picked up anything new lately. My eye fell on this iconic picture: Mom, on her fortieth birthday, head thrown back laughing, heading a table lined with and surrounded by friends from church, and high school, and work, family members, neighbors, the whole room full of people there to celebrate with her.

And me, but I was the one taking the picture.

At the time I didn't think a lot about it. If she'd been queer it would have just been a picture of our chosen family, but straight people don't think about things that way. The party had been a big deal, no question. We didn't have room to host something like that so one of my mom's aunts volunteered her bigger house, and while my mom didn't love accepting favors from folks, she was willing that time. She had a whole vision for this celebration that would keep her from being depressed about turning forty.

It had worked. At least I assumed it had. She came up be-hind me and nudged my shoulder. "That was a great day. All those people in one place, the food, the stories. I should have done another for my fiftieth, but it seemed like too much ef-fort."

"So we'll do one for your sixtieth," I told her. "Got a few years left to plan. Dec can make the food, you know how much he'd love that."

"Maybe we'll do something, but fewer people this time. I'm too old to talk to that many people in a day." She went to sit down, but I was still looking at the picture. It had been up in her house since she'd gotten the photos printed and I'd seen it thousands of times, but I'd never considered what it implied about her life. She was happy and surrounded by peo-ple she cared about and...didn't have a partner. A boyfriend. Not even someone she dated steadily.

"You seem deep in thought," she said from behind me.

I turned. "Did you never want to, I don't know, get mar-ried? Have someone around? Live together?"

Her eyebrows slowly rose. "I suppose I did. I must have. When you were younger. I did think you probably needed a male role model of some sort."

"I had male role models! I had my uncles, and Mr. Esposito next door, and—"

"That was the conclusion I came to, after a while, though there was still a lot of pressure to find a daddy for you. As if not doing that was a personal failure."

"Pressure from who?" I demanded.

She laughed. "Settle down, son. It was decades ago."

"Yeah, but you did a great job raising me. Look at me! I didn't need anyone but you and it pisses me off that anyone tried to make you feel differently."

"I wasn't all that impressionable," she said dryly. "You can stand down. I really didn't take that sort of thing to heart very often. And I certainly didn't marry the first swinging penis I came across in the name of having a man around the house, so I don't know what you're so mad about."

"I'm not! I mean. I don't know. Just." I leaned back against the bookcase, feeling too restless with all the stuff in my head to sit. "Did you ever regret it? For you, not me. Not having someone to share your life with?"

"I share my life with a lot of people." She nodded in the direction of the picture.

"Yeah, but you know what I mean. A partner, a companion. Someone to come home to."

"I like my space. And I have people when I want them. This way I don't have them when I don't want them, so it works out for everyone. Where's all this coming from? You've never been interested in my personal life before, Mason."

"Hey! I have! Not in a weird way. But I take an interest! I guess I just never really thought about it before."

She snorted. "Tell me again how you 'took an interest'?"

"Okay, yeah." I shrugged ruefully. "Maybe not much of one. But you always seemed happy?" My brain conspired with my vocal cords to turn it into a question, which I hadn't meant it to be.

"I was. I am."

"You're never lonely?"

"Oh, sure, sometimes. I think everyone's lonely sometimes." Her eyes narrowed in a familiar way and I knew any chance that she wouldn't dig into whatever was going on with me had just slipped through my fingers.

And you know? I wasn't actually that mad about it.

"But I'm not lonely the way you mean it, no. What happened?"

She didn't quite pat the cushion beside hers, but I went and sat down anyway. "I think I might have screwed up. But the thing I screwed up was impossible. So I don't know why I feel that way when I did the only possible thing I could have done, the only thing that made sense."

"In my experience there's never only one possible thing you can do. Tell me what happened."

Which is how I ended up sitting in my mom's living room drinking coffee in the late afternoon, telling her about Diego. And Claris. And how very impossible it all was.

I started strong, but by the time I was explaining their relationship—their marriage—I couldn't look her in the eye. Sure, Dec had told her about our coffee not-date, but this was a different thing now. I'd had sex with a married man. Fallen in love with him, maybe. Definitely had a whole-on affair with a married man, if that's how you wanted to look at it, and for a second I was worried she would.

But after I'd laid the whole thing out for her I didn't get the "You did *what*?" that I'd expected to hear. I got: "Hmm."

That was it.

I looked up at her, finally, trying to read her expression, but there was no righteous indignation. There were also no particular markers of sympathy. "What does 'hmm' mean in this context?"

"It means you haven't told me everything yet."

"I did!"

"Mason Alexander Ertz-Scott, do not take a tone with me when you know I'm right."

"But I…" Actually, dammit, she was right. "Nothing, just, Oscar said I'd regret it."

She snorted. "If Oscar's the one with the insight, boy, you know you fucked up."

"Mother! How can you use such vile language?"

A smile, this one soft. "I use it when it's appropriate. Why did you really break up with him? I can see how some stranger mistaking your relationship might be bothersome, even painful, but it's hard for me to make the leap to you breaking it off with a man you say you love."

I loved him. God. What a horrible, heart-twisting thought. I stared down at my hands. "It was just…that made me realize I could never have what I wanted as long as we were together. I can't believe you're acting like it's no big deal that he's married. You don't think there's something—I don't know—weird about a marriage like that?"

"Oh, Mason. Silly child. I'm old, I've seen a lot of people get married, and most of them end up unhappy or divorced, take your pick. You know what makes relationships work?"

I was hoping that was a rhetorical question, but when she didn't go on I shook my head. "What?"

"Communication. It's what dictates whether ending a marriage will end the friendship that started it too. Me, maybe I wouldn't want a marriage like the one your friends have. But I wouldn't want a marriage at all. And you—tell me why it is you wanted to run headlong into a wedding with Declan the second you could."

"What do you mean?"

"I mean exactly what I asked. Why did you want that? What did you like about it? Really think about that. Because if you still believe you were born wanting a church wedding and a picket fence, son, you're not as smart as I've always told people you are."

"Hey now, don't be mean."

My mom crossed her legs in the other direction and fixed me with her most *don't fuck with me* gaze. "Way I see it, people think they know what they want and sometimes they do. But sometimes what they think they know isn't the whole picture. I would have married your father and that would have been a mistake, no matter how hard it was to be alone raising you. And somewhere along the way I realized that wasn't even something I really wanted, it was just something I thought I wanted."

"Yeah, yeah, I know all this. But it's not like I've been handed life on a silver platter. I know getting married is what I want because I—because I've always—"

"Always wanted it. Exactly. You started wanting that about the same time you wanted to be Shaquille O'Neal."

"It's really not the same."

"I can see that. You interrogated one of those ideas as a grown-up, and the other one you didn't."

"Hey now," I repeated, more weakly this time. "But I do want it. I want to know someone's there for me. I want to wake up with them. I want to plan Christmas with them and nights out and see them after a long day and..." I trailed off, unable to help picturing Diego in a horrible Christmas sweater, sitting with a glass of wine in his living room, decorated tree in the background. "Can't I want those things? Don't I deserve to be someone's person? Why can't I have that, Mama?"

"Of course you deserve that. But why haven't you tried to get it? Because you've never brought a single person home since Declan. Not like that. Not like you were gonna introduce me to them as your partner."

"I've tried! But they weren't—no one ever got that far."

"*You* never got that far. And I understand that, sweetheart. Really, I do. You threw yourself into the idea of getting married and then it was pulled out from under you, it makes sense that you were afraid after that."

"I'm not," I insisted. "I wasn't afraid."

I don't know if all mothers have this look, or all women of a certain age, or what, but there's a *look*. When your mom puts it on you know the bullshit's over and she's about to tell you exactly what she thinks.

It was too late, but I opened my mouth like I could stop her, like I could change the subject, or provoke her, or something, anything, that would distract her from what I knew was coming.

"The only reason I've never mentioned it until now was because I didn't think you were ready, but here it is, my boy, and you'd better listen because I'm only going to say it once: when you want something, you go for it. There's not a single thing you ever wanted that you didn't go for. You wanted to join the baseball team, and even though you'd never played before, you learned, and drilled, and made the team. You wanted to be editor of the school newspaper, and you wrote as many articles as they'd give you until they hardly had a choice. You wanted to go to a good college, and even though you had the grades, you still studied your butt off and scored high on the tests." She put her coffee down so she could better gesture, which was never a good sign. "You wanted a wedding, and you proposed to the boy you happened to be with the second you could marry him. You didn't stop to think about how marriage would actually look, or if you were suited to each other, all you saw was that dream you'd had as a little boy when you realized that some kids had two parents at home."

This time she paused because her voice was getting watery and I swallowed, trying to ignore a stab of guilt for making my mom's eyes fill. Not that she cried. Not a crier, my mom. This was as close as she'd get: eyes a little shiny, voice a little wobbly.

"You are the smartest person I know. I am so proud of you. I am so proud you are my son. But that doesn't mean you know everything quite yet, Mason. So if what you want is to be with this Diego, then you'll figure out how. And if what you want is to not be with him, well, okay. Consider it a learning experience. But don't whine about how hard you've tried and how mean the world is, because it sounds to me like these people care about you, and that's surely not a tragedy." She stood and picked up both of our mugs. "I've got a salad with a side of chicken for dinner if you're staying."

She walked out. To the kitchen. To gather herself because she didn't say stuff like that. I always knew she loved me and was proud of me, but I couldn't really deal with the fact she'd said it out loud, so I was glad we both had a minute alone.

In my family you shouldn't need to hear a thing to know it was true. And I didn't. But hearing it kind of got to me anyway.

By the time she was back, I'd pulled myself together and she had too. "You staying?"

"How big a side of chicken are we talking about?"

"How can you have eaten that whole big brunch and still need a meal?"

"It was hours ago!"

"Not that many," she retorted. "It's a good healthy salad."

"Okay, okay. I'll stay for salad. Even though it's not really a meal."

"Now you sound like Oscar. Speaking of marriage, are we going to hear wedding bells for he and that what's-his-name? It's been a year now, hasn't it?"

"Not quite. And no way, even the mention of wedding bells would probably make them break up."

She made a noise—pure disapproval this time. "Foolish boy. I'll have to have all of you kids over for dinner soon. I miss the mess you used to make when you were still in school."

"We're not *kids*, Ma. We're in our thirties!"

"Still kids to me. Turn on the grill and set the table. I have lemonade if you want some. The good kind, not that hippie sour stuff they sell at Whole Foods."

So I ate salad (with a side of chicken) for Sunday dinner before heading home. At some point I'd probably get over the slight annoyance I felt that my mom was always right. That point had clearly not arrived yet.

Damn, though. I had the serious suspicion that at least in this case…she was right.

Chapter Twenty-Three

The first thing I did was tell the Motherfuckers that drinks were at my place.

I'd gotten the sectional and assembled it, and it definitely felt more grown-up, though Oscar and I still ended up on the floor—me because I didn't want to crowd my guests, and Oscar because he didn't want to sit that close to anyone, an arrangement that situated us comfortably around the new coffee table with enough elbow room that no one was banging into anyone else as we devoured the store-bought appetizers I'd picked up.

"Strategy session," I said after they'd all filled plates with carrot sticks and broccoli florets and pita chips.

"Is this roasted red pepper?" Ronnie asked, gesturing to a tub of orangish hummus.

"Yes."

"I have the garlic." Oscar nudged it in her direction.

"Oh good, thanks, you're a mind reader."

"Also," Dec added, "this is not traditional ranch, but I'm into it. It's got a little kick and I—"

"Excuse me," I interrupted. Loudly. "I need to win back a man so if everyone could just settle the hell down, that'd be great."

Mia made a face. "Wait, I didn't know we were doing a

whole thing! I didn't bring my notebook. You must have paper here somewhere—"

"I have some." Sidney pulled their bag over and began digging through it.

"Is winning back a man the kind of thing you need meeting notes for?" Jack asked, watching the whole thing with amusement.

I closed my eyes and counted to ten.

"You guys," Dec whispered. "Mase is freaking out right now."

"I'm not *freaking out*, I just would like everyone to *FOCUS*."

Dead silence. For half a second. Then my friends, my chosen family, my nearest and dearest, burst into laughter.

"Okay, okay, okay." Mia wiped her eyes. "Stop it, he's serious, come on. Project Mason Gets His Man hereby commences." She grabbed the notebook being held out to her, pen already tucked into the spiral. "Thanks, Sid. Next time someone's convening a strat session I'd like an agenda in advance, please, so I have time to gather my materials, but I'm ready now." She started actually writing a header.

It wasn't…nope, it was. She'd literally written MASON GETS HIS MAN at the top of the page.

Oscar, also peering upside down to see it, said, "Aren't you going to put your name and homeroom teacher on that so when it's graded you get credit?"

"Hush, I'm busy. So, what are our options?"

"You could call him," Ronnie suggested.

"Boring, wife, but okay, there are no stupid ideas." Mia began writing, smoothly dodging the elbow that came her way from her (boring-idea) wife.

"Make him dinner! Right?" Dec glanced around for support. "That would win back anyone."

"With *your* cooking, maybe," Oscar muttered. "The rest of us need other options."

Jack, still looking amused, shook his head. "All you did was show up and mock my house color, if I recall correctly. To be clear, dinner would have been nice."

"Shut it. You made it too easy to mock you."

I clapped my hands. "Can we try to limit the jaunts down memory lane? I have a man to win back." I gestured to Sidney. "You're the only one who hasn't come up with anything."

"I'm pro talk-it-out, I guess. Though a bit of a gesture never hurt anyone."

Dec leaned toward them. "Hey, remember that time I called into the show to ask your advice only it was funny because I was asking your advice about you?"

"Funny isn't how I'd describe it."

I rubbed my temple, where a massive headache was forming. "Thank you, team sidetrack, but does anyone have something I can *use*? Sid, come on, you must have answered this kind of question over the years."

"Oh. I must have." They paused, brows pulling in. "How did you leave it?"

"Um. Well. He…told me that maybe the problem was me, not the fact that he was married?"

Whistles around the room.

"Damn," Ronnie said. "That's…potentially accurate, but harsh."

Oscar was nodding with approval. "I like this guy more and more."

"Wait until you hang out with Claris." It took a few seconds for my brain to catch up with my mouth. "I mean. Um."

"It makes sense that you'd have to like the wife," Jack mused. "In terms of wanting to be part of a long-term dynamic with them."

"Him. Mostly. Well, I was already friends with her, so." To cover my sudden befuddlement I gestured at Mia. "Do you have anything I can use yet?"

"Maybe. While you were all tangenting I came up with some thoughts. Flowers, roses, chocolates? He's creative with dates, so you could come up with something equally creative. Alternately you could do something classic, like the beach. You could show up at his house with a boom box like a stalker lunatic and stand in the street—"

"Wait." Dec waved his hands excitedly. "Not the stalker thing, but you could just show up."

"I...think it's pretty stalkery if I just show up after telling him we couldn't be together?"

"Not at his house! At the show! It's tonight, isn't it?"

A flurry of activity while they all checked calendars and social media apps, but I didn't have to check. I knew exactly when GFW was. "No. I mean yes, it's tonight, but... I'm not dressed. It starts in an hour."

"This is the best idea we've come up with so far," Mia said, surveying her list.

"It's public, so not stalkery," Sidney added. "You can back off if he wants space. This is much better than the boom box thing."

"This is it, this is the plan!" Dec exclaimed. "Come on, you can get dressed in ten minutes."

I ran a hand over my chin. "But shouldn't I shave if I'm going—"

He jumped up and grabbed my hand, already pulling. "Bedroom. You guys pull up a map and see how fast we can get him there."

"No, but Dec—"

He flung open my closet like we were in a girlfriends movie and I was winning back my—oh wait. "What'd you have picked out? I know you had something picked out. Oh, pink looks good on you! Or this? Lavender?"

"That's my Ronnie-and-Mia's-wedding shirt."

His eyes gleamed. "So it's good luck!" He tossed it on the bed. "Take off your clothes, chop chop, we don't have all night."

Twenty minutes later I was in the back seat of Jack's car again, squished between Mia and Dec, half in Dec's lap, while both Mia and Ronnie had to tilt so much to get in at the sides that they only had one butt cheek each on the seat.

"We couldn't have taken two cars?" I asked, trying to straighten my clothes. "I'm wrinkling back here. I should have gone with Sid." Who had opted reasonably to drive their own car, which should have been the cue for everyone else to divide up equally, but nope. Not in this crowd.

"That would be no fun at all!" For someone crammed into a very small space, Mia seemed undaunted. "You have your ticket or whatever?"

"I mean, I know everyone working the show, so I doubt it'll be a problem to get in."

She sighed. "I think you don't realize how big the event is. Anyway, we'll figure it out."

"Ooooo." Ronnie tapped the window. "Look! There are so many people here!"

It looked like a freaking movie opening. Suddenly even my wildly fancy wedding suit wasn't looking quite up to snuff, though that probably had to do with all the *fashiony* people gathered in front of the theater. "Y'all, I'm not so sure about—"

"Dec, you and Mase get out here. We'll find parking and get back as soon as we can!"

"Yes, ma'am!"

Jack pulled to the curb some ways back from the door and I

realized that not only did I not recognize anyone, I also wasn't at all prepared to see anyone I did recognize. "No, but seriously, we didn't even workshop this idea—"

"No time for that, c'mon!" Dec half-dragged me out of the back seat.

Oscar leaned out the front window. "Being in love looked okay on you so good luck with that."

Dec blew an air kiss at him. "Oscar says the sweetest things, now go!"

I went. Sidewalk, bodies, a denser crush of bodies, me allowing Dec to tow me along behind him as he cut through the crowd. I wasn't just having second thoughts, I was having third, fourth, fifth thoughts. My sixth thoughts were having second thoughts. There was no way this was a good idea. Like at all. It was a terrible idea.

"Hi there," Dec said cheerfully to the young man working the door. "My friend is Mason Ertz-Scott and he needs to get into the show, he's expected."

The young man, to his credit, did not bother batting his long golden eyelashes in our direction. "VIP pass?"

Oops. "Um, no, but—"

"—but he's *expected*," Dec repeated. "He helped plan the whole event."

The eyelashes lowered slightly as the kid took me in. "Yeah? Then you should have been here an hour ago."

Somehow, absurdly, this dumb door kid made me blush. "I was...running late?"

"Uh-huh, well, as long as you have a valid ticket you can get in with everyone else when doors open, honey."

It had been so long since a twenty-year-old boy called me "honey" that I was suddenly less annoyed with him. "Look, it's just that—"

"*Mason*, oh my god, oh my god, Mason, thank god you're

here." Perri slipped from the shadows, or a doorway, or a doorway in the shadows, or possibly a wormhole that happened to
be in a shadow with a doorway, and touched the door kid's
arm. "It's okay, Romeo."

Romeo—and wow, *Romeo*—shrugged and unhooked the
legit rope stanchion for me to pass.

"Good luck!" Dec called as Perri spirited me inside.

"Did Claris call you? She said not to, but I should have
known she would anyway, she hates this kind of thing, you
know how much it means to her that all the plans go perfectly
and then when one gets screwed up she really—oh god, your
tie's going to clash with Diego's coat, hang on, we can find
something else—"

"But—"

"Corinne! Find Mason a tie that will complement Diego's
suit coat, please? Quick as you can!" Having dispatched that
order she pushed through an opening draped with curtains
into—

Pure chaos. Models everywhere, scraps of fabric on the
floor, voices rising and falling in various tones of panic, mir-
rors of all sizes arranged everywhere, most with clumps of
people in front of them doing final touches on outfits, a ca-
cophony of scraping, sliding, rolling, shouting, murmuring,
shifting, and any other kind of sound you might hear in a room
full of people getting ready for a fashion show.

"Twenty-three minutes, people!" Perri called loudly, star-
tling me. "Thank god you're here. Diego! Look, I've got
Mason, everything will be *fine!*"

I stopped walking. I couldn't face him. I had to face him.
He looked over, pins between his lips, sweat on his brow, glitter in his hair, and I just stared back at him, uncertain what
to say, or how to act, or if he wanted me there.

Perri grabbed my arm. "I know you're busy, but I need to

get someone in here with a mic for him, so just maybe fill him in until I get back? Thanks." And she whisked away, shouting three more orders as she passed people in the room before disappearing back through the curtain.

"Hi," I said.

He held up a finger and turned back to his pinning. Two more and then he took the others out of his mouth and said, "I think that's it. Walk for me? Okay, perfect. Hopefully hair and makeup are ready for you now. You look gorgeous."

The model blew him a kiss and walked away and I was momentarily distracted by just how good he looked, y'know, walking away. When I refocused on Diego, he was meticulously sticking his pins in a pincushion. "So," I tried again.

"Did Claris call you? She promised she wouldn't, but I guess when it comes to emceeing she's willing to lie. Not that I'm against it, I'm sure you'll be great, but we had a whole conversation and—"

"Claris didn't call me."

He stopped what he was doing and looked up. "Then why are you here? I thought—because Gregory, who was supposed to emcee, is in the bathroom puking, and—" The frown looked like it was going to fracture his forehead. "Why are you here?"

Which, now that I was there, standing in front of him, was a truly excellent question and I wish I'd taken some time, preferably back in my living room, to come up with an answer. This is the sort of thing we could have workshopped, damn it. "Um. I guess…"

"You guess? Mason, if you can't tell, I'm in the middle of a big fucking deal, the biggest show I've ever put on, so whatever this is—" frantic arm flapping between our bodies "—it's really going to need to wait until—"

I hadn't seen Claris approaching, but suddenly she had my

arm in a vise grip—and Diego's arm too. *"March,"* she said tersely, herding us. I was too disoriented by the surroundings to really know where we were going, but then we were behind a half-wall with curtains at each end and Claris loomed over us despite being shorter.

"You two get your shit together *right now.*" Her voice was low and sharp. "I did not work as hard as I've worked for the last nine months for the two of you to have a fit just before this event. You—" finger jab at Diego "—get out there, stop moping, and motivate the rest of these people, all of whom *are here because of you.* And you—" finger jab at me "—you're the voice of GFW and either you're gonna go out there and pretend it was your plan to emcee it all along or you're going to get the hell out, I'm not having you here complicating everything." Her fierce gaze took in both of us. "If you want to never speak to each other again, fine, it can wait until after the show. If you want to *not* be fools, then for god's sake, learn how to disagree like adults and pull yourselves together."

She let go of us and straightened up, her dress seeming to effortlessly flow around her like water around rock. "I swear, you're each as bad as the other. You have ninety seconds to decide, so figure out how you're going to walk out there—" finger jab at the curtain "—and act like you're not pissed at each other for the next three hours. After that you can do whatever the hell you want and I'm washing my hands of the whole damn thing."

Diego opened his mouth, only getting out "I—" before she swept around and went back through the curtain.

Leaving us standing there side by side like naughty schoolboys.

"Did she mean emcee as in…go out there in front of everyone and talk?"

"There's a script, so you just need to deliver it. I mean, not 'just' like it's no big deal. It's important. But you don't have to learn any of it by heart. Gregory only glanced at it as he was eating his ill-fated deli wrap. You'd be good. Emceeing, I mean." He wasn't looking me in the face, just vaguely in my direction. "And you're dressed exceptionally, though I don't think the tie will look good on film."

"It apparently clashes with you so Perri is finding me another one. Or sent a minion to do it."

"That sounds like Perri. Look, you can leave. You aren't obligated to stay here, not for any reason."

"I came to see you." I flushed, a state not helped by how warm it was in the room. "I mean the show. Your show. Everyone's pieces. I'm still invested."

"If you don't emcee, Claris will have to." He paused and probably both of us were imagining that. Claris was photogenic as fuck, but not exactly the person you wanted in charge of the tone of a family-friendly event.

Which didn't mean I was. "I'm not sure I can do this," I murmured, keeping my eyes down, trying to block out the sounds of the show going on around us.

"You're not sure you can do the show? Or you're not sure you can do *this*? Us?"

"I already screwed it up so much. Not the show. I did right by the show. But everything else? Is a mess."

He stepped forward and for a moment I thought he was going to walk out after Claris, leave me standing there, but then he took hold of my shoulders and pulled me to him, clutching me tightly, my arms automatically going around him in return. "We haven't talked in two months. Do you really want to break up? I'll respect your answer, even if I never understand it."

"No, but—"

"Then we won't." He pressed his face against mine. "She's

right, we're fools. We can't figure everything out right now, but you must see that we will be able to. You do see that, don't you? Mason?"

"But what if we *can't*?" My voice was barely a whisper. I wanted to believe him, believe them both, but how could I possibly? "It will end like it always ends, I can't do this with you, I love you too much—"

Then he was kissing me, desperately, one of his hands at the small of my back to hold me close, the other at my neck to keep me still closer, and I wanted him, *us*, in that kiss more than I'd ever wanted anything else.

"And I love *you* too much to let you go without a fight. But later. For now—hide here, go out there and host the show, hang from the rafters for all I care, but don't—" his eyes bored into mine "—don't you dare leave."

"I won't. I won't." I brushed tears from my eyes and carefully dabbed the ones on his cheeks. "Are you sure I can do this?"

"I'm sure you'll be absolutely fucking brilliant." Another kiss and he straightened my tie for me. "You look extraordinary."

"So do you." I took a deep breath to say something incredibly man-winning-back—

Perri's head stuck through the curtains. "Oh thank god, I thought you'd done a runner. Corinne! Dammit, where did she go? Mason, give me that tie, we have—"

"It's okay," Diego said. "I know it clashes a little, but we'll only be next to each other at the very beginning and the very end. Let Mason keep his tie."

She blinked. "Are you sure?"

"Positive."

"O-kay. I need him anyway." To me, she began, "I'm going to show you everything as well as I can but don't worry if things go a bit awry, we're just going to run with it. The models will nudge you toward your marks if you get in their way, everyone's been briefed, and Gregory is not coming out of the bathroom anytime soon, so this is it. Come on."

I looked back at Diego, the whole thing getting very real very fast. "But I've never—"

"Anything's better than Claris!" he said, smiling. "It's a low bar. And Mase? I'm bringing you home with me. You're not weaseling out of it."

"I don't want to."

"Good. Because you won't."

Perri shuffled impatiently.

Diego kissed me. "Have fun!"

Which seemed like it had to be facetious, but he wasn't joking. He meant it.

Fuck it, you know? How often do you get to randomly emcee a fashion show for charity? Pretty much never. *Here goes nothing.*

Chapter Twenty-Four

As many people as I'd thought there were outside, there were more now. Inside. Filling seats and making noise and taking pictures. "You want me to go out there in front of all those people?" I asked, my voice faint, my courage flagging.

"I'll take care of Mason, Perri." Claris took my arm and squeezed.

Perri pushed the handful of papers at me, apologized if they smelled funky, and skittered off to do more herding of cats.

"Now, darling, you'll do great. You know how you talked in all those videos you posted? Relaxed and comfortable, like a man who knows who he is and what kinds of clothes he likes to wear? That's who you are tonight, The Voice of Gentlemen's Fashion Week."

"I don't think I'm the voice of anything, Claris."

"You're clearly mistaken, since you're right here and you're about to be the master of ceremonies. When in doubt, ramp up the charm, works every time." She straightened my tie. "Sundays have been very empty without you, my metamour. I hope they won't be that way forever. Now then. Come with me and we'll harass everyone one more time before the thing kicks off and you have to be on stage." She winked.

"Shouldn't I be reading this?"

"Pish, it'll be fine. You'll read it for real in a few minutes, it's not like you have to study. Plus, it'd do the designers good to see you're here with them. Come on."

Everyone was ecstatic to see me. I got a variety of hugs and kisses and cheers. Even the models, whom I'd only spoken with to get photo releases or shoot quick videos, seemed happy I was there. By the time we'd made our rounds it was about time for the show to start.

"I have literally no idea what I'm doing," I said to no one in particular.

Brenda, who was up first, snorted. "Join the club, honeybuns."

The lights dimmed, the crowd quieted down, and Claris kissed my cheek—then wiped her lipstick off. "Go get 'em, tiger," she said, and pushed me through the curtains.

The show was a blur. A literal blur in my memory. All the lights and faces and darkness at the edges of the room. I couldn't make out much, but I started with, "Welcome to Gentlemen's Fashion Week. A much better master of ceremonies has been struck down with a non-lethal stomach ailment so now you're all stuck with me, for which I apologize." Which got a couple of polite chuckles.

Yeah, fuck that. I was going to get a hell of a lot more than polite chuckles if I was gonna do this thing. So in that moment, I decided to *do this thing*.

And it was amazing.

I guess I'd never really thought about performers getting high, that combination of fear and invulnerability tossed into a cocktail shaker with a little bit of adrenaline making you float inches off the ground. By the end of the show my face was tingling, my smile muscles were sore, my voice was rough, I was sweating profusely, and I felt like I could basically conquer the universe.

It was a hell of a rush.

"Drink," Claris ordered, shoving a bottle of water at me. "Everyone get out there!" The models and designers all filed back out, settling into a loose, laughing line, the audience on their feet and the applause riotous.

"Now you," she said to Diego, who grabbed my hand.

"But this is your moment—"

"Our moment, love. Come on."

We were the last on stage and, because he was the one who'd masterminded the whole thing, Diego went right to the middle of the line, all of the models cheering for him. He bowed, then gestured to me.

People shouted. Like. For me. I was standing there in that mass of super-talented people and I was part of it. Part of them. For this one moment.

"And everyone else!" Diego called, gesturing toward back-stage. The roar rose even higher and…

It was a fucking good night is what I'm saying.

The intensity of the performance didn't even have a chance to wear off before all of us were swept into the post-show, a swirl of hugs and kisses and laughter and swinging each other around in celebration, then dispersing into the crowd where chairs were being loaded quickly onto carts so that food could be brought out.

It wasn't at all the caliber of the BLM show—we had caterers, but only because Claris was good at sweet-talking people into donating their time and other people into donating the money to pay for the food being made by the people donating their time—but there was an almost family-reunion atmosphere to the after-party. More hugging and kissing and catching-up and excited introductions and cries across the room.

And my friends were there. Speaking of cries across the room.

"Mase! MASE!" Dec reached me and hugged me and clung

to me. "Oh my god, you were amazing, you were absolutely amazing, ahhhh, I can't get over your amazingness!"

"Thanks, Dec. Um." I detached him. "Dec, this is Diego. Diego, this is Declan."

"Ahh, it's so good to meet you!" He gave Diego a hug too. "Sorry, just, I'm so *energized* right now! Is it always like this?"

Diego laughed. "When it's good, it is, and wasn't Mase the best emcee ever?"

Sensing a kindred spirit, Dec moved in closer. "He was! I mean, I haven't been to fashion shows before but if I was doing any kind of thing that needed an emcee, I'd make Mase do it for sure. How did you get him up there? Last I knew we were doing some kind of Hail Mary grand gesture so he could win y—"

I clamped a hand down over his mouth and forcibly moved him away from my—er—from Diego. "Sid, would you maybe do something with this? Thanks. I'm kinda busy."

Sidney grinned and patted Dec on the head. "The first rule of strategic planning meetings is not talking about strategic planning meetings, datefriend."

"Omhghdyrright." He did a theatrical *eek* face. "Sorry! Anyway, nice meeting you!" He turned and muffled his *eek* face against Sidney's shoulder.

"Strategic planning meeting?" Diego asked, raising an eyebrow.

Ronnie, who'd just walked up with the rest of the Motherfuckers, sighed. "We can't bring you anywhere, Dec. You'd make a terrible spy."

I caught Diego's eye and both of us smiled. "Everyone, Diego. Diego, everyone."

We did more introductions and my friends—damn, they were the best. Mia gushed, Ronnie got a little choked up expressing her appreciation for the gender fluidity of the gentlemanly designs, Jack said super-clever shit about potential marketing venues, and Oscar stood at his side and didn't say anything rotten. Which I thought was about as close as he got to saying something nice until Diego stepped away to talk to other people and Oscar said, "I would wear some of that stuff."

We all looked at him.

"What? I would. Why are you all staring at me like that?"

"Um…" Ronnie paused. "Because I have to drag you kicking and screaming just to buy a T-shirt and now you're talking about actual fashion like it's a thing you're interested in? Which I'm here for! Don't get me wrong. I think we're just a bit surprised is all."

"I liked the midnight blue suit with the pop of hot pink," Jack said.

Oscar made a face. "Of course you liked the tightest possible thing."

"If you have it, flaunt it. That's what I say." Jack did an up-down with his hand at Oscar. "And you do. But I don't mind the decade-old T-shirts either."

"I can't stand you."

Jack kissed him. "I know."

"Okay," Dec said after a moment. "Now I've really seen everything."

"Right?" Mia echoed. "I can't even…"

My friends kept talking but I couldn't quite focus. My eyes scanned the room until I found Diego, nodding seriously and in deep conversation with a stunning drag queen. A feather from her beaded headband drifted down to his shoulder and I had this ridiculous urge to cross the room simply to brush it off.

Sometime later Claris pulled me against her and whispered, "I was so happy to see you, love."

Instead of staying with the side-hug, I moved all the way into her. "I'm still not sure we can make it work."

"I have faith in both of you. And, of course, I'm basically a genius and you have me on your side, you lucky boys. Now go be with him. I know he doesn't want to crowd you, but every time I look over you're trying to find him, so that indicates to me that both of you would be better off together."

I held her gaze carefully. "You don't mind?"

"Darling, when will you learn? His joy is my joy. And his joy is you." She kissed me on the lips, lightly, casually. "Go."

I went.

Chapter Twenty-Five

It was late. Super late. And it had been a wildly long day. And I was full of feels. Which is probably why I proposed that Diego take us back to my apartment instead of the house. It was some instinct of…sharing, or warmth, or recklessness, maybe. I'd tried so hard not to repeat any of my past patterns—like being The One With The Decent Apartment—that I'd never invited him over to my place at all.

But we'd dated for months and he'd never seen my space. Now, more than ever, it felt like the moment to share it with him. And the way he reached over and took my hand when I said, "Do you want to come to my place instead?" as if he understood what it meant to me? Yeah. Worth it. Emotional risk for the win.

Semi-win, anyway. The living room was still basically mid-drinks.

"Um, so, it usually looks way better than this, but like, welcome to my foyer. And the rest of my place." My brain ordered me to clean up. My body was fatigued and in that state of exhausted heaviness that wasn't unpleasant, but also wasn't motivated to move too quickly.

"It's amazing. And I like your foyer." He brushed his knuckles across the back of the new sectional.

"It's, um, actually?" I cringed. "It's mostly new. That's why it looks so Ikea showroom right now. I had a post-breakup crisis and refreshed my apartment."

He took both of my hands. "Mase. Most people have a post-breakup crisis and do something nuts like buy a sports car or quit their job. You…made your apartment look nice. Which is a thing you deserve to have anyway."

"I…well. I had been thinking about it for a while."

"It's lovely." He leaned in to kiss me, slowly, deliberately, until I felt my lips tingle. I was about to propose formally that I show him the boudoir when he took a deep breath, and said, "Now let's talk about *us*."

I actually pulled away and held my hands up in self-defense, like the words were, I don't know, a blow, or a bludgeon. "Shouldn't we do that tomorrow?"

"No!" He took the hands I was using as a shield and pulled me into an embrace that I didn't even consider resisting. It would take a stronger man than me to resist an armful of blissed-out Diego. "This is the moment. It's so perfect already. Let's make it *better*."

"You, uh, clearly have much more positive associations with the phrase 'let's talk about us' than I have. But if you think that's…a good idea…"

It was so far from a good idea that it was already sapping me of my own bliss, some vicarious, some organic to me. The evening had been…everything. From the moment we'd decided to go for it—go for the show, go for the relationship, go for whatever—until this moment now, which felt like the edge of a cliff.

Diego took a deep breath against me, our bodies pressed close, and I could feel the warm air on my neck. "Do you trust me?"

"I…" Why was this so hard? I did trust him. In my bones. Which was a strange thing to only figure out in this moment, when surely I must have trusted him all along, at least since we'd been dating, or courting, or whatever we'd been doing.

But it was right now, standing just inside my front door, Diego's words crystalline in the silence, and everything in my head was as messy as the half-eaten deli platter on the coffee table, the abandoned plates and napkins and hummus containers.

"I trust you," I said, and pressed my face against his shoulder. "I don't know what I'm doing. I don't see how we can do this, but I can't… I don't want to be the reason we don't."

"That's not how it works. You can't be wholly responsible for something both of us are creating." He leaned back. "Come on. Let's bring—I don't know—tea to bed? Or god, I'd kill for a cup of coffee. You don't have decaf, do you? And is it too forward of me to invite myself into your bedroom?"

From tense Relationship Moment to assembling coffee things and making him close his eyes while it brewed so I could tidy the living room. By the time I was pouring steaming decaf into my two favorite mugs, the evening was beginning to weigh on me, all the excitement gathering on my skin until I felt rooted to the floor in my kitchen, contemplating the scene. The mugs, my own kitchen counter, Diego's strong, dexterous fingers wrapped around glazed ceramic.

"It's not fair," I said suddenly. Then closed my lips over the words in a decent approximation of that old saying about barn doors.

He turned. "What's not fair? If it's the coffee, I assure you that sometimes when Claris isn't looking and I'm too lazy to go to Whole Foods I just get the normal stuff, even if it's not Fair Trade." And he winked at me, giving me a wide-open door to take it lightly. I sensed that if I wanted to put the whole conversation aside for the night, he'd let me.

But I couldn't. I owed him better than that. I owed him,

at the very least, my honesty. I refused to allow my shoulders to actually slump, but god, I really wanted to *slump*, like full-on, head-on-arms slumping.

I didn't, though. But I also didn't meet his eyes. "Sorry. I know it's wrong, but I just keep thinking if I'd met you first maybe this would be different."

He blinked, and I hadn't noticed until right this second that he'd worn some kind of glitter in his eyelashes. Glittery mascara, maybe? It caught the light and made me want to smile, except I couldn't do that either, because I'd just said something basically unforgivable.

"Worse, I think," he said after a moment. "Mason, you know I'm not polyamorous *because* of Claris, right?"

"Yes. I do. I mean. Of course. And I love Claris—not romantically, but I respect her, and I care about her. I don't actually want her to not exist. I just." I was clenching and releasing my fists, not like I wanted to hit something, more like they were an expression of my inability to explain. "It's just I had this whole idea for my life. And you are—I feel so much more for you than I ever thought I'd feel for anyone, but it's not how I thought it would be *at all*." Which was slightly misleading. I really looked at him, met his gaze. "In so many ways it's better. Being with you is *better* than I could have hoped. So I don't know why I'm still—" I broke off. I didn't have more words.

"Oh, that's easy." He reached up for my mug as well.

"Um." My turn to blink. "What?"

"You're so much like Claris. This is just a thing with you compulsive planner types where plans change and you have trouble adjusting. You'll figure it out."

"I…it…what?"

Mugs in hand, he gestured to the living room. "Should we sit for a few minutes? I've decided it *was* far too forward to invite myself to your bedroom for the first time. A gentleman should wait patiently."

I followed, mind muddled, and wished for the flickering firelight of his much bigger living room. Dawn was already tinging the sky very slightly lighter than it had been, but it was still more than dark enough for candles. I lit a few, thinking about that first night we'd spent together, how the candlelight seemed so full of promise.

We sat beside each other on the couch, bodies easily finding each other, coexisting without any awkward jockeying for position or shifting from discomfort. I sipped and tried to focus on the tiny flames, thinking about his tone, his…not quite a dismissal, but close to one. *Oh, that's easy. You'll figure it out.* What if I didn't?

"It doesn't feel easy," I offered finally, when I couldn't think of any way to feel less muddled.

"I'm not looking for other partners, Mase. This is all I need. My romantic inclinations are not infinite—or at least, they're infinite, but not for an infinite number of people. I share really different things with you and Claris, and I *like* that. That's a feature for me, not a bug. I want us to share different things. I want our relationship, yours and mine, to be something we've created together that's entirely different than anything I've ever had with someone else."

"I don't think I've had that many people to compare to. I've never been in love with anyone but Dec, and we were young and dumb and in love with the idea of being in love more than anything else, I think." His face glowed in the low golden light, making it hard to say more, but I tried. "I'm afraid you'll get tired of me."

"I haven't gotten tired of Claris yet." His lips turned up in a smile, though he wasn't looking at me the way I was looking at him. "That's not how it works anyway. I suppose theoretically we could fall out of love with each other, but that's true of anyone. It's not like I woke up one morning and looked at my sexy goddess of a wife and was like, *Yeah, I'm over this, time for a new model*."

I couldn't help laughing at the image. "Seriously, man, did you see her cornering that dancer, looming at him all domi-natrix-y?" I fanned myself. "Woman is hot."

"She already set up a kinky sex date with him, I asked. I do not know where she gets the energy."

"And she doesn't sleep," I added.

"Oh, she sleeps like a cat. Curls up anywhere safe and warm, happily sleeps through the whole morning if she's been out late. It's sort of adorable and sort of obnoxious. I can't imagine being able to nap in my car before touching up my makeup and going to a meeting."

"She doesn't," I said, momentarily diverted.

"She absolutely does."

I paused. "I can't tell if I'm more impressed or jealous."

"Same." He settled lower in the couch and sipped his coffee, letting his other hand rest on my leg. "Tell me about your plans. The ones I've frustrated by being way more awesome than you thought I'd be. Unless those are state secrets, naturally."

"They are, in fact. You say that as if my childish ideas about happy endings couldn't possibly be classified information."

"Did I say it like that?" The hand squeezed. "*Childish* sounds like a judgmental word to use. I didn't mean to imply childishness."

I decided his lower position felt right and snuggled against him. "I guess that's how I feel, like I had this dumb vision for how my future would be based on Disney movies."

"So *childhood*, not *childish*. I think that's an important distinction. Tell me about the fantasy future?"

"The classics, you know. Married. Kids—no more than two unless we adopted a sibling group with three, but probably four would be too many. Robust retirement fund. Financial security. Family vacations. Church with my mom because it would make her happy. Drinks with the Motherfuckers until we had kids, but try to time the kids with my friends having kids so they could all grow up together." I flushed, feeling like I'd revealed way too much. "Um, sorry. That was…a lot."

"I asked," he said gently. "And all of that sounds wonderful. Has that picture changed?"

"I'm not…sure. I mean." I frowned and hesitantly nudged his pinky with my pinky. "Doesn't it have to if we…if we're… I mean…"

"I think maybe you're framing this as *losing* things when it's actually *gaining* them. I love kids. I've always wanted to have kids. And I'd still be able to do it with Claris, she's willing to be in the lives of children, but she doesn't want to co-parent, and I guess there are queer people who single-parent in the same household as their spouse, but it didn't appeal to me as much as co-parenting does." His body went slightly tense beside me. "Not that I'm proposing we have kids together, oh my god, that's not what I'm saying at all, I just—"

"I'm pretty sure that's literally what you just proposed."

"I didn't! I just meant—I was only saying—I didn't want you thinking—"

I lifted his hand to my lips and kissed it, lingering over the scent of his skin. "I know what you meant. But how would that work in reality? If two people like us were together, and one of them was married to someone else—how would that ever be a situation you could bring a child into?"

"A lot of polyamorous people have children as part of their families. I actually did some research on it a few weeks ago." A line appeared in his forehead. "I was…thinking about maybe sending you an email. But then I worried that you wouldn't want to hear from me. I figured you'd probably already moved on and I'd just be getting in the way. But I did find out some stuff."

"I…" What would I have done if he'd sent me an email? Been pissed off that he'd interrupted the new normal? Or just sad that we couldn't have the things we wanted to have? "I tried to move on. Pretty hard. But I couldn't."

"Me neither. Though Claris would say I didn't try that hard. Case in point: googling how to structure families with poly-amorous parental relationships at two o'clock in the morning."

I held his hand to my cheek, not quite daring to kiss it again. "And what did you find out?"

"Well, legally it can be challenging, but it's not totally without precedent to have three parents on a birth certifi-cate. And of course it depends on the path you take, and how much money you have, your resources, that sort of thing. But we wouldn't have to reinvent the wheel. I mean. If hypotheti-cal people wanted to do that, they wouldn't have to reinvent the wheel. Plus, can you imagine Claris with a kid around to spoil? She'd probably lavish them with expensive gifts and fancy summer camps, the sciencey ones, that cost like a month of wages for your average doctor."

It was far too easy to picture Claris playing Daddy War-bucks. "Man, that's rich. But is it wages if you're a doctor? Isn't that a salaried position?"

"You bring up a good point," he said gravely. "That would change everything."

I elbowed him. "But where would I… I mean, you know, the other guy, the not-married one, where would he live? How would that work?"

He turned to me, half his face now cast into shadow. "How

do you feel about roommates? I can vouch personally for her cleanliness but she refuses to cook and won't eat leftovers."

"Diego, be serious."

"I am being very serious. I love my wife, but the woman throws away leftovers and it actually hurts my soul."

Another elbow.

"Okay, okay. Well, we—I mean they—could do it any way they wanted to. All of them could live together. There could be two homes they split between them. There could be a family house and a sweet sex den somewhere."

I giggled. "Okay, now we definitely need a sweet sex den. Unless you mean den as in bear fur rugs, in which case hard pass."

"No! How could you? I would never do that to a bear. Also, real fur creeps me out. Yes, it's soft, but also, it's *creepy*. Synthetics are just as soft and way less creepy. Anyway. My point was, we aren't limited in terms of options except by our own creativity. And that's not even counting Claris, who probably already has a list with at least ten options ranked in order of preference and she's just been waiting to share the document with us." His arm wound through mine. "I'm saying if we want to make this work, we can."

"But you…what if I can't take it? The two of you together, I mean. What if you go off to her bedroom and I'm just sitting there alone and…" I couldn't imagine it. I didn't want to. "I'd try not to feel jealous, but I would be really fucking jealous. Like, no lie, I would be upset."

"That's okay."

"Um." It didn't sound that *okay*.

He squeezed my arm. "I worded that wrong. I mean, okay in the sense that I've been jealous before. It's a thing that happens. We talk about it. But it doesn't derail everything I love about our lives. It was much harder at first, before we had years of practice going into it, but even now sometimes she goes off for the night and I know she's going to have this amazing adventure and I'm going to, like, drink tea and listen to an audiobook. But that's the thing: I *love* doing that. An audiobook, a cozy place to sit, a hot beverage, that's like heaven to me. So sometimes jealousy is actual jealousy, but a lot of the time it's basic FOMO that my brain tries to turn into something else."

"I don't like jealousy or FOMO."

"Me neither, but I acknowledge they're normal parts of the human experience. And Mase, do you really think that kind of thing is about me having a wife? Monogamous people get jealous too, you know. And if they feel less threatened by it, that's totally an illusion, since so many of them end up cheating."

"I mean…fair," I admitted.

"Can I suggest a possible…um…" He faltered. "I don't have to. Maybe we should wait. Do it some other time."

Yes. But no. "We're already here. And I don't want to repeat past mistakes, you know?" Which sounded so good, but part of me desperately wanted to put it off, whatever it was.

He looked at me with this intense sort of gentleness, like he was afraid to hurt me. "Listen. And I say this with so much affection. But do you remember when you told me about standing at the altar in front of all those people you cared about, and Declan leaving you there by yourself? I just wonder if maybe…it wasn't about the guy at the benefit who assumed we were married, but about all of those moments when someone from the outside has made assumptions about you, all the times you've felt like you had to live up to something. You share yourself so easily in some ways. Like tonight, jumping in to emcee, making people laugh, making people feel. Maybe this—" his fingers brushed over my arm as if encompassing everything between us in that one feather-light gesture "—is a thing you don't know how to share and that...makes it harder. I don't know, I'm not in your head, but I just...thought about that after we, um, you know. Stopped."

I couldn't look at him. I stared down at his fingers, still moving on my skin, and tried not to come apart. "I want to be seen as the type of..." I'd never ever tried to put this thought into words, but Diego deserved that much. "...the type of man who someone else chooses. Who someone else wants to...to be with. Not just because I look good, or because I can be funny, or whatever. I want to be worthy of that even when I'm...not those things. I want people to see that in me." It felt so petty and small, that I cared about how anyone saw me. But I did care, and even when I'd pretended not to, I always had. "I'm sorry. I know Claris doesn't care about anything this dumb, but—"

"Oh my god, Mase, Claris is always aware of what people think about her. She built her adulthood persona around other people's expectations and then just sort of expanded until she burst out into her own shape." He leaned in and kissed my cheek. "You don't have to be anything else. Not for me. You don't have to look good or be charming—though you always look good and I'm always charmed by you—but even if you didn't, or I wasn't, I would still love you."

I bit my lip. "It just..." It felt so wrong to argue with "I love you." And yet. "I just, and I know this is stupid, but if the three of us were on a sinking ship, you guys would save each other. You know? And no matter how much you love me, I think that's how it will always be." *Do not cry right now. Do not.*

"Oh, love, no. If the three of us were on a sinking ship, Claris would put you and me on a lifeboat, order you to take care of me, push us off, then go back for another batch of people to save." His thumb ever so gently wiped a tear from under my eye. "Relationships are all so different. I don't always love that Claris's first instinct is to make sure if she's not there to babysit me, someone else is. Because I don't want to be that guy that other people have to take care of. But honestly, if we were on a sinking ship I'd rather be tucked in beside you on a lifeboat than running around saving the women and children, which I know means I'm not that heroic, but here we are."

"Actually." I could picture that, my mental image of *sinking ship* basically the *Titanic* with deck chairs sliding into the sea and Kate Winslet looking Seriously Concerned in the background. "That's fair. I'd probably be relieved to have an excuse to be with you in a lifeboat. Also not that heroic."

"Only if Claris made you. If she didn't, you'd be running around saving people too, I know it." He offered a wry smile that slightly broke my heart. "I am apparently attracted to people who are really good at saving the less capable. I try not to worry about what that says about me."

"Oh my god, not at all." I pulled him against me with one arm and pressed a kiss to the side of his head. "How can you think that? Look at what you did tonight, what you did over the last year. You brought these people together and lifted them up; every time they had doubts or fears you showed them how to be confident, how to stand behind their work, how to make it the best it could possibly be. How can you say you're not capable? I could never have done what you did. And neither could Claris. You know that, don't you?"

He blinked at me, eyes glimmering in the dawn light. "I try to know that, but it's not always easy. This whole thing is about trying. Even when it's hard. Sometimes that's dealing with jealousy, or having a difficult conversation, or being vulnerable when you're afraid. But if we're both trying, and we're not shutting each other out, then I think we can make this work. I loved meeting your friends tonight. I loved seeing you with them, seeing how much they cared about you, how much they cared about GFW because it mattered to you."

"They've been desperate to meet you. Dec's really annoyed that Oscar got to meet you first."

He smiled. "I want to spend more time with them than just seeing everyone after the show."

"Yeah, um, me too. Them too. A lot. I don't know if you're interested, at all, but we have drinks once a week and..." I trailed off, realizing what I was saying. How could I do this? How could I invite Diego to drinks?

"You don't have to," he said quickly. "I mean, it's early, we don't have to do the like friends-and-family thing if you're not—"

"Oh, no, it's just, um. Okay, so I had this theory for a long time that there was a Drinks Curse, and that anyone I brought to drinks would basically stop dating me within a week."

He gave me a considering look. "Are you... I can't tell if you're inviting me or not inviting me to drinks with your friends."

I could not keep living under the stupid Drinks Curse I'd made up because something-something-bias. I cleared my throat. "I would be honored if you would attend the next gathering of my compatriots with me, good sir."

"The honor, and indeed the pleasure, would be all mine."

I grinned at him, happiness bubbling up inside me. "And if your lady wife is available, please extend an invitation to her as well." I meant it completely, and not as a concession. Claris would love my people, and they'd definitely adore her. And if Diego and I were together, Claris was a part of my life as well. My metamour, as she'd said.

"You don't have to invite Claris." His voice was uncertain.

"Well, I don't think I want to introduce her to my mom right away. But my friends? She's invited."

This time he kissed my hand. "She'll be thrilled. And everything else?"

The sky was noticeably lighter now. "We can talk about tomorrow. I'm probably going to have more moments of doubt. I don't think I'm like...cured."

"What, we haven't ironed out all of our couple issues in a single conversation? I definitely want my money back." He reached for my coffee mug and set both of them aside. "Cuddle for a few more minutes?"

"Sounds like the perfect end to a perfect evening."

"Oh, I bet we'll have a lot of other perfect evenings." He kissed me and then curled in against me, resting his head on my chest. "Thank you for having me in your home. It feels so much like you here."

"I want you here as often as it makes you happy. And you are officially welcome in my bed anytime."

He nuzzled against me. "Super hot. Can't wait to take you up on that when I have more energy."

"Me too." I didn't know how I could feel so much better when nothing concrete had been *resolved*, but somehow, I did. We sat there as the candles burned low and eventually went to bed.

Chapter Twenty-Six

Insistent ringing. Oh my god. Ringing. So much ringing. The world would never stop ringing. Until it did.

I had just enough time to think *Thank god* before Diego's phone started up. He stirred against me. "'S Claris. You get it."

My laughter was more of an amused huff. "This is how you're going about proving that we're equals in our relationship?"

"Mm hmm." His hair was a mess. His eyes were closed. One of his bare legs was sticking out from under the sheet. "Plus, 's for you."

"Last I checked, Claris was your wife."

He yawned massively and pulled the pillow over his head, mumbling something I thought was, "Go see."

I reached for the pile of our clothes, unceremoniously stripped off beside the bed, and not in a flurry of passionate kissing either. Stripped off in an "almost too tired to bother" sense, which added to the confusion of belongings. I finally managed to find the culprit and hit answer. "Um, it's Mason."

She laughed warmly in my ear and said, "Check your front door. And thank the curvy young jogger in 2D for letting me into the building when you get a chance." Then: *click.*

I glanced at the screen to confirm that she had actually hung up. Okay, then. I padded to the door, wrapping a robe around myself and listening for footsteps. Silence. I slowly peeked out.

A fancy-looking box that, fancy though it was, also looked a bit well used. I pulled it inside with some trepidation and set it on the kitchen island to open.

One wide ribbon, tied neatly. So dramatic, so Claris. Inside was a neat little tray with pastries and a press full of coffee, two mugs, a bowl of strawberries, and a note.

My darlings,

We'll be at Perri's, but wanted to drop this by first. You were both brilliant last night. I'm sure in more ways than one, wink wink. I got us a table for three at the Grill for nine. Time to start planning for the Next Big Thing!

Kisses,

Claris.

I padded back to the bed with the tray. "Coffee, babe."

"Mmmm coffee." He unearthed himself and sat up, rubbing the sleep out of his eyes. "She even left a note? She must be feeling sentimental."

"She got dinner reservations so we can plan The Next—"

"—Big Thing, of course she does. Woman can't rest for five damn minutes."

I settled in beside him and selected a chocolate-dipped croissant as he poured the coffee. "And you can? What would you do if Claris came home and told you she'd decided you guys should take some time off?"

He laughed. "Wouldn't happen. She's never taken time off in her life. She spreads that story that I'm the one who works too hard, but have you seen her pause for a minute?"

"Maybe that's what she's doing with Perri."

"Claris has many virtues, but putting work aside for the sake of sex is not one of them. Though she does sometimes have epiphanies at strange moments."

I looked over, coffee cup halfway to my mouth. "Tell me she has not had work epiphanies while having sex."

Diego grinned and clinked his mug against mine. "Some of her best work is done naked."

"Oh my god. I can't—I mean, I *can*, but—oh my god."

"Now that we've covered that little tidbit, I wonder what the NBT is." He sat back and picked up the other half of my croissant. "She was really excited about your work with our social media presence. I wouldn't be surprised if she comes up with something along those lines. New forms of engagement, that kind of thing."

"To what end?" I asked. "I thought you were making money on your line."

"Sure, that's money. But Claris wants to save the world. Didn't she tell you? She wants a foundation, like the Gateses. Only ideally without the divorce."

"Ooo. And yes, no divorce, good plan. What would the foundation do?"

"A lot of things, but she wants the main focus to be objective scientific studies into things like poor medical outcomes for women of color and the actual health risks, if any, of weighing more than our body-shaming culture says you should."

I blinked. "Whoa, okay, that's not where I thought this was going. I figured it'd be curing cancer or AIDS or something like that."

"There are a lot of people doing those things. But it's hard to find studies that aren't funded directly or indirectly by corporations with a stake in their findings. It's not super sexy, funding research studies. Except to Claris. And then the key is publicity, if the findings don't correspond to the popular narrative." He waved a hand and said sleepily, "It's a whole thing."

"It sounds like an idea with a lot of merit. The Diego Flores and Claris Russell Foundation?" It didn't have an immediate ring, but I thought I could get used to it.

"She says that only works if you have massive name recognition. She really wanted to call it the Phoenix Foundation, but *MacGyver* already took that." He said it with a slight smirk.

"Did you make fun of Claris for wanting to call her foundation after the secret government agency in *MacGyver*?" I asked.

"I may have done."

"You're a terrible man."

"I am." He nestled up against me, smelling like coffee and pastry. "A terrible, horrible man. Let's spend the whole day in bed, okay?"

"We have dinner reservations at nine."

"It's not a church week?"

"My mom will understand. And um, if you want..." I almost faltered, then didn't. "If you want, maybe you can come with me next Sunday?"

He kissed me until both of us were breathless. "I would love to do that. I would love to meet your mother. Are you sure she'll be okay with rescheduling?"

I imagined the way her voice would sound when I told her I was bringing Diego and smiled at him. "Totally sure."

"Then until nine, let's stay here."

"So you can demonstrate what a terrible, horrible man you are?"

He smiled and kissed my jaw, my cheek, my ear. "Mm hmm. Over and over again. We'll conduct a study about it."

"Ohhh, is that right?" I set my coffee down and took his as well. "An objective scientific study about what a terrible man you are?"

"Among other things." He coaxed me lower, throwing his leg over mine, speaking in between kisses. "Will you be my research subject?"

I nibbled his earlobe. "I think I can manage that."

"Oh good." His hand cupped my cheek and the sunlight

caught on his skin, making him glow. "I have such a lot to learn about you."

"We have time," I said. "So much time."

And, as if that was the most romantic thing anyone had ever said to him, his eyelashes fluttered, eyes going glassy. "So very much time."

We kissed. And kissed again. And forgot about everything outside that shaft of golden light.

★ ★ ★ ★ ★

Acknowledgments

All my thanks to the following folks, who helped me out immeasurably with this book and this series: Courtney Miller-Callihan, Stephanie Doig, Lennan Adams, Alexis Hall, and of course, always, General Wendy. Special shout-out to my kiddo, who named the plants at the studio (as we name all of our plants, naturally). And all my love to everyone who read *The Love Study* and *The Hate Project* and let me know how much this particular chosen family meant to them!

As executive chef at one of the hottest restaurants in DC, DeShawn Franklin has almost everything he's ever wanted. Until a scheming grandma and the divorce that never went through conspire to bring him back to the one man who got away: his not-so-ex-husband, Malik.

A marriage lost is found again in this cheeky new romantic comedy from acclaimed author Jayce Ellis. Keep reading for an excerpt from If You Love Something, *out from Carina Adores.*

Chapter One

DeShawn

The faint strains of a familiar tune wafting in from the front of the restaurant made me pause my usual hurried pace to my office. Was the pianist playing…? I tiptoed down the hall, keeping as quiet as possible, and listened.

Yep. That was definitely the Divinyls' "I Touch Myself." Wow, he was on one tonight, and I bet the esteemed patrons of this starred establishment, one of only two in DC, had no clue.

I covered my mouth to muffle a snicker and snuck back to my office before someone found me and made me perform. I wish I could flout propriety like the pianist but—I paused, looking down at my arms, covered in tattoos that always peeked out of my coat—I guess I got away with enough.

I slipped out of my over-expensive, toe-pinching loafers into the far more comfortable clogs I wore while working. My butt had just hit the seat when Maribel, our head chef, burst through the door, her normally light tan skin flush with exertion.

"Janice is sick," she said, referring to our first line cook. "Or, rather, her wife is, so she's gone home to take care of their kid."

Whatever joy I'd taken in the pianist's subversive musical selections faded, and I was left with nothing but a nervous energy I couldn't parse. One of our other line cooks was on paternity leave, and rather than get someone to fill in, the CFO had decided we could make do. We had, but we were on the rails, and as executive chef, that was always my fault.

Bel cleared her throat and stepped toward me. "I'll work her station, and you can play head chef for the night," she began, but I waved her off.

"No. I'll handle her job. You keep doing what you're doing." Yes, that was a better idea, one I liked. It might even be fun.

"DeShawn, the line cooks are scared of you."

I snorted and fixed her with a withering look that she knew was all jokes. "They are not. I'm friendly with all of them."

"Friendly, but you're still *the* DeShawn Franklin, god of the kitchen, and we are but mere peons." She fluttered her lashes and kissed the air, and for a brief moment in time I wished I had those godawful loafers back on, because clogs didn't give me the satisfying clunking sound as I tapped my foot.

"Hush, you." I grabbed my black chef's jacket and cap, smoothed it over my locs, and followed her out the door and to the kitchen. "You go on and be the big bad boss, and I'm gonna be one of the guys."

She huffed and mimed flipping her hair, except it was pulled back into a tight bun with a white cap over it, so not a strand moved. "We'll see about that."

I laughed, the banter with her just what I needed to loosen up. I loved this job, being an executive chef at one of the hottest restaurants in town, but I'd be lying if I said I didn't miss actually getting to cook every now and then. That was dead last on the list of my responsibilities, and while I understood, it still grated. I missed the simplicity of chilling in the kitchen all night, shooting the shit and joking with the other line cooks and sous chefs, even when we were slammed. I wasn't nearly as fond of being bogged down by glad-handing patrons who barely touched their plates.

I slid into Janice's station next to Graham, an absolute lumberjack of a guy who made my already short five-six look positively tiny, and he started to grin, then gulped and his body went fainting-goat stiff. "Oh, Chef, I didn't know it was you."

Good Lord, was Bel right? Were people actually afraid of me? Impossible. I refused to accept it.

I elbow-nudged him and gave him a grin, the one that made folks love me or whatever. "You know I don't like being called Chef anyway. Call me DeShawn and let's get to work."

Graham, eyes still saucer-round, nodded, then swallowed so hard his jaw clicked. He gripped his knife *way* too hard and I tried to muffle my small squeak of alarm. Apparently, that was enough to make him take a deep breath, loosen his grip, and began cutting.

I waited for a few beats, then pulled Janice's card and went to work chopping onions. So many onions. Diced for the mirepoix, sliced for salads and a few of the entrees. Next to me, Graham's shoulders finally relaxed, and I watched him from the corner of my eye. He was a beast with the scallions, slicing with an efficiency I'd never been able to master. Huh, maybe he should give classes.

The door banged open, not an unusual sound, but the loud, nasally, "Chef DeShawn" made my heart sink. Mine, and probably more than one person around me.

Still, I tried for a halfway decent grin as I turned and smiled tightly at Christopher. "Yes?"

Christopher—my agent slash publicist slash general pain in the ass—stomped over to me, his warm, slightly sweet cologne a sharp contrast to the pungent onions we were cutting "We have multiple VIPs waiting to meet you. Powerful, influential. I need you out there ASAP." He paused and frowned, like he'd just realized where he was, or rather where *I* was. "What are you doing here anyway?"

"Helping," I said. "Janice is out. We're short."

"Your job does not involve chopping onions," he hissed.

I straightened and turned. Christopher looked on the verge of tears. He wasn't supposed to be in the kitchen anyway. Served him right that his eyes were watering. Because I'm a G, I didn't smile. "My job always involves service. If they'll wait a few minutes, I'll be right out."

"These are VIPs," Christopher protested.

"And?" I ignored him and chopped half an onion while he stood there. "Every patron wants the same thing, right? The best food, the kind that got us a star, as quickly as possible. In fact, I think they'd appreciate I'm not above jumping on line and helping out."

Christopher didn't answer, but I felt his eyes narrow on my back. We were supposed to work together for things that benefited my career, and his by association, but that glare made me feel like a recalcitrant schoolchild. He waited until I finished before muttering, "Are you ready now?" and turning away before I could answer.

He sounded every ounce the sullen little boy, and I groaned internally. I shouldn't enjoy frustrating my agent, no matter how much he irritated me. After conferring with Graham that he'd be fine on his own, and getting a squeaked "yes" in response, I followed Christopher out, slowing my step to get myself together. I ignored the knowing glance and tiny smirk Maribel gave when I passed, flicking her off as I walked out. By the time I pushed through the door, I was ready, my smile fixed in place. Christopher led me to a series of raised tables, where people who were there to be seen more than to eat sat.

"Took you long enough," one man grumbled, his face flushed, both a half-full tumbler and a full glass of wine in front of him. I smiled, the smile that made me so popular in the city, and stared at him until he dropped his eyes and coughed slightly, then mumbled he was just joking. Of course he was.

I took my eyes off him and beamed at rest of the table, then gave a slight bow. "My sincerest apologies for keeping you waiting. We're somewhat short-staffed and I'm a cook at heart."

"I'd think you had better things to do than that," one woman commented, adjusting her posture so I couldn't help but notice the deep scoop neckline of her spaghetti-strap dress. For reasons forever unknown, I got that a lot. My being openly gay hadn't changed it a bit.

So I smiled and even gave her a little wink, making her blush. "I hope to never be so big in my britches that I'm above helping out the line cooks who bring my fantastical ideas to life and make your excellent meals possible."

That got a series of coos from her and the other women there, and even begrudgingly respectful nods from the men. I inquired about their meal—what, if anything, they particularly enjoyed—and, as usual, the restaurant comped their desserts. Throughout it all, Christopher stood next to me, his smile so wide and fixed it bordered on Jack Nicholson's Joker.

After another quick bow, I decided to take one quick circuit through the main room to speak to our other patrons. Once I made it back to the kitchen, it was unlikely I'd leave before the night was over.

Christopher wasn't interested in that, his face drooping the minute we were out of sight of the Very Important People. "We have to get back," he insisted, swiping at my sleeve.

I ignored him and shook hands with the "regular" customers at another table, spending time with them, listening to their stories and answering questions, before moving to the next one. Ten minutes later, Christopher scowling at my side, I headed back to the kitchen.

"I brought you out here to meet VIPs," he hissed in my ear.

"I did. What? You didn't want me to make anyone else feel like a VIP, too, Chris?"

"Christopher."

"My bad." As much as I thought he was a pretentious douchebag on the best of days, I wasn't an asshole about names. Given the number of times my own had been butchered over the course of the past forty years, I was better than that. "What else do you want, Christopher? As you can see, I have work to do. You saw how short-staffed we are, and I made this round because I won't make it back on the floor tonight. What can I do for you?"

"We have a series of events lined up, some television gigs you'll need to be at in the next few days."

I crinkled my nose, well past trying to hide my distaste. "Christopher, why can't Bel do these instead of me? She's as photogenic as y'all say I am, and she actually likes that stuff."

He was shaking his head before I finished speaking, even though her agent worked for Christopher's agency and they usually swapped us in and out like playing cards. "Perhaps, but she's not..." He waved his arm vaguely at me. "You," he finished.

In someone else's world, that was a compliment. In mine, it was a pain in the butt. Once upon a time, I'd been thrilled by the idea of doing TV. That'd changed pretty quickly when I saw the amount of bullshit hand-wringing it involved, the excuses to maintain the status quo rather than innovate, and I'd tried—without success—to avoid it ever since.

I rolled my shoulders, knowing I wouldn't win this argument. Nothing to it but to do it.

"All right. Fine," I said. "We'll work it out. Let's schedule a time later this week."

For once, Christopher just nodded, and I pushed into the

kitchen, intent on making my way back to my temporary station. Bel caught me as soon as I entered.

"DeShawn, I didn't want to come out and tell you, but your grandmother called while you were out. She says you need to come home."

Coming home didn't happen for two more days, until Janice got back and I finally put my foot down and forced the CFO to get a temp line cook. I'd called Grandma to explain, but she'd always been asleep, per her BFF Miss Maxine. She'd assured me it wasn't critical, that Grandma just needed to talk to me. "Cryptic" might as well have been both of their middle names.

I made the drive to Baltimore and pulled up to the small, single-story house located smack in the middle of the street, and climbed out, taking a deep breath to let the calm wash over me. Here I was just Lil D, Grandma's baby, the sorry one whose mama had passed having me. It'd taken me a long time to not feel guilty, but I'd been loved beyond measure. That knowledge led to a different kind of regret. While it was common for me to talk to Grandma a few times a week, it was rare she beckoned me home, and I hadn't made the drive up for close to six months.

I climbed the front steps and fished my key out of my pocket, leaning against a post I needed to have fixed for her. I should have come home more anyway, though. She was getting up in age, and I didn't know how much time we had left.

I opened the door and called out immediately. "Grandma? It's me."

The door shut behind me, and I took a moment to hang up my jacket on the coat tree. I turned at the sound of footsteps. Miss Maxine stood in the hallway, her arms open. I wasted no time crossing the distance and engulfing her in a hug.

"Hey, Auntie," I said.

She pressed a kiss to my forehead and patted my cheeks. "Hey, baby. Larry's in there with her now."

I walked in and smiled at Maxine's son. We'd grown up together, but he'd become an adult and gone into law while I played in the kitchen for a living. He sat next to Grandma, who was reclined comfortably in her bed, the adjustable-frame mattress I'd bought her apparently being put to good use, and grinned at me. "Hey, D. What's good?"

"Not much, man. Always looking for a reason to escape the city." I leaned over and kissed Grandma on the cheek. "Hey, pretty lady, how's it going?"

"Good, baby. Take a seat, because we have some things to discuss."

No lie, that sounded pretty ominous, and I paused in front of the chair I'd been about to plop down in. "What's up?"

She wasted no time. "The cancer has metastasized and I'm not doing no more treatment."

If I'd been holding something, I would've dropped it. I sucked in a big gulp of air, but it wasn't enough. My hands tingled, like ants had taken up residence, and my shoulders ached with the sudden weight.

Not this. Jesus Christ, *not this.* She'd been in remission ten years, and I still remembered like it was yesterday the fear in Grandpa's eyes when he thought he might lose her. When the doctors told us she was cancer-free, Grandpa'd cried. Broke down on the hospital floor thanking the Lord for saving his wife. I could've handled just about anything she told me. I wasn't sure if I could handle this.

I gripped the top of the chair and fought to stay upright. "Grandma, what?" Someone had taken a meat mallet to my voice, and I barely got the words out.

"I'm tired, I've done what I set out to do, and I'm ready to go when the good Lord is ready to bring me home. Now sit down, because I'm not finished."

I'm glad my legs obeyed her, because they sure as hell didn't listen to me. Or maybe it was the combined efforts of Larry and Miss Maxine pushing me into Grandma's old sitting chair. My fingers fumbled for the little patch of threadbare fabric on the arm that I'd been picking at since I was six. It was harder to pluck at it now than then, but way easier than to accept what I'd just heard.

Larry re-took his seat, cleared his throat, and spoke. "Your grandmother has redone her will and wants you to know what's in it."

I nodded, still a little too numb to speak. That made sense, I guess. I knew she'd done one during her first bout with cancer and chemo, but once she'd gone into remission, I'd stopped thinking about it.

Grandma speared Larry with a look, but he just smiled indulgently at her before turning to me. He was a super bigwig at a downtown DC firm. He'd come into the restaurant a few times during lunch and always left huge tips. The servers adored him. "Grandma has left the house to you. She wanted you to have a place to, and I quote, get away from the madness of the city."

I blinked at him, then at Grandma, who gave me a quick smile. I adored this home, the quiet comfort it always brought me when the world got to be too much, but I'd assumed she'd leave it to my uncle Robert. Even though we were twenty years apart, we'd both been raised here and, I don't know, I guess I thought he was attached to it like I was. Knowing my uncle, that was probably a naive thought, but still.

I reached out to grab her hands. "Thank you," I said, ignoring the slight warble in my voice. "Corey will love it."

"That dog loves anything. But I want you to love it, too." She sniffed, but she doted on my bulldog as much as, if not more than, I did.

"We will. But he'll especially love having this entire place to himself."

She cupped my cheek and I placed my hand over hers, tears springing up and a few strays spilling over. She wiped them with her thumb and I sat back, then shook myself and let out a hoarse cry, the reality of the situation overwhelming. Grandma telling me her final wishes. I wasn't ready. Internally, I berated myself to get it the hell together, but it still took a few more deep breaths before I could face them.

Larry waited until I was done, his eyes warm with brotherly concern, before continuing. "Now, the actual cash, savings accounts, checking accounts, those liquid assets?"

I raised a brow. Me and Robert were the only family Grandma had, so if I got the house, he had to get the cash. He'd blow through it, like he blew through every bit of money he'd ever gotten his hands on, but it was kind of what he did. I'd long ago given up on Grandma saying no to him. Of course, she could also give it to charity. She was big into her church, and...

"Those are all going to Malik Franklin."

I paused. Closed my eyes, swallowed hard, fought to keep the name from thunking around my eardrums. Fought to keep the memories from swallowing me whole. "Malik? My ex-husband, Malik?"

My throat closed all the way up, and I hacked hard enough that Larry scrunched his nose at me and sat back. Miss Maxine came over and rubbed my back until I found my voice. "I... Sure. I mean, it's your money. Do with it what you want."

Honestly, I don't even know why I was pretending. No one in the room believed a word out of my mouth. I didn't have to perform for them, and with that in mind I blew out a deep breath and focused on what she had to say.

"So," Grandma started, drawing the word out, "that's really why I needed to talk to you. To tell you what we found."

My confusion? Sky-high. "What, Grandma? What did you find?" *And why is my gut performing Kegels?*

She cleared her throat, and that really didn't help. "So. You and Malik's divorce…"

My nostrils flared at the word, and I had to take a moment before I could respond. "What about it?"

"Well, there was a problem with it."

"Okay. What problem?"

"Honestly, I'm not really sure."

Not. Helping. "Grandma, what are you telling me?"

"That you guys did something wrong and aren't divorced."

"What!" I leaped off the chair and stared at Larry, then at Grandma, then back to Larry. "What are you talking about, we aren't divorced? We've been divorced for years." Seven of them, to be exact. Seven years, three months, and eighteen days. Give or take. Maybe nineteen.

Larry winced but shook his head. "No, you're not. Not only are you not divorced, but they closed the case out years ago. If you want a divorce, you have to start over."

I collapsed back in my seat and closed my eyes, pinching the bridge of my nose. "How long have you known about this?" I asked Grandma, and felt like shit when her eyes got big and she shook her head rapidly. Hell, I hadn't meant to accuse her of anything.

"Not long, baby, I swear. They sent the paperwork here, but your grandfather had just died and I—"

I couldn't get to her fast enough, to sit on the bed and pull her close. She didn't need to explain. Grandpa's passing had been sudden, had shaken our whole world to its very core. I'd been in Barcelona and had broken down at least three times on the flight home. If I'd been here, there's a good chance I would've missed the paperwork, too.

Miss Maxine picked up where Grandma left off. "We found it when we were cleaning. We didn't want you to have to go through all her stuff the way she did Cornelius's, so we were trying to get that done now, and…"

She trailed off, and my mind circled all the way back around to losing Grandma. To her deciding to let go and let God. And as much as I wanted to plead with her to fight, not to give in, I also thought that her making this decision and doing it on her own terms was pretty badass. Which was Grandma in a nutshell.

"So now what?" I asked, trying to keep my voice light. "You telling me I don't get the house and he doesn't get the money unless we reunite and are remarried within six months or something?"

She laughed, long and loud, and it was music to my ears. And I wondered if this was the last time I'd hear it. I clenched my fists, digging my stubby nails into my palms to keep the tears at bay.

"No, nothing like that. Besides, I asked, and Larry says I can't do it." She winked at him, and he chuckled, his unbridled affection for her evident.

"No," she said again, settling her gaze back on me. "There's no ultimatum. I'm telling you this so you're prepared. Robert's going to fight it tooth and nail, and you need to be ready. And you need to be there for Malik when Robert goes after him, too."

I frowned, thinking about the terms she'd laid out. "Grandma, are you cutting Uncle Robert out?"

"Yes." She punctuated it with a sharp nod. "I've given him more than enough, and I know he waits for my death with bated breath to get the rest. But I've assisted him enough in this life, and it's time for him to make his own way."

Wow. I had no words, couldn't think of when I'd heard her this passionate. I mean, except for her extremely vocal disapproval of my apparent non-divorce. But yeah, Uncle Robert was going to come out swinging to challenge this.

I looked up at her. "I don't know how to reach Malik. I don't have his number—we haven't spoken since the divorce."

Grandma smiled at me gently, like she was dealing with a toddler and not a forty-year-old man, then glanced at Larry. He cleared his throat and leaned across the bed to hand me a folded sheet of paper. I opened it to find Malik's name and telephone number, and couldn't help but chuckle.

"Why do you have this?" I asked her, though I didn't know why I was surprised.

She snorted. "You two may have divorced, or tried to, but I didn't. That boy's been my grandbaby as much as you since the moment you brought him home."

God, Malik had loved her. Had adored her almost as much as he had me. And as happy as I was that he still spoke to her, hadn't let that die when we had, the sour tinge of bittersweet recriminations would haunt me tonight.

"Yeah, okay," I said, staring down at the paper in my hands. Wondering what I could possibly say. "I'll reach out to him."

"Don't dillydally, DeShawn." Grandma's voice was gentle, but she was serious. "This is important, and you need to reach out to him soon."

"I will, Grandma. I promise."

Don't miss If You Love Something *by Jayce Ellis, out from Carina Adores!*

www.CarinaPress.com

Copyright © 2021 by Jayce Ellis

Also available from Kris Ripper

Catalysts

Copyright © 2015 by Kris Ripper

Will Derrie likes girls but he isn't honest with them; he wants kinky sex and lots of it. When Hugh offers to dominate him, no sex required, Will realizes it might not be so easy to separate the two.

Hugh Reynolds holds the world at arm's length. He lives alone, works alone, and he thinks he's as happy as he'll ever be. But Will gets under his skin and once he's gone, Hugh realizes he doesn't want to go it alone forever.

Truman Jennings hits on a cute guy at a conference and he's smitten by the end of their first date. Hugh's not the kindest or the easiest boyfriend Truman's ever had, but he brings one thing to their relationship that no one else could: kinky, adventurous, sweetly submissive Will.

Sometimes you can't find the right man till you find the wrong one. Three men. Three sides to love, and intimacy, and laughter. Three people who didn't know what they were looking for…until they found it in each other.

Discover another great contemporary romance from Carina Adores

As executive chef at one of the hottest restaurants in DC, DeShawn Franklin has almost everything he's ever wanted. Until his grandmother calls him home and drops three bombshells:

1) She has cancer and she's not seeking treatment.

2) She's willing half her estate to DeShawn's ex-husband, Malik.

3) That whole divorce thing? It didn't quite go through. DeShawn and Malik are still married.

And when DeShawn's shady uncle contests Grandma's will, there's only one path back to justice: play it like he and Malik have reconciled. They need to act like a married couple just long enough to dispense with the lawsuit...

Don't miss
If You Love Something by Jayce Ellis,
available wherever Carina Press books are sold.

CarinaAdores.com

CARJE0122TR

Discover another great contemporary romance from Carina Adores

Accomplished, take-no-prisoners art historian Adrianna Coates has built an enviable career since museum courier Charlotte Hilaire saw her last. She's brilliant. Sophisticated. Impressive as hell and strikingly beautiful.

Hospitable, too, as she absolutely *insists* Charlotte spend the night on her pullout sofa when a blizzard strands Charlotte in Spain for a few extra days.

One night becomes three and three nights become a hot and adventurous long-distance relationship when Charlotte returns to the States. But when Adrianna plots her next career move just as Charlotte finally opens a door in academia, distance may not be the only thing that keeps them apart.

Don't miss
Meet Me in Madrid by Verity Lowell,
available wherever Carina Press books are sold.

CarinaAdores.com

CARVL1121TR

IF YOU ENJOYED THIS BOOK
WE THINK YOU WILL ALSO LOVE

Carina Adores is home to modern, romantic love stories where LGBTQ+ characters find their happily-ever-afters.

**Discover more at
CarinaAdores.com**

CARADORES2021TR